Widow's Walk

by

Wendy Webb

Widow's Walk

Cover Art by *Abigail Owen*

The Wild Rose Press, Inc.
PO Box 708
Adams Basin, NY 14410-0708
Visit us at www.thewildrosepress.com

Publishing History
First Fantasy Rose Edition, 2020
Print ISBN 978-1-5092-2880-5
Digital ISBN 978-1-5092-2881-2

Published in the United States of America

Dedication

To Steve;
To the Dark River Writers past and present;
and to the memory of friends greatly missed.
You are why.
Special thanks to editor Claudia Fallon—
You showed me how.

Chapter 1

Annie Cameron yanked a suitcase out of the car trunk, smoothed the rolling hem of her denim skirt back into place, then looked to the far end of the dock where a little launch bobbed up and down in the water. A slender, gray-headed boatman waved as if he had known her for years. She waved back, pulled her hair into a ponytail, and leaned into the back seat of the car.

"Charlie? Grandma? Time to get your things together. We're going for a boat ride."

As usual, there was no answer or a response of any kind.

"Charlie, honey? Come on now. I don't think that man on the boat will wait forever, and there's no other way to the island."

Her ten-year-old son nodded, pushed his glasses further on his nose, hesitantly unloosed his seatbelt and that of his grandmother, then reached for the door.

"Of course, he'll wait. That's his job." David Cameron exploded from the driver's side of the car, slammed the door shut then walked to the trunk to wrench more suitcases out. "That man can wait all day with what we're paying him."

"I thought you were in a hurry to get back to Atlanta to meet the contractors. That's what you said."

"I'm well aware of what I said."

That familiar tightness formed in her husband's

jaw as they approached the same uncomfortable topics. "You said you had a meeting with the contractors. You meant *contractors*, didn't you? Not a meeting with someone else?"

David pulled the last suitcase out. "Do you really want to discuss this now?"

"No, David, I don't. Not in front of Charlie anyway."

"You coddle the boy too much, pamper him like a puppy. Always have. That's why he's the way he is."

"That's not true, and you know it."

"No, Annie. I don't know it. All I know is what I see."

"You're never home. How can you see anything?"

She caught a motion out of the corner of her eye. Grandma, as frail and brittle as a dying twig, had come around the car to put a protective arm around Charlie. She glared at Annie and David with clarity in her brilliant blue eyes as penetrating as it was rare.

Clearing her throat, Annie changed the subject and forced a lighter tone to her voice. "We'll be fine down here while the house is being renovated."

"You won't recognize the place."

"And I'll make sure Charlie keeps up with his school work."

"What's that?" David tucked a suitcase under each arm and grabbed for more.

"His assignments. From school. I'll see to it that he gets the work done."

A smirk crossed his face then instantly disappeared. "Of course you will. And I'm sure Charlie will be at the head of his class."

"'Heigh, my hearts!'" The booming voice

commanded immediate attention. "'Cheerily, cheerily, my hearts! Take in the topsail.'" The man offered a hand to David then to Annie, Grandma, and Charlie. "The name's Winston Mann, and as soon as we get boarded, we're ready to go."

"Yes, sir, Mr. Mann," Annie said, popping to mock attention. "I'm Annie Cameron, from Atlanta, and I think we're ready now."

"Well then," he said with a broad, friendly smile, "let's to it." He scooped up luggage into his leather-brown arms and headed to the boat at a brisk pace that equaled his banter. "'Tend to the master's whistle. Blow, till thou burst thy wind, if room enough.' Watch your step. This dock has got to be older than dirt. There you go."

Stepping easily onto the bobbing craft, he worked effortlessly with the weight of the densely packed suitcases. It was if his slight frame had to be held in check. Standing back, arms akimbo, he surveyed the result of his work and nodded with satisfaction.

"Yup. I think that'll do it. Let me help you get on, Annie Cameron. Your mother can sit aft." He winked. "That's the seat in the back."

"That seat'll do just fine, thanks. She's David's mother actually. I take care of her."

Annie glanced at David on the dock, caught the hardness in his gaze, then returned the look and immediately regretted the pettiness of it all. Being cold to others wasn't in her nature, but somehow, recently anyway, this was a disturbing new wrinkle to her otherwise easy way. She would have to work on doing better and now was as good a time as any.

"Is this seat okay for me and Charlie?"

"Charlie, huh? A name fit for kings. That seat's fine. Mr. Cameron, you can have the seat right there."

"No, thanks. I'm not going on this trip."

Mann paused at this news, glanced at Annie, then David then back to Annie. "That right? Well, you just let me know when we might be expecting a visit—you got my number—and I'll be here quicker than a June bug on a cow-pie."

"Soon, I hope," David said, shrugging. "I'm not sure. I'll let you know."

"A long weekend, maybe?" Annie asked. "That would be nice."

"Maybe."

And then David was gone, across the old dock, and back to the car without so much as a wave to his son or a kiss on his mother's cheek.

They watched him go until Mann broke the silence. "You gonna be okay, Annie Cameron?"

She nodded mutely.

"I see." Mann turned the key to the engine. Nothing. He turned it again. *Errand Two* can be as ornery as the wife when she wants to be."

Or a husband. It was David's idea, his insistence, that the family stay at another place while the house was being renovated. That meant all of them together, one happy family, and in a place a damn sight closer than four hundred miles and a boat ride away from the renovations, school, and the usual obligations.

She shook her head and decided not to dwell on David's behavior or the now convoluted reasons that brought her to this place. There was an adventure ahead of them, and adventures didn't happen very often in her mundane routine, so she was going to enjoy every minute of it if it killed her.

"*Errand Two*? Does that mean there was an *Errand One*?"

Mann cranked the engine. A rumble came from under the boat, then a gurgle of water from behind.

"Yup." He paused as if deliberating whether or not to continue. "She crashed against some rocks in a storm a few years back."

The engine coughed then roared to life in a cloud of blue smoke. He engaged the gears, and they backed away from the dock and turned parallel to the shoreline of the lunchtime busy town.

"'...though the ship were no stronger than a nutshell, and as leaky as an unstaunched wench.'" He pulled out a baseball cap from the dashboard and wedged it onto his head.

"That line is from *The Tempest*. One of Shakespeare's finer plays. You might have noticed I tend to quote from that work when I'm out and about doing boat duty." He glanced at them. "Or maybe not. Fortunately for us," he yelled over the din of the engine, "we haven't had any bad weather to speak of pretty much since. Folks on the island have gone a little soft about preparing for a storm. I guess they think something like that can't happen again. And maybe they're—" He stared at the shoreline.

Annie twisted in her seat to follow his gaze.

There, on a park bench that looked over the water, sitting as still as a weatherworn statue, was a woman dressed in moonless, midnight black. She was clothed from the black veil that hid her face to the simple dress, gloves, and opaque stockings that covered her legs and ended in severe pointed black shoes. As the boat passed, she rose slowly, as if by a mere inch at a time, until she had reached her full height and stood tall and unwavering as the wind shifted and blew from inland to island and sea. Her dress rolled gently about her and revealed a body that could be little more in girth than a skeleton. There was no other gesture or sign of recognition on her part, save for the motionless affect of her posture when she stood at their passing.

Mann pulled his ball cap off, rubbed an arm across his sweat-covered brow, and turned the boat away from their sight of the woman and into the inlet that led to the island. "Something like that can't happen again. It can't."

"Who is that woman, Mr. Mann?" Annie asked.

He dismissed an answer with a wave of his hand and pulled the cap back on his head.

"Mr. Mann?" This time there was not even a wave forthcoming. Annie turned for another glance at the woman and saw she was gone. The park bench was occupied by a couple sharing a strawberry ice cream cone. Scanning the waterfront town, she saw nothing but the bustling activity of townspeople on a lunchtime break.

There was no woman in black. Anywhere.

Instinctively she pulled her over-shirt tighter around her and reached for Charlie's hand. He did not close his fingers around hers as usual but stared at some distant spot that only he could see. If Annie didn't know better, she would have guessed Charlie was unaware she was there. But she did know better. She knew better than anyone how tenuous Charlie's hold was on the world. He was wired differently; she explained simply to those who bothered to ask. A definitive diagnosis was impossible to come by, but the end result of losing him forever to his internal world was always a threat.

She saw the old woman's sweet face a picture of peace by way of a quick doze. Eyelids fluttering, perhaps Grandma was dreaming pleasant thoughts. She shifted slightly in her seat; her lips moved without benefit of sound.

Charlie's hand twitched in Annie's.

Grandma mouthed another voiceless word.

Another twitch of Charlie's hand, and then it stilled.

Annie looked from one to the other then dismissed the act as a trick of fatigue after a long drive. Raising her son's hand to her lips for a kiss, she mumbled a word of thanks he and Grandma had each other. The two were so fond of each other.

Mann steered the boat into shallow water filled with a maze of marsh grass that broke the brown surface. The scent of salt, of decaying fish, of aged gasoline, and rancid oil punctured the air and left a bitter taste.

A flick of Mann's wrist on a lever dropped the decibel level of the engine and the speed. Now there was only the tick-tick-tick of the engine as they gently navigated the marsh grass and dark surface of the inlet waterway.

"Gotta be careful here. Low water can be hard on the hull. Not to mention the undercurrent that can creep up. These can be dangerous waters if a body doesn't know what they're doing." He sighed deeply and looked up. "Buttermilk sky."

"What's that?" Annie asked.

"Some say it means rain, maybe a storm."

"A storm?" Annie watched the sky with suspicion. "I don't like storms." Nervously she rolled the curling hem of her denim skirt back and forth and brushed away a strand of brown hair that had escaped her ponytail. "Not anytime soon, I hope."

"Hard to say. On an island in September, it's always best to expect the unexpected."

"How often do the unexpected happen?"

"Hard to say, 'cause it's—"

"Unexpected. I should have guessed not to match words with someone who recites Shakespeare."

Mann nodded sagely, then cupped his hands around a pipe and tried to light it. "Worse one was a Maritime High. Kinda like a hurricane nearing the offseason. Good news is we haven't had one of those in an awfully long time. It's an unusual thing, and very rare, a Maritime High."

"But you've had other storms?"

"Yup."

"Bad ones?"

"Depends on who you ask."

"I'm asking you, Mr. Mann," she said, wrapping her arms around Charlie.

He looked up at the sky again, a buttermilk sky, and then at Annie. "Nah. Maybe a little rain, a soft rain. Nothing more."

The air turned fresher, a little crisp. The marsh grass became sparse, the water open.

Mann pointed over the front of the boat. "Lullaby Sound is just around that little island up ahead and to the right. In no time, you'll be able to see Mico Island." He tried lighting the pipe again then puffed victoriously. "You like horses, Charlie?" There was no answer. "Not much of a talker, are you? Well then, I'll just have to do the talking."

Annie smiled. There was no doubt in her mind Mr. Mann relished the idea of being the talker.

"Jekyll Island is to the north of us. That's where the rich folks used to live before WW Two. Called their summer home a cottage, but the damn things were bigger than any house I ever lived in. Down south of us is Cumberland Island. There are lots of horses there, wild ones, and wild pigs, too. The official term is feral pigs and horses, but that's too fancy, so we'll just say wild, okay? Okay."

Annie smoothed back the hair on Charlie's forehead and kissed him. "You like horses, don't you, Charlie? Sure, you do." She tweaked his nose then looked over at her mother-in-law.

Grandma was awake now and intent on the workings of her hands. Open, close, open, close; she was like a pianist preparing to perform. The blast of clarity in her eyes before she got on the boat had turned empty and hollow again. Her senility was getting worse.

Annie finally recognized the void in Grandma's eyes for what it was. No amount of excuses, no matter how good they sounded at one time, could hide the sad facts of what it would mean to take care of Grandma. An overwhelming pity surrounded Annie then a nagging guilt at realizing the pity was not for Grandma.

Charlie shifted his position and buried his head deeper into Annie's shoulder. His eyes never wavered from Winston Mann.

"Yup, Mr. Charlie. Your whole family is running

me ragged with conversation. Would you like to hear a story?"

Motionless at first, Charlie just perceptibly nodded then pushed his glasses higher on his nose.

"Okay, then. Did you know there was a King Charles? No? Actually, there was more than one. And I'm kinda thinking that they may have even gone by the name Charlie. Well, maybe not, and none of this really has anything to do with my story, but I did want to get your attention. Have I got it? Good." Mann pushed the boat into a higher speed now that the water was clear and smooth. "We're headed to Mico Island, right? Well before you got here, even before me, if you can believe that, there were plenty of others who came to this island. Spanish folks came and built missions, Indians lived here, too, and there were forts built by the English. Now, none of these folks live here anymore, and there's no forts left, but they were here just the same."

"How do you know?" Charlie demanded.

Annie's eyes widened at her son, talking to a total stranger. Why could Winston Mann evoke a response out of Charlie when no one else could?

"Know what?" Mann asked.

"If there's nothing left, how do you know people were here?"

Mann stroked his chin. "Mr. Charlie, you are one tough customer. People wrote things down, which is a good thing 'cause if we had to remember everything, we might get our facts wrong. The wife insists I do that all the time." He leaned conspiratorially to Charlie. "Keep that in mind when you get a wife." Mann nodded slowly then continued, "Anyway, Mico Island wasn't just for the Spanish, English, and Indians; it was a great hideout for smugglers and other unsavory types who didn't want to be found. You don't know anyone like that, do you?"

Charlie shook his head.

"I didn't think so. Someone with the same name as a king would only know the best people. The Indian Mico, or chief, became good friends with an English king, and so everyone lived happily ever after, and Mico Island finally had a name."

"That's some story, Mr. Mann," Annie said. "I'm not sure the history books would recount it quite that way."

"Well, Annie Cameron, I don't let facts get in the way of a good story if I can help it. I guess that means my wife is right. She'll be so pleased to hear that."

"Is all that true or not?" Charlie asked.

"As true as I can make it, Mr. Charlie. Ask me about this tomorrow, and I'll have even more to say on the subject." Mann chewed on his pipe. "I like a good story now and then, don't you?"

"I think so," Charlie said. "I guess so."

"Good. You're a man after my own heart."

Mann slowed the engine down to a crawl as they approached the island, and waved at a very tall fisherman reeling in an empty line. The man waved back then exaggerated the size of a fish he had just missed catching. Mann roared with laughter.

"That there is my old friend, Stretch. Bet you can't guess why he's named that, huh? Fine man, Stretch. And he's our chief volunteer fireman to boot. His wife—Peggy's her name—is a top-notch woman in her own right." He glanced over his shoulder at Charlie.

"Maybe when you're all settled in, your mother there, will let me take you fishing. What do you think, Mrs. Cameron?"

"We'll see, okay?"

"You're the boss. Okay by you, Mr. Charlie?"

"Yes, sir. I guess."

"Good." Mann eased the boat along the shoreline and pointed at the lone dock up ahead. "There's where we'll get off. It's just a spit from here to Manchester Place. You ought to be able to see it real soon."

Annie narrowed her eyes and scanned the shoreline for sight of the house they would occupy for the next few weeks. There was a small beach that evolved from high water erosion and tidal idiosyncrasies, but it was fine for her. Beyond the beach was a veritable forest of lush underbrush, healthy pines, and majestic Live oaks draped with silver moss.

"I see it!" Annie said. She caught her breath. "It's beautiful."

The white-frame house rose from the flat of the land like an eruption. Columns rose from the bottom of the first story to the top of the second. Large picture windows peppered this side of the house for an unobstructed view of Lullaby Sound, and there was even a window from the gabled room that marked the third story.

"It's the most beautiful house I've ever seen. Are you sure this is ours?"

"As sure as I can be," Mann said, easing next to the dock.

"Look at that porch." Annie couldn't take her gaze off the place. "It must follow the entire front of the house."

"Verandah goes clear around. Watching a sunset from this side is a sight that will change your life, I can tell you."

"That on top, is that a verandah, too?"

"In a manner of speaking. The one on the far side, with the walls and no roof, is an unfinished room. Old superstition held that a completed house predicted dire misfortune for the family living there. That room makes the place unfinished, you see. On this side is the widow's walk."

"Widow's walk?"

"Yup. Folks say that in the olden times, the wife of a sailor would walk it while waiting for her husband to return from the sea. The guy who designed this place thought it would be a nice touch."

He looked at Annie, and something flickered across his eyes.

"You can't get up there even if you wanted to. No door." He turned away as if concentrating on docking the boat. "It's just something nice to look at from down here. That's all."

A hint of disappointment nagged her. The view of the sound from up there would be something else. Well, it didn't matter anyway, not when she had all the rest of it, at least for a little while. She smiled. Things were going to work out better than she had ever hoped. Here was a great house on a beautiful waterfront, and it was all hers—she glanced at Charlie and Grandma—it was all theirs. What more could anyone ask for?

"Watch this," Mann said with a grin.

He pointed at a young man sleeping in a lawn chair on the dock then pumped the boat horn. The sound punctured the air and rocketed the sleeping man out of the chair. Mann laughed uproariously and grabbed his sides.

"Good old Richard. Sleeping on the job, but here just the same. Lawyers, can't live with him and don't know what I'd do without him."

Richard yawned, rubbed a hand across his eyes, and scanned the passengers. His gaze settled on Annie. He smiled at her, hitched at the blue jeans that covered his well-built frame, then grabbed the rope Mann tossed him.

"Welcome to Mico Island," he said directly to Annie. "We're glad you chose us as a vacation destination."

Mann snorted and rolled his eyes theatrically. "That was a fine tourist board presentation, Richard. And if we ever get a tourist board, I'll be sure to nominate you for president." He climbed out of the boat and offered a hand to Annie, but was knocked sideways by Richard.

Annie climbed out of the boat without assistance while staring at the great house. Nothing more she could ask for, there was not a thing, except maybe a loving husband to share this with. But that, too, would come in time. She could feel it. This place might even afford the second honeymoon she had always wanted, a starting over of sorts.

She looked up, higher still, at the widow's walk and the two-hundred-year-old oak that gently caressed the walk with its branches. Things would be different now, she knew.

Things would be different.

Chapter 2

Sybil Mann filled a cup with steaming dark tea, brushed a strand of gray hair out of her eyes, and pushed a plate of homemade butter cookies toward her husband. "Well?"

This was his cue to fill her in on the new tenants of Manchester Place, he knew. Sybil was nothing if not overly inquisitive; some even said she thrived more on gossip than on breathing. He was all too familiar with their game of question and answer, and if the truth be known, he loved playing it so fully that it was almost a guarantee to get a rise out of her.

"Seems like a nice family," he said.

She poured tea in her favorite mug then wiped the chipped rim with her fingers. Dropping a spoonful of sugar into the cup then another, she stirred then dipped a cookie into the tea. "And…"

"They're nice, that's all." She chewed slowly, deliberately, and with a patience he knew was severely limited.

"Nice."

"At least they're not off, like the last bunch."

Wiping her hands on the pink cotton housedress, she spoke with a voice that was beginning to thin. "You're too kind as usual. They were a bunch of nuts. Have a cookie."

"No, thanks. Not hungry."

"Winston Mann," she pointed an arthritic finger at him, "I will not have you wasting away on my account. Eat."

He reached for a cookie and chewed at it distractedly. New thoughts had pushed away enthusiasm in playing the game.

"I think the husband and wife are having some problems. He didn't come out with his family. Doesn't seem right, that's all." He shrugged. "Maybe it'll be okay. We'll see."

"They didn't bring a load of photo albums, did they?"

"Photo albums?"

She cocked her head and glared at him as if he had lost his last thread of sanity.

"What...?"

Oh, yes. The last tenants, a couple, had brought crates of photo albums holding hundreds of grim pictures inside. He laughed, spewing cookie crumbs across the green Formica kitchen table.

"No. No albums this time."

"Thank God. That's all I can say is thank God." She shuddered at the thought.

"It could have been worse, Syb." He wiped his mouth with a crumpled napkin then swept the wayward table crumbs into the palm of his hand. "There could have been pictures of naked people dancing around, or worse."

"Naked people are okay. I'm naked myself on occasion."

She looked at the reflection of herself in the faded yellow refrigerator door. Her hands smoothed down the bulky material of the housedress to reveal a small bulge in her middle. Taking a deep breath and holding it, she pulled in her belly and stood as tall as her five feet would allow. A side glance to her reflection forced the breath out with a loud disgusted sound.

"Although I'd look a lot better if I got rid of a few pounds."

"You're fine, Syb. I love you the way you are."

"Picture of a dead woman lying in her casket. Make-up an inch thick. And here I am trying to be all sympathetic. 'I'm so sorry,' I say. 'A relative?' And them shaking their heads. 'No. We were just passing through. Thought it'd make a nice picture for our collection. Isn't that a gorgeous dress?' they say. 'Too bad it had to be buried with her.' Honestly, Winston, boxes of photo albums filled with dead people they didn't even know. You couldn't get those people out of here fast enough to suit me."

"We needed the rent money."

"I scrubbed that place down for a week. Didn't want the tiniest bit of craziness left. It might be contagious or something." She refilled his cup then forced another cookie on him. "We can manage without the money if it means nuts are renting it."

"As far as I know, being crazy isn't contagious. But I've always wondered if you could inherit it."

"Winston." Her voice was softer now. "That happened a long time ago. You weren't even born. Even the original house is gone. Most of it anyway."

He shrugged. Some things never leave, and some things seem to return to sit on park benches dressed in black when they should never come back. Mann blinked, grunted—Sybil could never know about the woman in black—then changed the subject. "The

17

mother, Annie's her name, there's something about her. Something—I don't know." He rubbed a leathery hand over his eyes. "She's sweet, vulnerable, I think, maybe even lonely. Her husband didn't come, but her mother-in-law did. Don't you find that a bit off?"

"Well, it's not photo albums, so that's something. If she's a mother, that means there are children."

"One. A son. About Phillip's age." His voice cracked. Turning the cup around in tiny circles, he rubbed his finger along the floral pattern. "Phillip's age before he...before he was...hurt."

Sybil got up from the table, came to him, and wrapped her arms around him.

"Does it ever stop hurting, Syb? Twenty-seven years and I can still see him as if it were yesterday."

She rubbed his shoulders, his neck. "I think about him too. What he'd be doing right now, how handsome he'd be. He had your chin, you know, your blue eyes. And your stubbornness. Phillip could dig his heels in with the best of them."

"He could be a mean one if he wanted to, couldn't he?"

"That he could."

"Remember the time he locked Scram in the suitcase?"

Mann wondered how many times they had this conversation, but settled into the comfort of its familiarity anyway. "We had told him time and again to leave that cat alone, but would he listen? 'I just wanted to see if Scram would fit,' he said, 'just in case I go someplace, and he goes with me.' I thought we'd never get those locks undone. The cat yowling and carrying on in there. I thought that piece of luggage was a goner for sure."

"And when we did open the suitcase, all I saw was an orange ball of fur heading out the door like he was shot from a cannon."

"That cat never showed up around here again."

"Can't say as I blame him. Probably found himself a home where there were no suitcases."

"Probably did."

Sybil kissed him, then gathered up the cups from the table. Mann saw her hands shake, and the everyday china wobble dangerously. He reached out too late and cringed at the crash of china meeting peeling linoleum.

"Damn, damn, damn."

"It's okay, Syb. I'll help you clean it up."

"No, I'll get it. Damn. Look at this mess."

"These things just happen. It's not your fault."

She stopped, whisk broom and dustpan in hand, and looked at him incredulously. "Excuse me for being daft. But if it's not my fault, would you mind telling me just whose fault it is?"

"Gravity."

"Beg your pardon."

"It's gravity's fault. Gravity did it."

Her eyebrows shot up to her hairline. "Are you trying to tell me that anytime something breaks, we can simply blame it on gravity?"

"Sure. Why not? If it wasn't for gravity, things wouldn't fall. And if things didn't fall, they wouldn't break."

"Winston." Her hand dipped into the torn pocket of her housedress, missing a snap about the level of her navel. "Gravity didn't pick up the cup to begin with. How do you account for that?"

"Okay, so in this case you were gravity's helper."

"I don't believe you're telling me this, and I'm not going to listen to any more nonsense." She leaned down to sweep up pieces of the shattered cup.

"Think about it, Syb. It makes sense."

"The only thing I'm going to think about right now is dinner. Chicken or pork chops?"

"Chicken. But watch out for that gravity." A grin formed on her face as she deposited the cup fragments into the plastic garbage can. "It'll get you every time."

Her face turned somber suddenly. "Yes, I imagine you're right. You can't be too careful about some things. Most people just don't take gravity with enough gravity. If you know what I mean."

"I do, Syb. I do."

"Glad to hear it." She opened the refrigerator door and peered in like a bird of prey closing in on its victim. "Green beans or salad?"

"Green beans. You know, I'm glad we had this talk. Most couples claim they don't have anything to say to each other. That's not the case with us."

"Some might argue with you after this conversation."

"Just think, we've got an untapped source of topics in physics alone."

"The mind reels. Potatoes—mashed or baked?"

"Mashed. Keep the skin on."

"I always do." She deposited the vegetables in the sink and turned on the water. "Supper'll be ready in about an hour."

"Okay. I'll be here."

"I'm counting on it."

"Mind if I rest awhile in the study? Or can I help

you with something?"

"A snooze might do you some good. But watch out for the couch." She winked at him. "The cushions slide, you know. Wouldn't want you to help Mr. Gravity any."

"I'll keep one eye open." Mann stood, stretched, then moved to the door. "Syb?"

"Uh-huh."

"Thanks."

"For what?"

"For lots of things. See you in an hour."

"I'll call you."

He walked down the hallway and into the study. Sybil Mann was something else. No one could ask for a better friend or a more perfect wife, but what she saw in him, he couldn't begin to guess.

He flipped on the light and glanced around the dark-paneled room at his book collection. How many times had he stared at those books? A thousand? A million, maybe? But every time he walked into the study, it was different. Something new would catch his eye. That was the nice thing about words; they took on new meanings with every read.

The cracked, deep brown leather bindings of his Shakespeare collection felt soft and comfortably worn under his fingertips. He brought them to his nose and deeply sniffed the rich scent. Sybil had saved for months to get him the old books, had practically threatened the antique man with bodily harm if he didn't relinquish them—and her needing new reading glasses with the little money they had. Dryness touched his throat as he tried to swallow the lump that formed there. She was something all right. No doubt about it.

He moved to the next bookcase. Poetry, plays—Ibsen, now he was an interesting writer, a man ahead of his time—books, the classics. Mark Twain. How long had it been since he had read Twain? He pulled out one of the gray-green books at random. *Tom Sawyer*.

His chest tightened.

Phillip.

The tightness in his chest turned to a dull throbbing ache. Of all the books in the study, why this one, and why tonight? He blinked against the burn starting in his eyes.

This book had become Phillip's favorite, read and re-read until the pages had browned with the little boy's finger smudges. Even sick with pneumonia, fever so high that he could barely lift his head off the pillow, he'd insisted on hearing the story again.

"Read it to me," Phillip had said.

"Okay. But not for long. You need to rest." Mann eyed his son for a sign of sleepiness and opened the book. "Chapter one. 'Tom!' No answer. 'Tom!'"

Mann read until his son closed his eyes to fight the sickness in his sleep, but it didn't stop there. The request for a story came every night, and it was only for the one book.

"I like the way you change your voice for Tom and Huck. How do you do that, Dad?"

"I don't know. You just do."

"Read some more."

And Mann did, over and over and over. Phillip never tired of the book until there was no need to ever read it again. For the past twenty-seven years, the worn book had stayed closed.

Until now.

Until tonight.

Mann rubbed his hand over the faded leather cover to feel the coarseness that once used to be gold lettering. Opening the book to the table of contents, he inhaled the musty smell of age and the lingering hint of a little boy's soap. Some pages had fallen loose from the binding but clung to the brittle, brown glue that bubbled on one side, and still somehow remained together as one piece. He flipped through a few pages and saw the book was still readable.

Books aged gracefully, people didn't. Books lasted, that is, if they were taken care of, but people didn't last no matter how good the care was. He and Phillip had been taken care of, Sybil saw to that, but Phillip was gone now, and the book was still here.

The throbbing in his chest worsened. He reached for the little bottle of medicine in his pocket, opened it, and slipped the tiny pill under his tongue. Too much activity for one day; that was it. The day had been a bit too long for an old man like himself.

He was old, wasn't he? Old enough that some referred to him as "Old man Mann," old enough that he could give Methuselah a run for his money, so it must be true that he was old. Sixty-eight, give a year or two, was somewhere in the documented range since counting them didn't seem to matter anymore. But to hear some people talk, he should be picking up seashells on a beach in Florida somewhere, or spend the better part of his time chasing ladies from a nursing home wheelchair; anything but trying to make ends meet by renting out an old house to tourists who needed a vacation.

The pain arced. He closed his eyes against it. It

would go away in a few minutes; it always had before. He'd just rest a bit now, and tomorrow he'd take it a little easier, but the day after and every day after that, Winston Mann would show everyone that age was just a number on a birthday cake.

She was calling him, a voice from far away. Almost as if it were coming through a tunnel, the sound reverberated off walls until the words were colorless, faint.

"Doorbell. I think it's Richard."

The pain was easing now. Another minute and it would be gone.

"Be there in a second."

He hoped he sounded convincing. There was no need worrying Sybil with his problem; the wife had enough on her mind as it was. Money was tight. Her arthritis had flared up again; there was enough to cope with without a cardiac cripple on her hands, too. Yes, some things were better left unsaid. He'd just keep this little secret to himself.

The pain had disappeared, all but a twinge as a reminder to slow down as the doctor ordered. Tomorrow would be as good a day as any to take off, so that's what he'd do. It would give him a chance to spend some time with Sybil, maybe do a few things around the house.

Richard could run some errands, that is, if he wasn't too busy studying for his law exams. The young man could use some extra spending money, or so the argument went. Richard refused payment most of the time, stating simply that he just liked to help out.

Mann shook his head at the thought of the running argument. If the young man practiced law that way, he'd starve before he reached thirty-five, so there was nothing for it but to talk to Richard about the errands later on tonight. This time Mann would be firm about the money.

"Winston. The door."

"Coming."

He looked at the book in his hands. Maybe one day he could open it without thinking of Phillip, maybe, but somehow he doubted it. The book had out-lived Phillip, and he knew that it would still be here when he was gone too. Perhaps in the interim, another little boy would hear him read aloud. Sighing deeply now, the twinge of pain had gone, he reached out to replace the book on the shelf.

A paper fell from between the pages of the book, drifting soft, quiet, on small air currents until it settled on the floor and opened.

His eyes widened. The hair on the back of his neck rose. First the woman in black on the park bench and now this. Mann turned away from the paper but knew that he would have to look again.

It was in crayon. Blood-red. Phillip's handwriting.

He closed his eyes against the words, hoped they would go away, but knew they wouldn't. "No. Not Phillip. Please."

Darkness surrounded him. He knew he was falling. In the dark, he saw only red, the blood-red scrawl of a ten-year-old boy. He drifted into unconsciousness with the words burned into his mind.

Help me.

Chapter 3

A breeze off Lullaby Sound brushed the thin white curtains aside, reached out across the room to caress Annie's bare shoulder, and brought with it the soft scents of salt, orange blossom, and rose.

She tugged on the soft blue comforter until it touched her chin, and settled back into the fortress she had made of plump, down pillows. The mahogany four-post bed groaned when she moved.

Taking a deep breath, she tried to sort the faint smells that touched the room; cedar for sure, probably from the closets; a remnant of violet soap, or maybe sachet; and the crisp, fresh smell of the sea in early morning, of dawn creeping up on the horizon. Then there was the orange blossom and rose. She hadn't noticed a garden anywhere, or any location that was groomed for such vegetation, but found the smell pleasant in any case.

But there was something else, something old, acrid almost. Smoke? Nose turned to the air she sniffed and tried to zero in on the odor, but it was gone as fast as it had appeared. She sniffed again then wondered if she had smelled smoke at all. Perhaps it was her imagination. Minds played tricks when they were tired, didn't they?

It had been a rough day yesterday, enough to make anyone tired. An early start on the day, six hours in a hot car, then getting everybody settled into their rooms after a quick dinner and a bit of cursory unpacking was a bigger undertaking than she had bargained for. She yawned, stretched, and rolled to one side where she curled into a tight, comforting ball. It was no wonder she imagined strange smells after a day like this past one. Finally, though, everyone had been tucked into bed to fall fast asleep. Everyone that is, except her.

Maybe it was just the excitement of being in a new place that brought on this insomnia. On any given night at home in Atlanta, she'd be asleep before her head touched the pillow. Of course, there were the household duties, her teaching schedule at school, then later working one-on-one with Charlie, and the care of her family that beckoned her to sleep every night. And she did it without any help from David, thanks to his myriad excuses why he was a poor choice or simply didn't have the time. Or interest. But she chose not to dwell on that right now.

Last night, in this beautiful island house, she felt like she'd been running for a week straight, and yet, she wasn't the least bit sleepy when she collapsed into the four-post bed. She wasn't sleepy now either. There was just so much to do, so much to think about that her mind refused to settle down.

She closed her eyes and willed her body to sleep.

Her mind played pictures of Live oaks with fuzzy silver moss hanging from the branches. Then it was the house itself, the columns, the big picture windows, and the branches of the oak caressing the widow's walk that faced out over the sound. A head-to-toe investigation of the house proved to her the widow's walk sat perched over what was now the dining room. Take away a wall or two, and the living room, kitchen, and dining room combined could easily have been designed for parties— grand parties.

What kind of parties would they have been? Elegant ones for sure, large fancy ones with live music reverberating off tabby walls and flowing out among the lush green walled garden filled with palms, rare clove, olive trees, and the soft scent of blooming orange blossom, rose and magnolia.

The walls in the dining room, like the rest of the house, were made out of tongue-and-groove wood. But the thought was here, as clear as if she were standing next to the off-white, shell-cement wall of tabby. She reached out to touch it, to see if it was as real as it seemed. It was. She breathed deep the garden filled with fragrant blossoms and knew it was true.

The musicians touched talented fingers to instruments and made their music. Her feet tapped to the rhythm. How she loved to dance, she always had, but it had been such a long time. She looked around to see who else attended the party.

The men were quite handsome in their waistcoats and high collar shirts. Men from all over the world had come to this special place for a moment such as this. They lingered and charmed and held out hopes for future invitations, and there always were. The women were treated like royalty by their husbands, and they were treated like rare and fragile jewels by their suitors. Their long Empire gowns, made out of imported pastel silks, fell in soft trains behind them as they danced.

A hand touched her lightly on the shoulder.

Then, as quickly as it had appeared, the scene

shimmered and faded away.

Annie blinked and looked around the dark bedroom. The light of the full moon cast shadows across the antique furniture, and the intricate hand-carved woodwork spilled ominous shadows that hung and shimmered like unwelcome wraiths. A moment ago, she was at a party full of light, warmth, and infinite possibility. Now she lay quiet in the darkness of a rented house. Confusion filled her, no explanation of what just happened was immediately forthcoming, so she decided it was fatigue that led to the strange dream.

She sighed deeply and wiggled further into the feather pillows. This was an impressive house. She'd never seen one quite like it before and dared not think she'd ever be so lucky as to stay in one again. Tomorrow she'd walk every inch of the verandah, and when she was through, she'd walk it again. Later, after a little time with Charlie and his schoolwork, she'd pour herself a glass of wine and watch the sunset color the horizon behind the sound. That would be nice, real nice.

The people who owned this house were fools for renting it out. Not that she had any idea who owned it; Mr. Mann was quite clear the owner wished to remain anonymous, and wouldn't budge on any additional information even when she pushed him. If she owned this house, she would never let anyone have it, not for a month, not even a week. It would be hers and hers alone. A sanctuary, a place where imagination took hold and let the mind drift where it would, that's what this house would be if it were hers.

She tried closing her eyes again and decided that it was no use, might as well get up and be done with it.

Maybe fix something warm and soothing; hot cocoa might be nice. Easing out of the warm bed to the cool wood floors, she tussled with the dark fuzzy blue robe. She grabbed one end, twisted it around, then heard the sound of a tear, and knew that the hole in the armpit was larger. The old robe was so battered it was hard to know which way was the right way to wear it even in a well-lit room. It didn't really matter anyway since the old robe was comfortable and warm, and no one would see her in it outside family. Not that she could convince David of these attributes; she could rarely convince him of anything.

Every year for Christmas, her gift from David would be as much a surprise as the choice of shirt he wore to work—long sleeve, blinding-white, moderate starch, Oxfords. She peered through the dark at the lump of pillows in the bed. The lump could have just as easily been her husband for all the attention he paid her.

But that was then, and this was now in a whole new place that whispered adventure, and a personal mission: Project cocoa. She was doing something for herself, something she wanted to do without anyone staring at her or waiting for her to take care of their needs. This time was hers to do as she wished. In the quiet of the house. Her house.

At least for now.

She reached out until her hand touched rough, splintering wall, then followed it along to where she knew the door should be. Her ankle grazed the leg of a footstool, and it tottered. She knelt to stop its fall, then stood and felt for the wall again and gasped when her hand touched something icy-cold. Relief turned to a nervous giggle when she recognized the enemy as a narrow brass doorknob.

She cringed at the squeal of hinges needing oil then slipped quickly into the hallway.

With the door to the bedroom ajar, she listened for a moment. The narrow wooden stairs leading up to the small attic room groaned as if some unseen weight walked it. The door at the top remained firmly closed, and she reminded herself that Grandma would be safe there. The stairs would deter Grandma from unattended forays around the house, and the sparsely furnished room would protect her from injury if she should trip and fall. The rusted hinge, all that was left of an old lock, creaked when the heavy wooden door to the attic opened and closed. No one would be able to go in or out without being noticed, much like a hospital call buzzer.

It was quiet here. Not a creature was stirring, except for the house. She liked the quiet and the dark, and as soon as her eyes adjusted a little better, she would try the stairs that led to the foyer and the living room and finally to the kitchen beyond.

Turning on hall lights would be far more efficient, but it might stir Charlie, notorious for his light sleeping and sour moods when awakened suddenly. She had left him with a small nightlight, and the door to his room cracked so she could hear if he needed something. She tiptoed past Charlie's door, then stopped to listen. His breathing was deep, even, gentle enough for dreaming whatever little boys of ten dreamt about.

Annie held herself in check with the urge to go in and give him another goodnight kiss. He pushed away her attempts at affection so readily, waking him was not worth the days of acting out it would undoubtedly bring. Charlie had withdrawn into his own darkness for lesser crimes before. Maybe the toy she had left him to find in the morning would soften him a little. So she opted for a quick peek then cracked open his door another inch.

The next door was closed. It led to a room full of old books and connected to Charlie's room by way of a narrow passageway. The many wonderful books in the library were a bonus she hadn't expected, and she hoped Charlie would find the surprise equally pleasant.

He didn't. His refusal to even look at them, prompted no doubt by the pain of his reading problem, became another project they would have to work on. Still, it was nice to know the books were there in case he changed his mind.

Better the room was now a library than the nursery Mr. Mann said it used to be. Charlie was adamant; he was not a child anymore, and no one would win that argument with him. Annie had long since learned to pick her battles when it came to a child with special problems like Charlie.

She moved to the top landing and felt more than saw the sudden open and hollow expanse surrounding the foyer and the high ceiling of the living room. Her whispered "hello" barely echoed then fell away. Using her foot to gauge the distance of the landing's edge and the stairs' beginning, she took the first step. The next one was easier then the next, until she reached the middle landing and could release a held breath.

A human-like, misshapen figure loomed in front of her!

Annie gasped, stood frozen. Her throat tightened with words of bravado she didn't feel. "Who are you?"

The shadowy outline stood still.

"I've got a gun," she squeaked and fumbled for the pocket of her robe.

The figure fumbled with its pocket.

She blinked, squinted at the menace in front of her then lowered her arm.

It lowered its arm.

Raising her hand slowly in front of her face, she did the first thing that came to mind, she waved.

It waved.

With realization, she laughed out loud, then covered her mouth with the back of her hand and looked up the steps to see if anyone had heard. No one had. She looked back to where the figure had stood and shook her head at the sheer ludicrous turn of this event. Her reflection in the full-length mirror was as good as any hunchback imitation. She touched the wooden frame, the beveled glass within it, and met her reflected finger—just to be sure.

"It's a good thing you weren't a prowler," she told the mirror in her most stern voice while digging deep in the robe pocket. "Or I'd have been forced to use *this*." A wad of tissue wagged at the image in the mirror. "Sad, but true. You would have been wiped to death."

She continued down the steps until she reached the front door and stopped to peer through the stained glass windows on either side. The wind danced shadows from the eerie glow of the moon across trees in the yard to the road beyond, and turned the bright green sunlit shrubbery into shades of gray. Branches swayed by a touch of the breeze created shadow puppets of human-like forms. She shuddered at the sight then turned the brass knob to make sure the door was locked. It was.

She chastised herself at the silliness since the island had only a handful of inhabitants who all knew each other, but couldn't help an extra jiggle on the knob for good measure. A small current of air drifted in from under the door and tickled her toes then crept up along her body until it settled around her neck. She recoiled at the tickle then pulled her robe tight around her.

There was nothing to be afraid of. It was safer in the old island house than in the densely packed subdivision back in Atlanta. Whoever came up with the idea of safety in numbers never owned a house in Willow Bay, that's for sure. She didn't even know most of her neighbors, didn't care much for the ones she had met, and had yet to find the bay or the willow the development was named after.

The chill passed. Rational, logical thinking could be effective when the mind tended to wander. *Well, it sounded good anyway.*

She loosened her tight grip on the robe, felt it settle about her, and headed for the kitchen. Maybe she'd have Mr. Mann figure out how to fix the draft under the door the next time he was around. No sense in everybody coming down with summer colds.

Annie squinted against the bright lights then went to the sink to dig through the clean supper dishes until she found a coffee mug.

A glance out the picture window showed her morning was not far away. The reflection of the moon over the sound had begun to fade with the impending approach of dawn. Color was making a slow return to the foliage, and birds started their morning songs.

Cocoa, or considering the time, should it be coffee? She opened the first cabinet and spied the dark brown container, cocoa it would be. The gas stove popped into flame with a touch of her match, and she waited for the pot of water to come to boil.

What would her Atlanta neighbors be doing today in Willow Bay? *I don't really care.* Their lives were just as boring as hers, except now she was living in Manchester Place—even if it was only for a month or so. It was September, the end of one season, but it felt like the beginning of something other than a new season. A change of some sort had started, and whatever it was, she hoped it to be for the better.

Sinking back into one of the cane-backed oak chairs that surrounded the kitchen table, she propped her feet up on the edge of the old red brick hearth and listened to the house and the sounds of an island awakening.

Within the next week or so, those vacationers who remained on the island would pack up and leave; then her quiet would extend to the entire island. The vacationers would go back to their nine to five schedules, the kids back to school, and the husbands back to a life that didn't include their wives.

But what those people had to do didn't matter to her. What mattered was simply herself, Charlie and Grandma and their time together. They would be happy here at Manchester Place; she would make sure of it.

A new chill crept up her spine, tickled the hair on her neck, and brought back a memory of another drafty house, the house where she grew up. She closed her eyes tight, trying to force the angry faces and raised voices away, but they were there as clear as if they happened yesterday.

Her parents were fighting again. Her mother's

voice grew higher and higher until it became shrill and poisonous as the angry words her voice produced. Father stared at her as if she were a stranger, a dangerous intruder, and said nothing. His jaw tightened with her mother's escalating pitch and staccato verbal assault, tight, tighter until the muscles below his ears pulsed with rage.

In their combined fury, they had forgotten Annie was there. Pulling herself into a tight ball, she sank deeper into the armchair. Her pink polka dot dress was pulled and tugged until it covered her knees. She began to curl the hem back and forth, back and forth until tiny wet fingerprints stained and frayed the material. Maybe they wouldn't see her.

Mother's words battered Father, a flicker of pain crossed his eyes, the pain suddenly turned icy cold, detached. The look was all too familiar and meant a decision had been made. Father's decisions always turned into physical action.

He grabbed Annie by the arm and jerked her out of the chair, pulling her to him. Her arm seared with pain, but she didn't dare cry out. A soft trickle of tears oozed down her face. He stroked her hair, comforted her. She felt only roughness and a deep sick in her belly. His pent-up rage turned into a bellow then a torrent as if he had been saving the words for years.

Mother froze with the onslaught and looked away. Annie didn't want to see the hurt anymore, had never wanted to see it, but found she could not turn away from it now. It was her fault, wasn't it? Maybe if she had picked up her toys that morning, Mother and Father had told her to do so, this wouldn't be happening now.

Her fault, her fault, her fault. "I'm sorry," she mouthed, *but they weren't listening. Tears splashed onto the pink dress, made tiny stains with every drop, she looked at the dress then her feet. She gasped. Her parents stopped suddenly at the sound. Father loosened his grip around her then began to tremble.*

"Now look what you've done," Mother said. "You can't stop hurting us, can you?"

Annie toed the long brown strands of hair with her shiny black shoes as if she were an onlooker and not really there. The distance was comforting, safe, and then the dull ache started where her hair had been pulled out.

"You're not going to hurt me anymore. Or Annie." Her mother grabbed Annie's arm and pulled.

"Since when did you decide to be a mother to my child?" Her father grabbed her other arm. "It's too late now," he said through clenched teeth. "Too late. She's mine."

"No, please," Annie screamed. "I'm sorry. I didn't mean to."

"You'll never see her again," Mother said. "Never."

Annie shook her head, tried to erase the horrible moment of her childhood. "Come back, Daddy. Please. David...come back."

David? Where had that come from?

Fire leaped up from over the edge of a wall and reached heavenward. The cool water of the sound was just out of reach, and her feet hurt, burned almost. She smelled smoke.

I'll wait for you. The words were whispered, almost imperceptible, far away. *It's been taken care of.*

You'll see.

Annie bolted awake in the cane-back oak chair. Smoke billowed out of the empty pot on the stove. She grabbed the handle barehanded, flung the pot into the sink then turned off the gas flame. The pot sizzled when it met the cool dampness of porcelain, popped then sputtered and quieted.

She held on to the countertop, tried to calm the pounding in her chest. What was happening to her? First, the bitter memories of her long-buried childhood David didn't even know about and now whispered cryptic words in a voice she didn't know. And if that wasn't enough, she had practically burned the house down. At this rate, she would be completely useless by lunch.

Another glance at the clock told her that Charlie and Grandma would be up soon. Wiping a sweaty palm across her robe, she took a deep breath and decided breakfast and the usual morning rituals were the best courses of action.

There was too much to do around the house to be carried away by crazy thoughts. Routine had a way of keeping one's perspective intact.

Annie opened the refrigerator door and deliberated the menu. This was a special morning, being the first, and deserved a special breakfast.

Eggs, bacon, and scratch biscuits for Grandma, pancakes and syrup for Charlie, or would he want waffles? She'd make him both this morning. He deserved it.

And cocoa to drink, he'd like that. She reached into a cabinet and produced another pot.

"I'm going to watch you like a hawk this time."

She filled it with water, ignited the gas stove, and placed the pot over the blue-yellow flame.

The words rushed back to her then, stronger, loud.

It's been taken care of, you'll see.

Chapter 4

Charlie dreamed. Grandma pulled the quilt up under her chin and smiled. Animals. He was dreaming about all the animals he would tend to if he were a "peterinary," as he called it. Charlie liked cats the most. It was their independence and self-reliance that attracted him. He envied them so and wished he could be more like them.

"Grandma," when I grow up can I be a cat?" he had said,

"I don't think so, little one. Kittens grow up to be cats. Little boys grow up to be men. You know that."

"Yeah, I guess so. But it sure would be cool if I were a cat."

"Isn't it fun being a little boy?"

Wrinkles appeared across his forehead. She knew that meant he had to think a minute.

"Sometimes," he said slowly. "Not always. I think it would be more fun to be a cat."

"Draw me a picture of what you would look like if you were a cat."

Charlie scrambled for a piece of paper and a pencil. An outline was sketched first then a series of gray shading in various parts of the picture. He worked his tongue over chapped lips when he came to the more difficult detail of the drawing.

He always spent more time on the eyes than on

anything else, but the final rendering was always masterful and well beyond his years. What he couldn't express through written words or understand by reading, he more than made up for with his extraordinary talent in drawing.

He stood up from his place on the floor and rushed over to the mirror. Staring at his reflection for a moment, he had pulled his eyelids in various angles until he found the right expression, paused, then stuck his tongue out at himself before he headed back to his place on the floor.

The house in Atlanta had a carpeted floor.

Grandma blinked, stretched, and looked at the planked wood flooring of the simple small room she occupied now. This floor would be much too hard and cold for little boys to sit on.

She tugged at the quilt again and gathered the neckline of her heavy flannel nightgown. *Why would a room be so cold in the middle of the summer?*

The doctors said it was old age, her constantly being cold. Maybe it was, or maybe being in an attic of a house that was older than herself was the reason. One excuse or another, it was still cold, and it was dark, even with the light of early morning.

The only natural light came from a small, oval glass window across the room from the heavy wooden door. She had seen windows like that before, as a little girl growing up in Savannah, and knew they were never meant to be opened. Although the window was pretty enough with its natural distortion, the occasional bubble around the edge, and the barest hint of pink, it wouldn't allow enough light in to suit her.

She slipped a hand out from under the cover and

pulled the cord on a bedside lamp. The single bulb hissed, sputtered, and dropped yellow light around her. Dark, figure-like shadows occupied the corners and clung to the walls where the light failed to touch.

Hung from the ceiling was a strand of wires that ended in another lone bulb swinging with an unseen air current. It was if someone had set it in motion to taunt her then moved on. There was no switch in here to turn on the overhead light. Like in many attics, the switch was probably outside the door.

She was in the attic with its many narrow steps that were hard to climb and even harder to climb down. Annie knew how difficult it was—there were so many steps—yet she insisted Grandma stay in this place. It was dark here. She hated dark places and the secrets that seemed to hide there. Her preference was for light, lots of it, but Annie knew that, too.

Unless Annie didn't care. No, that wasn't true. Her daughter-in-law worried more about everyone else's well-being than her own. There was not a selfish, unkind bone in Annie's body, not one. It was David, who was the problem.

The money had not been enough to live on, her house ramshackle, and there were times when an hour or more would go by without any recollection of what had occurred. She didn't eat much and would eat less if need be, and the house kept the rain away for the most part, but as much as she tapped the side of her head and willed it to work right, things didn't get any better. Her only child, David, insisted on a nursing home, but Annie would hear nothing of it.

"Have you ever been in one of those places?" Annie had asked David. "They reek of urine and who knows what else."

"Are you suggesting she live here?" he asked incredulously.

"Where else? She needs someone to take care of her, to watch out for her."

"We have too many people here as it is."

"Your wife and your son make for too many people? David, if you want isolation, build an igloo in Iceland."

"This is my home. I don't want her here."

"David, she's your mother. Don't do this to her, to me. I will not let your mother rot in a seedy nursing home like you insisted my mother do. No amount of your fancy talk will sway me this time."

"Fine then. She'll live here, in the guest bedroom. And you'll take care of her. I don't want to know anything about it or be bothered in any way."

David and Annie didn't know Grandma had heard the conversation. They were unaware Grandma knew David's renege in coming to the island before he told anyone, or that Annie was about to get a letter that would change her life. They didn't know a lot of things about her and what she could do with what was left of her mind.

But Charlie did. He was the only one who bothered to ask, and more important, Charlie understood and accepted her the way she was because he could work his mind around things, too. So Annie cooked and cleaned for her, and David tolerated an occupant in the guest room.

Grandma rolled over in the small, wood-frame bed and curled into a ball. She rubbed her feet together for warmth that was not forthcoming and worried about her forgetfulness. Sometimes days would go by and she didn't even know it until later, until things got clear again. And the times when things got clear grew further and further apart. Forgetting was disturbing certainly, maybe even frightening to those who watched from the outside, but was it bad enough to warrant such hate from her son?

She was a burden to him, to them, and what better place for a burden than the attic.

The thoughts came to her then, quiet, like a whispered conversation in a faraway room. Her mind wrapped around them.

A packed box carted by the family from one location to the next, unopened, that's what she was. One day the box would be rediscovered, and with the excitement of Christmas morning, it would be opened and met with disappointment at what was inside. They would wonder why they had carried the box around for so long. Wonder why they had taken her in.

No. She refused to believe that. Annie and Charlie were family, they loved her, as did David in his own way, and she loved them. She couldn't help the way she was and tried to be more helpful, to be less of a problem, but sometimes her body refused to cooperate with her mind.

Awake, she sensed thoughts, feelings, but in her sleep, her mind played tricks on her. Pictures of things appeared from nowhere, with no warning, pictures she didn't understand. Sometimes they scared her, and other times she just forgot.

That was no reason for them to think of her as an old box filled with useless things, was it? There were so many things to tell them, to share with them. If only they would give her a chance.

If only she could remember what those things were.

And then it came to her, something strong and growing stronger, something dark like the shadows that hovered in the corner of her room.

The thing told Grandma she didn't belong.

She was an old box that needed discarding, a problem.

It hadn't come from Charlie, of that she was sure. David? She closed her eyes and tried to see him, but he was too far to reach now. She turned her attention to Annie and saw a flicker of disjointed memories and conflicting emotions that passed almost as quickly as they had come. The thoughts had not come from Annie.

Grandma's fists clenched into hard knots.

Where was it coming from? Here?

Yes.

There was something, someone in this house. Someone she didn't know.

Grandma? His thoughts touched her mind, clear and unmistakable.

Charlie?

I'm scared.

Chapter 5

"Coffee?"

Mann opened one eye to peer at his wife.

She stood at the bedside with a no-nonsense look in her eyes and a laden wicker breakfast tray in her hands. Steam billowed out of a mug, a pale-yellow froth of orange juice oozed over the side of a tall glass, while the rest of the containers held mixtures of yet undetermined liquid. "I said, coffee?"

"No, not right now, thank you. Maybe later."

"Good." There was triumph in her voice. "I brought you some of my special herb tea instead." She placed the tray over him and punched the corner of chintz-covered pillow near his head. "I had a feeling you wouldn't be wanting any coffee."

"I don't want any tea either. Especially not any of that herb stuff."

She straightened the matching chintz bedspread then tucked it securely around him like a strait-jacket.

"I'm telling you I don't want it," he said, pushing the tray away and kicking the bedspread. "That tea gets stuck in my teeth."

The tray came back. Glasses wobbled and clinked. "How in the world can tea get stuck in your teeth?"

"It's not the tea itself. It's those damn fool flowers you put in it."

He shoved the tray again, setting one glass into a

dangerous sway then sat up in bed. She caught the glass like a pro baseball player and held it firm until he had arranged himself.

"They gum up my teeth something awful." He frowned. "Practically have to use a crowbar to get 'em out again."

"Why not use a toothpick instead?"

"And if a body was to smile after drinking that stuff, he'd look like a walking botanical garden." Mann wrapped his arms across his chest and pushed his lower lip out in protest. "I'm not going to drink it."

Sybil leaned over him, hands on hips, and bared her teeth. "You *are* going to drink it. You're going to drink every drop on this tray. Besides, if you'd bothered to look, you would see that there's no wildlife in your tea. It's plain tea. No sugar, no cream. No flowers." Glaring, she slid the tray back in front of him. "Drink."

It was a command tone he knew, a non-negotiable order. If life as he knew it was to be on a more normal keel, there was no choice but to obey her command. He took a tentative sip of the tea, ran a tongue over his teeth to check for foliage, and decided what she said was true. The tea wasn't bad really, kind of bland, but definitely drinkable. He sucked down a long, liquid slurp for effect.

Her arms relaxed by her side. "There, you see? Tea. Plain and simple. Although the flowers would have been good for you, fiber you know." She busied herself, straightening up the room while throwing comments over her shoulder to him. "And when you're through with that, there's orange juice, pink grapefruit juice, and pineapple juice."

"What's the green stuff?"

"Honeydew melon juice."

Mann paused, mug suspended halfway to his mouth. "Honeydew melon?"

That did it. The mug slammed into the breakfast tray.

"I'm sorry, Syb, but I draw the line there. No green melon mush is passing these lips."

Her back stiffened, and that meant war. He was ready for battle stations.

"Where in the hell did you get it anyway?"

"I made it."

"Oh." Now the words would have to be chosen carefully. "I'm sure it's wonderful, a real culinary treat. Perhaps when I'm feeling more myself I'll be better able to judge its fine qualities."

He picked up the glass and eased it onto the bedside table—out of sight, out of mind. First, to the bedside table, then out of the room.

"I just hate to waste it, you know, not feeling well and all."

"Drink."

"Syb, darling, be reasonable. There's enough liquid here to fill a fish tank."

She spun on her heel toward him. Anger lashed out as if she directed a bolt of lightning at him through her pointed arthritic finger.

"And just how reasonable were you last night?" Her head shook, her finger wagged, and her mouth struggled for the right words. "There you were, lying on the floor, as cold and wet as if you'd just stepped out of a shower."

"Well, that explains these pajamas."

"At first you didn't say anything then when you did

start talking, Richard and I couldn't understand a word you said. Neither could the doctor. A bunch of nonsense is what it was."

"Don't be angry with me. Please. I wouldn't hurt you for anything; you know that."

The tension in her face relaxed a notch. She stared at her outstretched accusing finger as if it were the first time she had ever seen it, clenched her fist, loosened it then dropped her hand to her side. "I'm not angry, just scared. You scared me last night, Winston. Do you know what that feels like?" Her voice softened.

"Well, I—"

"Don't interrupt. I'm not finished." Sybil sat on the edge of the bed to caress his feet through the bedspread. "I was afraid that you had…that something horrible had happened, that I was going to be alone."

She cleared her throat and sat up straighter. Ever so slightly, her chin jutted out. He knew she was pushing the incident out of her mind in preparation for more important issues.

"The doctor said it was the heat. Dehydration. That you needed to rest and drink."

"I'll take a scotch on the rocks."

"You know what I mean. The doctor said drink, and that's what you're going to do. Juice, not alcohol. He said, 'push fluids,' and that's what I'm going to do."

"You're saying he gave you the okay to be pushy?" He grinned at her but got nothing in return. "All right. I'll finish the tea. I'll even drink the pink grapefruit juice. But I will not, and get this, Syb, I will not drink the melon-honey whatever it is. That green stuff."

"Fine."

"Good. At least that's settled."

"I'll make banana-raisin juice instead. It'll be good for you."

"You're kidding, aren't you?"

"I'm kidding."

"Good."

"Fine." She patted his feet then picked threads that had crept out from the seams of the bedspread. "Winston?"

"Hmm?"

"You're not hiding anything from me, are you?"

"Hiding anything?" He looked deep into the dark tea and hoped he could still maintain the legendary poker face while her eyes bore holes into him. Maybe she wouldn't notice his hands shook. "No. Why do you ask?"

"Just something the doctor said, mumbled, under his breath last night." She pulled a thread. The material gathered then she smoothed it out again. "He listened to your heart a long time. At least it seemed that way to me. There's nothing wrong, is there?"

He forced a smile. "Nothing the fountain of youth couldn't cure."

From the look in her narrowed eyes, she wasn't buying it.

"Aw, c'mon, honey. Doc was just doing his job. You know how those young guys are. They just keep looking and looking until they find something. This time it was being out in the sun a bit too long."

Doubt lingered on her face.

"It was probably everything he could do to stay awake while he examined me."

"All right, Winston. I believe you." Her tone of voice and expression proved she would be a lousy poker player. "That is until you can think of something better." She stood up with one last tug and a pat to the bedspread.

"There is one thing, Syb."

Her body tensed as if preparing for bad news.

"Did you happen to find a piece of paper in the library? Near where you found me?"

"Piece of paper? What kind of paper?"

"Nothing important. A shopping list." He bit his lip at the poor lie, so much for poker. "It was written in a red marker of some kind."

"A shopping list?"

He nodded.

"Written in red?"

He nodded again then shrugged.

"Winston Mann, since when have you ever written out a shopping list? You wouldn't know a shopping list if it flew up and hit you in the face."

"It's not my list."

Her eyebrows shot up.

He would have to think fast over this one. "It's Mrs. Cameron's. She gave it to me yesterday. Some things she needed. I better attend to it right away."

The covers whipped back with a crack, and he popped up on the side of the bed like a jack-in-the-box.

"You're not going anywhere, mister." Standing in front of him like a fortress, she dared him to move. "No. Where. Got it? Besides, Richard has taken *Errand Two* over to the mainland. Nice boy, Richard, even if he is almost a lawyer. Ought to be in town about now as a matter of fact. Now *he* has a shopping list. Anything he forgets, and Mrs. Cameron needs in a hurry, I'll pick up at Kenzie's. The miserly old goat. And that filthy place he has the nerve to call a store."

"You're sure you never saw the, uh, shopping list?"

"Honestly, Winston. Do you think I'd give one whit for a piece of paper, with you lying unconscious on the floor? No, I haven't seen it, and aren't you glad about that? You could have been a stone by now if I'd decided to rush out and stock up on canned peaches instead of attending to you."

"I'd better check the library."

Sybil stood tall and silent. With a slow, deliberate movement, she walked over to an armchair and pulled it across the floor until it sat almost touching the edge of the bed. She eased herself into it and folded her hands under her chin.

His gaze held hers until he finally had to turn away. The grandfather clock struck the half-hour with a soft resonant chime. Its sound vibrated and echoed through the house then dissipated into silence.

"The paper. What is it?"

"Nothing. Just—"

"No." A half-smile appeared on her lips. "You can't fool me. I know you better than that."

He leaned toward her. "It was a message. Written in crayon and tucked into a book where I was sure to find it." His throat tightened. "But I didn't, Syb. I didn't find it until last night. If I had found it twenty-seven years ago, maybe—" His voice cracked. "Maybe Phillip would be here today. He was asking for help. He needed me, and I wasn't there."

"What makes you think the message was from Phillip?"

"There's no doubt in my mind. I know his

handwriting."

Sybil kneaded the skin on the back of her hand and shifted in the chair, leaning to one side, then back to the other. A myriad of emotions crossed her face but passed too quickly for him to read, or guess, what she thought and felt. Her hand turned red from the ceaseless rubbing; it would bruise by tomorrow.

"It was an accident."

"But suppose it wasn't. Suppose—"

"An accident, Winston."

The kneading came faster, harder. His hand ached as he watched her movements.

"That's all it was. An accident."

"How do you account for the message?"

"A joke."

"A joke?"

"Someone put it there as a joke. To catch you off-guard."

"C'mon, Syb," he pleaded. "You don't believe that. I know you don't."

"And what would you have me believe? That you should have stopped the boat from crashing into the rocks?" Her eyes narrowed to slits; her voice rose higher with every word. "How were you going to do that, Winston? Tell me. How?"

He raised his hands weakly from his lap then dropped them back. "I don't know."

"Besides, if Phillip knew he was in trouble, why didn't he just tell you?" Her voice became strained with emotion. Her eyes darted this way and that as if trying to find and grasp something elusive, something kept hidden for years. "Why didn't he tell *me*? Why the message?"

"I don't know."

He rubbed a dry hand through his gray hair—it was so thin now, so old and brittle—and wondered after all these years if Sybil was strong enough for this conversation. Was she ready now to place the blame where it really belonged?

"I was gone a lot then. Remember?"

Sybil rubbed her eyes, her temples.

"The storm was all but on us, and I was out getting things ready for it. I didn't see him much. And when I did...it was too late."

"Are you telling me Phillip knew what was going to happen to him?"

"Maybe. Maybe not. I don't know. There's one thing I do know. Something scared him bad enough to make him run. He tried to leave, to get away, but he didn't make it." Mann paused then tried to prepare for her reaction when he told her. "*She* kept him here, Syb. Somehow—I don't know how, she kept him. Then she killed him. It had to be her."

Sybil leaped out of her seat and paced the room. "Oh, for God's sake, Winston. Have you listened to yourself, really listened? You're talking like a madman. First, it's some kind of cryptic message found in a book; now it's murder committed by a dead woman. I suppose, next you'll be telling me that the Ghost of Christmas Past is sitting right here in our bedroom. Maybe even in my lap, and I just haven't realized it yet."

He looked away from her piercing stare and the angry words and concentrated on the hypnotic, almost insistent rhythm of the Grandfather clock.

Tick...tick...tick.

The mechanism moved on oiled gears, hummed softly, and released its sound.

Tick...tick...tick.

Maybe Sybil wasn't ready to think through the step-by-step events of that night. Perhaps this conversation was best left for another time or, maybe, not at all.

"Don't." The word was quiet, ominous, one tick of the clock. "Skeletons belong in closets. Not out in the open where we can see them."

"Or face them?"

"What's done is done. It's over. Almost two hundred years now. Nothing left of her but an entry in the family bible."

"Three entries. Hers, the boy, and Phillip." Only it wasn't three anymore; it was four. And Sybil could never know about the last one.

"Let them alone, Winston. Let them rest."

"But she can't rest, can she? She always wants more."

"I don't believe that."

"You have to," Mann said. Sybil had to believe because it was true, as true for her as for the woman on the park bench dressed in black.

"I don't have to anything." Sybil's chin jutted out. Her cheeks, pale minutes ago, flushed pink with new rage. "I won't believe that some dead woman reached a hand from the grave and took my son. It was a boating accident. Nothing more."

She reached past him to pick up the tray, moved to the door then stopped.

"Please, don't do this to yourself. To us. To me."

He nodded, then forced a smile.

"Get some rest. I'll be in to check on you after a while."

The door closed behind her.

A hand from the grave. Or was it more than that?

He walked over to the window, blinked at the bright sunlight that streamed into the room, and made the flowers on the wallpaper dance then looked out over Lullaby Sound. The floating dock that tethered *Errand Two* when it was home, bobbed with gentle waves.

It was a view much like this that she would have seen. By night she paced the widow's walk to look for a boat bearing a lantern, a boat that would bring her husband back to Manchester Place after years at sea.

He had no choice but to seal the door to the widow's walk. By hiding it behind plasterboard and wallpaper, he had made it safe. No one could get up there now. No children with prying fingers, not even an adult with a crowbar could get up there. No one. They would be safe.

At least he hoped so.

Chapter 6

Grandma? Charlie called to her in his mind.
I'm scared.

Glowing yellow eyes stared at him from the dresser. He lay still, afraid to move lest the thing would get him. The eyes wiggled on currents of cold air drafts from a rock fireplace near his bed. The damper clattered up and down in a hollow, tinny sound in the chimney. His gaze never wandered from the glowing eyes. He hoped more than anything if he didn't move, the thing connected to the eyes wouldn't move either.

He blinked at the early morning light that filtered in through high beveled windows and stopped short long before the thing on the dresser could be fully revealed. The eyes were the thing to watch, always the eyes. Rubbing a sweaty palm across the front of his red pajama top, he felt more of the superheroes picture peel off. A superhero, just about any of them, would be good to have around about now. But no superheroes were available except for those left in the group picture on his pajama top, and most of their vital parts had long since peeled off.

There was no one left then, except him.

And the thing with the eyes.

He needed a plan and quick. Maybe he could slide out of bed before the thing knew what happened and scoot out the door to the hallway. *Yeah, that might work.* Tightening his body like a coiled spring, he got ready to jump then stopped. Going out the main door to the hall meant passing dangerously close to the dresser and the thing. It was too lethal a mission. He flopped back into the bed.

He spied the fireplace, considered crawling up the chimney, but gave up the idea almost immediately for fear of getting stuck. Next plan.

The book room through the alcove next to his room might work. He could creep out of bed, sneak past the dresser then bolt down the skinny hall that connected his room to where all the books were. This plan had possibilities.

Looking at the dark alcove that led to the book room, he considered the move. Once he made it there, it was a simple matter of racing down the hall steps, then out the front door, and as far away from the glowing yellow eyes as possible. If he timed it right, he could be out of there in nothing flat. Piece of cake, no problem, and the thing with the eyes as well as all those books would be far behind him. As difficult as reading books were, it was as good a reason for escape as the thing with the eyes. If he couldn't be caught, his mother couldn't make him read.

Gauging the distance between the old bed and the floor, he knew he would have to jump. The high bed practically needed a stool just so he could climb into it; getting out would be more challenging. First jump, then run, then never look back. But he would need his glasses to make the most of this plan. Reaching under his pillow, he felt for his glasses, found them, and slid them onto his nose.

Enough morning light had filled the room now so

that if he squinted hard, he could make out more detail on the thing. It was small, fuzzy, and along with the eyes, a mouth with a big toothy grin.

A paper mouth.

It was a toy with eyes that ogled him then bounced independently of one another. The eyes were on stalks of some sort, maybe pieces of coiled metal. A toy. Relief turned to anger.

It's a toy, Grandma, he shouted in his mind, nothing but a stupid toy.

He balled up a sock and tossed it at the creature that tumbled to the floor with the impact and released a high-pitched, hysterical laugh.

The stupid toy laughed at him.

He cringed behind a blanket then pulled it tight over his head.

The laugh changed pitch, became lower, then high again. With a scratching sound, it finally stopped.

Charlie listened for a moment to the silence then slowly lowered the blanket from his face. The fuzzy thing, it was blue maybe, or green, fell over on its side, one eye staring dully at the ceiling, the other eye vibrating on the end of the coil for a moment then stopping to fix its unblinking gaze on him.

This was not one of the toys he had brought from home. And never in a million years would he have ever asked for something as lame as that.

It was green, definitely; he could see that now in the growing light. The short, stubby toy body was covered with fuzzy green hair, kind of like a troll, but the laughing, that was something he'd never heard before.

A note hung from the green thing. Holding onto the

headboard, he twisted his body from one side to the other until his toes touched the floor. He smoothed out his bunched up pajamas top, felt another piece of the superheroes picture flake off then approached the toy with cautious steps. Eyeing it from all sides, he decided it was probably harmless and picked up the toy. His face wrinkled in concentration, his lips moved to make sense of the words on the note:

To Charlie,
Thought you could use a good laugh. Surprise!
Love,
Mom

She had left the thing after he had gone to sleep. Looking at the tag underneath the note, he mouthed the name of the toy.

Gig...ga...les. Gig-les. Giggles. Mr. Giggles.

A stupid toy with a stupid name and it was a stupid trick to make him read. He slammed the toy on the dresser, then covered his ears to drown out the raucous laughter that filled the room.

It was laughing. *Laughing.* He hated it when people laughed at him. Toys were even worse, and this toy was the worst of all. It was a mean laugh, a knowing laugh, like the toy somehow knew all his mistakes, his problems, and was teasing him with the grating sound.

"I'm not dumb. I'm not!" he shouted at the laughing toy.

He talked over it; he sang; he tried everything he could think of to distract himself from the paper grin, the eyes—*did the toy just wink?*—and the horrible laughing.

"Stop!"

It did.

Slowly, he released the grip over his ears and glared at the intruder that sat on the dresser, wishing he could throw it away. But any movement might make it laugh again, so he didn't dare disturb it.

"I will never touch you again, Mr. Giggles. And you'll never laugh at me again."

The toy sat motionless. Eyes at the end of their wire coils stared at him.

"I hate you."

The toy sat.

He had to get out, had to think about this new problem. Charlie slid out of his pajamas and into a worn pair of jeans and a camouflage T-shirt. After jumping into his sneakers, he crossed the Velcro straps then bolted for the door to the main hall.

"Where are you headed in such a hurry?"

The rubber of his shoes squeaked on the wood floor. With a shrug, he came to an abrupt stop in front of his mother.

"Breakfast is ready. Pancakes and waffles. I bet you're starving." She leaned over to kiss him.

He backed away from her. "Can I go outside?"

"Now? You haven't eaten yet."

"Not hungry."

"C'mon, Charlie. Just a bite or two?"

"Not now."

"What about your schoolwork? We can't get behind."

"Later. I promise."

She hesitated, then ruffled his hair. "Well, all right. But be careful."

He nodded then half-ran, half-jumped, down the

steps to the middle landing, using the smooth oak banister for leverage.

"Don't forget to come in for lunch," she yelled.

Catching a glimpse of himself in the landing mirror, he was glad Mom didn't have a comb handy or remembered he needed a bath.

With a great leap to the foyer floor, he grabbed the handle to the front door, twisted the lock, and scrambled to the porch. Another jump from the weather-beaten wooden porch to the soft sand three feet below landed him on hands and knees. He pulled himself up, rubbed his hands across his thighs, then spat out salty sand that clung to his lips and tongue.

Charlie looked left and right down the long, perfectly straight, dirt road that fronted the house and the bayside of the island. Then listened for the sound of oncoming cars. There was no sound, no activity of any kind, except the wind whispering through the moss-laden Live oaks that lined the road. Maybe tomorrow he'd explore where the road went, or find the path that led to the ocean. Today he would check out the bay.

He turned the side of the house, walked the circumference of the huge oak tree that hung branches over the widow's walk, and slapped the fronds of tapered palms on his way. The thin yellow-green leaves of the palms bounced at his touch and rustled softly as they resumed their original shape.

Densely packed trees and underbrush gently gave way to smaller, sparse growth and grasses as he neared the water. Bright morning reflected the sun in the bleached sand, and he squinted. The white sand that seemed to cover everything was so different from the rich, dark, dead smelling stuff his mother bought at the nursery to put around her houseplants, or the red clay that surrounded Atlanta. The sand was everywhere, white sand with green plants and trees and grasses growing from it.

The tread of his sneakers left a clear, crisp imprint in the white ground. This would be a hard place to play spy or hide and seek.

A glimmer of something shiny caught his eye. A small metal piece peered out from the earth a few feet ahead. He ran to it, but the resistance of his shoes in the dense sand pulled and slowed him down.

Pouncing, he examined the object closely. It was a coin of some sort with a picture of a lady on one side and some kind of flower on the other. About the size of a dime, it didn't look like any dime he'd ever seen before.

Charlie tried to read the writing on it but gave up deciding that the sun was too bright for reading, and tucked the coin into his jeans pocket for safekeeping. Or until he could find a gumball machine that took funny coins. Brushing sand off his hands, he headed toward a steep embankment that led to the water.

The air was cooler here, more wet. A thin mantle of sticky moisture covered his face as he approached the crest of the embankment. The smell of salt and dead fish forced him to pinch his nose closed while he looked around for the source of the potent odor. Sand shifted under his feet. He sank in the damp sand, stepped back out of instinct when his feet suddenly went out from under him.

Twisting and writhing with the sudden downward movement, he grabbed anything that would stop the fall. There was nothing. His eyes widened, his mind tried to register the cause of this event. There was no time; it was happening too fast.

He looked down. The dark water of the bay loomed in front of him, rose to meet his fall.

The undercurrent. Someone had said something about dangerous waters.

He grabbed sand clotted with black algae, long blades of grass that poked from the slimy surface, anything to stop the inevitable fall into water. His feet, now unrecognizable with the covering of muck, dug into the pliant ground in a futile effort to stop the slide.

A tree root rose out of the soil like a cobra rearing its head and snagged his pants. His momentum slowed, and the sound of tearing material punctured the air. Dampness crept down his leg and he knew that the double strength knee patch on his jeans was gone for good. He hoped his mother wouldn't be mad.

The root twisted and turned as his body bumped over the gnarled wood. Skin tore and abraded at every touch of the root. Coarse sand crept through his clothes and covered the wounds with burning salt.

The root, now free from his body, lashed out with a stinging blow to his face and scratched his glasses. He grabbed the root with both hands and clung to it. It cracked and threatened to break, but his fall abruptly stopped short with a jerk. Air caught in his lungs released in the beginnings of a relieved sigh.

Then the root broke.

He fell another foot, maybe half a foot and collapsed in a heap on the shore. Breath came in painful gasps while he scavenged for his glasses then surveyed his position. He rubbed the sore place on his face; the swelling had already started and stared up at the hill where he had stood just seconds ago. The embankment was a good ten feet high if he guessed right, maybe higher. He marveled at the uneven track his body had taken on its way down and that he escaped worse injury.

Charlie's breathing slowed, and the stinging in his face lessened. There was one thing for sure, he wouldn't take that route again anytime soon, even if it meant walking clear around the island to get home.

Small waves, as if made by a boat, washed up on the shore with quiet lapping noises. He was surprised to see the water only four or five feet away. Minutes before it had seemed closer, ominous somehow. Now it was different. Now it was warm, peaceful looking and almost inviting.

A small, conical shell twitched, stopped then cautiously moved again. Thin, brown, pointy legs sprouted from under the shell, followed by the thicker crab body. Charlie pushed his glasses up on his nose, grinned then poked the crab with his finger. It disappeared into the shell then moments later emerged again. Hesitant at first, the creature crept across the beach sideways with the shell firmly planted on its back, and paused now and then for a look around with its stalk eyes.

The crab lived in a shell house that it carried wherever it went. Cool.

His wounds forgotten, Charlie watched the crab inch its way to an empty seashell and begin to fondle it. The spindly legs reached inside the shell, felt around, then did the same to the outside. Over and over, the crab repeated its action until it seemed satisfied with the results. In a fraction of a second, the crab hoisted its body from its own shell and moved into the new one. Charlie watched the crab make its way down the beach to disappear into shallow water.

Really cool.

He picked up the abandoned shell and shook it to see if anything fell out. When nothing did, he held it to the scratched lens of his glasses and looked inside. It was clean and smooth, unlike its marred and chipped surface.

Maybe the crab was too big for the smaller shell, or maybe the crab was just looking for something a little better, a change of some sort. Charlie considered keeping the shell for a souvenir but decided to give it back to the beach in case another crab came by looking for a change. He dropped it in the sand and walked down the narrow shoreline of the bay.

Even crabs needed a change now and then. If it was all right for them, maybe it was a good thing for him too. His mother had said their lives were in a rut, so like the crab, his family changed houses, too. But it was only for a little while, and when everything was fixed at home, they'd go back.

He stopped at the gaping mouth, and fixed eyes of a half-eaten fish that had drifted to shore then kicked sand over it. Tiny crabs ran for cover from his sand storm. Some of the crabs wielded a single giant claw, and others had nothing but a regular old leg.

If he were a crab, he would want to be one with a claw; then maybe people would listen to him now and then. If they didn't listen, he'd pinch them until they did. That would show them. He'd even pinch his parents if he thought it would make a difference.

He continued down the shore, prodding clumps of

grass with his shoe.

If he were king of the crabs, he would make sure that his grandma had a claw, too. She needed one almost as bad as he did. Maybe more than he sometimes did. A pang of guilt at not stopping in to see her before he left nagged. Grandma liked to hear about his plans for the day.

And on the days she couldn't talk very well, he could see the interest by the way her eyes crinkled. Sometimes her mind and her mouth wouldn't work together right. Other times he couldn't get the words out himself. But they still talked, sometimes only with their minds, but there was always lots to say.

When he got home, he would see her, tell her about his day, and how he fell. And about the crabs.

A boat tethered to a dock up ahead bobbed with the rhythmic waves of Lullaby Sound. As he got closer, he recognized it as the one that brought his family to the island. Mr. Mann had called it *Errand Two*. Charlie wondered what the name meant and tried to remember to ask Mr. Mann about it some time.

"Hello there."

Charlie spun on his heel. A tall man, with two or three days' worth of beard, smiled.

Richard's smile disappeared. "Good gravy, boy. What happened to you?"

Charlie backed up a few steps and looked down at his torn and dirty clothes. He rubbed a mud-streaked hand over his face. The stinging started again. An ache in his back traveled to his legs. He was hurt worse than he thought, or he must be since the man seemed to think so.

Richard stretched out his hand and waited.

Charlie nodded almost imperceptibly, and laid his muddy hand into the warm, strong one.

"We'll get you fixed up before you know it, young man. Looking good as new."

Chapter 7

"Richard? Bring my medicine kit, will you? It's on the bottom shelf underneath the bathroom sink. Oh, and some clean towels. Lots of them."

Sybil turned to the muddy child who sat before her and clucked under her breath while tilting his chin up for a closer look at his face. "Word, boy. You are one mess. Now don't even think about crying. Auntie Syb is here to fix you up before you know it."

She patted the top of Charlie's head then wiped her muddied hand across the front of the flowered apron covering her green house dress. "Richard? What in the world is keeping you so long? Richard!"

Richard's voice sounded muffled as if he were shouting from a closet. "I don't see a medicine kit. Where'd you say it was?"

"Under the sink. Next to the johnny brush. The towels are in the hall closet. Be quick about it; there are folks waiting."

She ran water into a big iron kettle and put it on the stove to boil. "A dab of aloe on those scratches and a cup of my herb tea will make you as fresh as the day you were born."

Sybil eyed Charlie wondering what had happened and decided she'd find out soon enough. She had a knack of getting the truth out of people, sometimes without them realizing they had said a word. This boy had a lot to say. Plenty to say if she guessed right and she always guessed right. All this child was missing was a sympathetic ear and a shoulder to lean on. Her shoulders were big enough for Winston, the child, and then some. There was even one to spare for Richard if he ever needed it, but ever since he started law school, he didn't seem to need anything. Where was Richard anyway? Couldn't he see that she had a job ahead of her?

"Richard. Get in here—"

"Found it, Mrs. Mann. I didn't know you could put so much under a bathroom sink."

"What I have under my sink is of no concern to you. Soak some of those towels in warm water. You can start on his hands. I'll take his face."

She reached for a washcloth and rubbed it across Charlie's forehead. Tears sprang to his eyes at her touch, but he didn't make a sound or try to move away. It was almost as if he had given up and had lost what little fight was left in him.

Had it been a fight that caused all those wounds? She looked at his slight frame, the jeans, and T-shirt that clung to it, and ruled out that possibility. He wasn't the type to settle arguments with his fists; he was an intellectual sort, a boy who did his fighting with his head, or, better yet, avoided confrontations completely. Besides, the injuries looked like the result of a particularly, arrogant briar. That, and a roll in the mud to loose himself from thorns would account for the mess.

"Richard, see if you can't find an old shirt or something in the box out there in the carport. I will not let this boy sit here a minute longer in wet clothes." The screen door slammed. She caught Charlie's slight movement, as if to protect himself from her plans.

"Don't worry, son. The clothes out there are old, but they're clean. The ones you're wearing will be safe in a plastic bag until we can give them a good washing."

"This okay?" From the other side of the screen door, Richard held up a faded red and blue flannel shirt with the pocket torn off.

"Perfect. Bring it in." She turned to Charlie and whispered the confidence. "Washed that one in hot water by mistake. Winston would have to lose fifty pounds to squeeze into it now. Hardly worth it, don't you think? So I've just acted like it disappeared into thin air."

She reached for the warm, wet cloth and approached his chin with a softer touch. It was then that she realized he hadn't said a word since he'd been in her kitchen.

"What's your name?"

Nothing, he uttered not a sound and acted as if he hadn't heard her. Richard had been no help at all with the child's name, remembering only that of his mother.

"I know you have one. And I'll bet it's a nice name." Dropping the soiled washcloth on the table, she reached for a clean one then started on the side of his face with light, slow strokes. "Do you like cats?" A flicker across his eyes, maybe? "We had a cat once. His name was Scram. Scram was a big orange tom-cat."

She glanced sideways at Richard to remind him she needed help in the cleaning. He moved to her side and reached for Charlie's hand.

Distance crept back to the boy's eyes; she would

have to work harder.

"Would you like to hear a story about Scram and a suitcase?"

A slight nod.

"All right then. And when we're through talking, we'll have some hot tea and some fresh gingerbread right out of the oven. Sound good?"

Another nod.

"Fine."

Sybil finished with his face and started on his neck while keeping up the monologue with the enthusiasm of a college cheerleader at a homecoming game. With a final dab of aloe applied to a scratch on his chest, she stood back, hands on hips, and surveyed the results.

"Not bad if I do say so myself. Now, we'll use what buttons are left on this old shirt, roll up the sleeves, and there you are. Feel better?"

He nodded tentatively, and squeaked a barely audible "yes."

"Good."

She stuffed the dirty shirt into a bag and put it in the corner. The boiling water in the kettle on the stove whistled then whined. She switched the heat off and reached for a mug.

"Time now for some of my herb tea. And some of that gingerbread I promised you."

"Don't do it, Syb."

She turned to the sound. Anger rose at the sight of Winston standing in the doorway. Hadn't she been forceful enough in her command he stay in bed and rest? A tirade of words came to her lips, but she held them when she saw recognition and relief cover Charlie's face at the sight of her husband.

"Hello, Mr. Charlie," Winston said. "Good to see you again." He scrutinized the dirty towels, the medicine kit, and the boy's clothes. "Sure is a nice shirt you're wearing. Used to have one like it myself. But I'll be damned if I can figure out where it got to. You have any idea, Syb?"

"Not a one."

"Didn't think so. How 'bout you, Richard?"

Richard looked at Sybil for any hint of how to answer, saw none. "I plead the fifth, Mr. Mann."

"Yes, I imagine you do. Well, it doesn't matter, I suppose. I guess me and Mr. Charlie here happen to have the same fine taste in clothing."

Sybil stepped to the oven to pull out the gingerbread. So the boy's name was Charlie. At least that mystery was solved. She flipped the gingerbread out of the pan, sliced it into large squares then scooped three pieces onto individual plates. A mug of tea and a plate slid to the table in front of Charlie.

"The wife's gingerbread is the best anywhere. I'm only glad I got here in time to save you from the herb tea."

Charlie scrutinized the mug of steaming tea.

"Charlie knows me as Auntie Syb," she said.

Mann's eyebrows shot up then a half-smile formed on his lips.

Sybil glared at him. "There is not a thing wrong with my herb tea except that *Uncle* Winston doesn't like it."

"It's not just me, Syb," Mann said, with a defensive edge in his voice. "Richard said himself he only tolerates it because it makes you happy."

Her gaze shifted to Richard.

He squirmed then stepped back until the wall blocked his retreat. A kitchen-witch hanging from a ceiling hook swayed in a long lazy arc and batted him in the head.

Richard grimaced, developed a small tic in his right eye, but didn't move away as he spluttered an excuse. "That's not completely true, Mrs. Mann. I think the tea is great."

She glared at him as he fidgeted with a button on his shirt.

"I mean, I think it's nice." He twirled the button this way and that.

Sybil snorted.

The button popped off Richard's shirt and rolled across the floor. He made no move to retrieve it.

"All right, then. It's okay. I think I'd like it better if it didn't have all those flowers floating around in it."

"There. You hear that?" Mann said with triumph in his voice. "The man said he didn't like the flowers. If you can't trust a lawyer, who can you trust?" He pulled out a chair from under the kitchen table and sat. "Tea's okay. If you like such. Problem is," he tapped his front tooth with a fingernail, "flowers get stuck in your teeth. You tend to look like a walking vegetable garden. You ever see a human squash, Charlie?"

Charlie shook his head and grinned.

"How about a human tomato or walking cucumber?"

Charlie giggled.

"I say we all have lemonade instead. Sound okay to you?"

"Sounds great to me, Mr. Mann," Richard said, then quieted at the look on Sybil's face.

"I'm not talking to you, Richard," Mann said. "How 'bout it, Charlie?"

"Um-hm."

"What's that you say, young man?"

"Yes, sir, Mr. Mann. I mean, Uncle Winston."

The smirk on Mann's face became plastic.

Sybil suppressed a laugh, waited for a second or two, and his cheerfulness was restored. "Okay, you talked me into it. Lemonade all around." She shot one last look at Richard. "You can join us at the table if you like, but I'd be a little careful about the first sip. You never know what I might slip into my potions."

Lemons were carefully lined up on the counter next to the sugar, and she started in.

"I can't lie about the gingerbread, Mrs. Mann," Richard said. "You make the best."

Her hands went to her hips at Richard's empty plate. "Didn't your mother ever tell you to chew your food at least a hundred times? What would your colon say if it could talk?"

"Now, Syb. Don't get started," Mann said.

"Don't know, Mrs. Mann," Richard said, winking at Charlie. "Guess I never asked it."

He pressed the remaining crumbs onto his fingertips, then licked them with exaggerated relish.

Charlie laughed then mimicked the behavior with equally liquid noises.

Winston watched the two of them in mock outrage, but she knew there was laughter in his eyes. He was enjoying himself, and down deep, she knew he wished for a little boy at his table every day.

Richard was as near to a son as they had now, but he had come to Mico Island, a young adult considering a future in biology, and ended up staying through his off-time from law school. He said he stayed because of the island life, but his real-life had become Winston and herself. And their lives had become dependent on his friendship and love as well.

As special as Richard was, she wished for a little boy at this table again, too. She dabbed at the angry, red scrapes on Charlie's face with a cloth then stroked his hair.

He pulled away ever so slightly, looked up at her, then returned his gaze to the empty plate in front of him.

The hollowness in her stomach filled with a sudden surge of emotion at the emptiness in his eyes. He was lonely, problem-plagued it seemed, but there were also the seeds of trust in him. She saw that trust and felt grateful. Whatever it was she had done to earn that trust, she would try that much harder to keep it. He needed her, and somehow, over the past hour, she had grown to need him.

She cleared her throat of the tightness that had gathered there. "I don't need to ask if anyone wants another piece. I can see it for myself."

There were nods all around and mock moans of ecstasy as she slid the gingerbread on the plates.

"One hundred chews a mouthful. I'm counting."

Richard stretched a foot under the table and made an empty chair move as if by the hand of a poltergeist. When they all turned to see the cause of the sudden movement, Richard whisked away Charlie's plate and hid it.

Charlie glanced back to find his plate missing and stoic expressions of disbelief from the men. When the plate was replaced, Charlie wolfed down his piece and shot the men a doughy grin for their efforts.

"I won't be having you boys act like a bunch of no-mannered animals," Sybil said, knowing they hadn't heard a word she said, and not really caring.

It had been years since she'd taken the role of disciplinarian. Years. Even when it came to something as innocent as horseplay and table manners. Certainly, she couldn't count on Winston to wield a stern hand when it came to Phillip. When their child needed it most, Winston would shrug and look at her with a sheepish grin. So she became the lawmaker, the enforcer, the one everyone counted on in a crisis.

She sighed at the antics at the kitchen table. Richard was busy being amazed at himself with a trick that looked like he was separating his thumb into two parts. Winston and Charlie concentrated on the maneuver and then tried it out on their thumbs. There was little surprise the trick only seemed to work on Richard's thumb, that is until he finally gave in and showed them how to do it.

If only she could make problems disappear with a little sleight of hand. Abracadabra—and they wouldn't have to worry about renting out the house for living money. If only they could sell it and be done with it. But that wasn't possible since the islanders knew too much about its history and had loose lips for any ear that would listen. That is if the owner of the ear was a local. Visitors were more likely treated to the brochure version of the island's history.

Still, it was only a matter of time before the Camerons got wind of the ghost stories and decided to leave a little earlier than planned. She had seen the pattern too many times to think it might be different this time.

Presto-chango—a snap of the finger and Winston's heart problem would go away. Not that he would ever admit he had a heart problem so they could talk about it and get it out in the open. Winston didn't know she had badgered the story out of the young doctor months ago and knew the truth. Doc had made her promise she wouldn't tell Winston, mumbling all the while under his breath about patient confidentiality and other such medical mumbo-jumbo, so she promised; not for the sake of the doctor, but for the sake of her husband who had tried to spare her from an ugly truth.

They'd been married too long, had been through too many things together to be playing silly newlywed games of keeping secrets, but she grudgingly respected the doctor's wishes and acted ignorant about the matter.

In the process, though, her role had expanded from disciplinarian/enforcer to keeper of secrets. She wondered how many more secrets she could bear. This last one was by far the hardest.

Winston was working his best to master the thumb trick. He wouldn't go back to bed now short of being bound and gagged, not with Charlie sitting there. They were enjoying each other's company too much.

When had Winston's hair gotten so gray, his eyes so tired? It was as if he had aged years in just a matter of hours. The message thing from Phillip had affected him more than she realized, so there was nothing to do but constantly remind him that his theory simply wasn't true. There was no hand from the grave, no hand-scrawled message begging for help when it was too late, it was all simply some strange aberration as a result of the heat. That was it, end of discussion.

Sybil excused herself from the mischief in the kitchen and drifted down the hall to the library. With the door closed, and a pause to make sure she hadn't been followed, she ran her fingers along the collection of Mark Twain books until she came to *The Adventures of Tom Sawyer.*

She flipped through the pages then shook it. Shook it again, harder this time. The binding cracked, but nothing fell. There were no more messages scrawled in crayon.

"Syb?"

The book slammed back into the shelf.

"Just tidying up a bit. Need anything?"

"Not a thing," Mann shouted from the kitchen. "Richard's got some studying to do, and I'm going to escort Mr. Charlie home. I imagine his mom might be a tad worried by now. Especially when she gets a gander at those scratches. We're planning a fishing trip soon as he's up for it. Need anything while I'm out?"

"You think that's wise? Going out and all?"

"No problem. Richard says he'll carry me piggyback if need be. Isn't that right, Richard?" There was muffled dialogue, followed by laughter at what must have been a response. "I'll be fine."

"Wear your hat."

"Will do. Say bye, Charlie, just the way we told you."

A pause then the young voice: "Bye, Charlie." There was another howl of laughter followed by the sound of the screen door opening.

"Come back to see your Auntie Syb."

She hoped Charlie had heard her before the door

creaked shut. He was a nice boy and one that needed fattening up. Maybe she'd make some sugar cookies. If nothing else, it would give her an excuse to visit him at the house to meet his mother. It might also be a good time to find out if any of the ghost stories had drifted to the new tenants at Manchester Place.

Like the one about Winston's aunt, how many great-greats generations past, burning herself and her son to death then coming back to take Phillip. The very idea of such a thing was ridiculous.

Past ridiculous, it was totally absurd. Absurd thoughts were for crazy people who were better left in institutions where they could take medication and push the pain so far away, so deep, that she could forget it ever happened, could remember it never happened, and then convince herself life would go on without ever seeing her son grow up to be a man.

No, there would be no thoughts of that now, nor of the book that brought this back to her and her husband. Her eyes narrowed to tight slits. Somehow a story that once brought pleasure had turned against them.

It wasn't going to bother them again. Not if she had anything to do about it.

Grabbing the book from its shelf, she walked to the kitchen, her footsteps angry, slapping sounds that mirrored her emotions. She was glad for the anger, allowed herself to fill with it lest fear filled her instead.

She went to the sink, turned the water on full force then flipped the switch to the disposal that gurgled and whirred. The mechanical mouth chewed and swallowed chapter after chapter.

Ink splattered from the maw and dripped down the sides of the porcelain sink. Some secrets should never be revealed. Secrets ruined families and sent people to institutions where they were kept sedated so they wouldn't think bad thoughts. Secrets kept people locked up when they should have been at home taking care of their husbands.

The disposer engine coughed, hesitated, then gnawed some more.

"Huck Saves The Widow."

The widow. Burned to death by her own hand after she killed her son. Sybil's only regret was that she hadn't been there to start the fire herself. The woman deserved what she got, and more since the only thing left from the fire was the four-foot thick tabby foundation that now sat under Manchester Place, and a hornpipe found in the ruins.

Her hand shook. The book finally emptied of pages. The pitch of the disposal engine heightened suddenly as if ready for whatever else she could give. She reached deep into the front of her dress to pull out the piece of paper.

Folding it tight, tighter so she wouldn't see the red crayon scrawl as it was destroyed, she tossed the paper to the drain.

The mechanical teeth of the sink shredded the note then quit. She flipped the switch to "off", knowing that it didn't matter anymore, the machine would never work again.

Phillip's message was destroyed, and one more secret was buried deep within her mind. They would get on with their lives and forget any of this had ever happened now. That was it, end of discussion.

She spied the bag and Charlie's dirty shirt within it. *The woman killed her son first then burned to*

death by her own hand.
    Charlie.
    No. It was over.
    Or was it?

Chapter 8

A letter. From David.

Almost forty-eight hours after their arrival on the island, the start of the third day, and there's a letter.

He had to have mailed it before the packing was complete, knew it was on its way while his family climbed into the car to drive four hundred miles with him, and offered not a hint, not a word it was coming even as they boarded a boat to head through murky waters to get to an unfamiliar place.

Annie stared dry-eyed at the open letter that sat on the kitchen table and made a personal vow she hoped she could keep. There would be no tears for a man who didn't keep his promises; the promise of visiting his family for a weekend was forgotten, the promise of "'til death do us part," gone.

The worry, the hopes he thought of them, and what they were doing, or if he cared, was over. There was nothing left in her but anger, and she had plenty of that; anger at his lying and his cheating, anger at his cowardice in sending a letter before they had even left the house, and after twelve years of marriage, and anger at herself for not seeing it coming.

She opened the dishwasher to put the clean dishes away then wondered why she bothered. Things would be different now; things would be done her way.

A plate with a loud yellow-brown floral pattern

beckoned her. The small chip on the edge of the plate made one of the flower petals odd. Imperfection in other things, in other people, in him, was something she would no longer tolerate.

With a flick of her wrist, the plate crashed to the floor. Small ceramic pieces scattered over the linoleum.

The next plate belonged to a different set. Cartoon-like bluebirds sitting on vapid blue branches was something she found particularly distasteful at the moment. The one she had chosen for her wedding pattern—if David hadn't already gotten rid of it—was much more to her liking, so why keep this one? She flipped it into the air, and it slammed into the floor. It broke easier then the first one, the impact turning fragments to blue powder. A tight smile touched her lips as blue dust settled among yellow-brown pieces.

David would pay. First, for the dishes, then for his meetings with the "contractors," then for everything else in their miserable marriage.

Assuming the position of an Olympic discus thrower, she hurled another plate into the bare front wall. It struck with a dull thud, tore away a piece of wallpaper, and bounced back into the room to splinter in mid-air.

The next plate was even easier.

Annie tried another one out on the aluminum screen door to see what kind of a flying disk it would make then shrugged as it rattled to the floor and fractured into two even halves.

The glasses would be even more satisfying than plates, especially the big tumbler size. She sent them shattering in machine-gun precision fascinated as the picture window wall absorbed the onslaught with only an occasional dent and scuff on the wallpaper as evidence.

Turning to the hearth, she fired at the brick opening. Too high. The glass splintered against the mantel, spewing pieces across the floor. She imagined David's face in the hearth opening and fired another.

Bull's-eye.

Another glass, then a juice tumbler over the shoulder to the front wall where it hit with the second hollow thud and rolled intact back toward her feet, a piece of wallpaper stuck to it.

She reached back to the dishwasher, saw that it was empty of ammunition, and grunted with disappointment until she spotted the silverware. Spoons, forks, or should it be knives? Knives it was. Sharp instruments couldn't be more appropriate for someone who had just been cut to the quick. Grasping a carving knife with a tight fist, she wheeled on one foot then aimed the blade.

A knock on the screen door stopped her mid-arc.

His tall, lanky body was taut with tension; his handsome face stared at her wide-eyed.

"What do you want?"

Richard slowly stepped back from the door.

"Well?"

He looked over his shoulder as if to see what his chances were for a quick escape.

"You're not going to sell me something, are you? You've got that look."

"No, of course not," he blurted. "I'm not selling anything. It's not really my line of work, although some might argue that point. Mr. Mann sent me over to see if you needed anything."

"You're sure about the selling thing," she said,

wagging the knife.

"Trust me. I dropped my demo vacuum cleaners and magazine subscription order forms in the bushes when I saw your knife."

She returned to the counter to place the knife in a drawer.

"So, uh, anyway," Richard spluttered, "Mr. Mann sent me over here to see if you needed anything."

"You said that already."

He paused, looked over his shoulder again. "Yes, I suppose I did. Need anything?"

"No."

"Some new dishes, maybe? I mean, I know the dishwasher is old, but I didn't know it was that bad. Not that I'd be selling the dishes."

Looking around her as if seeing the place for the first time, she realized how horrible it must have appeared to him. It would take hours to clean up the place, maybe longer. But one good thing came from this momentary dip into insanity; there were no more dishes to wash.

The humor of the situation touched her then, dark at the edges but getting lighter with every second. No more dishes to wash, but if she needed a vacuum or magazines, she could always find them in the bushes outside. She smiled. A rumble grew in her chest that bubbled out in an explosion of snickers, and she finally laughed so hard she had to hold her sides from the aching.

Confusion crossed Richard's face, and Annie laughed harder. She collapsed in a chair then waved him in.

He refused to budge from his position on the other

side of the door.

"Come in," she said through cackles. "The knife is safely put away. See for yourself." She pointed at the closed drawer. "No one will be hurt, not a soul. At least not anyone who matters anymore."

Playful doubt crossed his face. "Promise?"

Her laughter changed pitch suddenly, heightened, choked, and turned to sobs. Tears ran down her face. "Promises are made to be broken."

The door opened. He came to her side and patiently waited while she cried.

The tears stopped finally, but her nose ran, and she hiccupped. Crying and hiccupping in front of a total stranger, it couldn't get much worse than that unless it had been David who saw this display of weakness.

Richard cleared his throat. "As I, uh, was saying, Mr. Mann sent me over to—"

"I know," she said, voice cracking a little. "To see if I needed anything."

"Look, I've asked you twice now if you needed anything—"

"Three times," Annie added, dabbing her nose.

"Three times, so it's obviously not the charm, and I'm beginning to feel a little foolish. So why don't I just leave."

"I'm not a nut."

Richard didn't answer.

"I just got some bad news, and I didn't do well with it." She rubbed her runny nose and sniffed. "Although why I had to get the news today, and in this place of all places... You probably think I've lost my mind."

He handed her a paper napkin and waited while she

blew her nose.

"And you'd be right. I did lose my mind, but I'm better now." She pulled another napkin from his hand, dabbed her eyes, and stood up. "Would you like some coffee, Richard?"

"Have you got any cups left?" he asked with a grin.

She smiled. "A few. Not all of them needed washing."

"I don't want to bother you."

"No bother. Please, sit," she said, pulling out a chair. "Oops, not here. That's a pretty sharp piece sticking out of the chair. Sitting on it could cause a man the unkindest cut of all."

Richard appeared shocked at her statement at first then laughed, and found a safer chair to occupy. "Thanks for the warning."

"No thanks needed. I told you about it for purely selfish reasons."

"Oh?" he asked, hopefully.

"I'm taking that chair home for my husband."

"Oh. Well, in that case, coffee would be nice." He tensed as if preparing for bad news. "You don't put flowers or anything like that in coffee, do you?"

"What?"

"Never mind. It's not important."

She filled up the kettle with water, put it on the stove to boil then reached for two cups.

"A death in the family?"

Annie turned to him with the comment. "I beg your pardon?"

"The bad news. In the letter, Mr. Mann brought over this morning. A death?"

It should be so simple; David run over by a truck

on his way home from work. Or better yet, getting the worst case of crabs recorded in medical history by way of a "meeting with the contractors," and then scratching himself to death.

How ironic that David chose to let her do the dying instead. A slow, painful death filled with tainted mirrors that reflected her inadequacy as a wife and her failure as a mother. Evidence of her failure lay all around her. Charlie couldn't read simple words from a baby book, and Grandma didn't know what day it was, or what year most of the time.

Annie accepted guilt for the dissolution of her parent's marriage, and if that wasn't enough, she got to see what it felt like firsthand in her marriage. A slow death. Second to minute. A six-hour drive to three days on an island to twelve years of marriage down the tubes. And all of it summed up in one neat, clean, pre-mailed letter.

"No," she said. "Not a death, although I'm working on it." For David, or herself?

Richard waited for her to say more, but there was no more, not now anyway. There was too much to sort out, too many things to decide before talking would do any good.

Grabbing hold the broom for something to do, she swept broken pieces of glass and plates into even piles across the floor. Sweeping faster, harder, the bristles of the broom brushed the floor with slow, rhythmic scratching sounds. Over and over, she brushed until the sound became isolating and hypnotic-like waves on the shore.

The sound of water washing up on white, uncluttered sand.

The sand of a beach.

The boat was readied and waiting. Evening approached by darkening clouds that drifted across the Lullaby sound, the blue of the water turned shades of gray. He was setting out to sea. It would be a long trip.

Who was he?

Someone was coming then.

Annie backed up to let them pass, but knew it didn't matter; they wouldn't see her. This daydream was yet another mental escape for dealing with stress. She'd become good at playing mind games with herself in the past few months, even better in the past three days, but this time it was different. This time the story was being played out for her benefit, separate from her imagination.

The man was large, muscular, and bore the splitting-seamed, heavy duffel bag as if he were carrying nothing at all. His wife followed three steps to his one, a lit kerosene lamp in one hand and a loaf of bread tucked under her arm. The dim light of the lamp cast uneven swaying shadows in the dusky light that surrounded them. There were no words between them, no sound except that of footsteps in the sand, and water touching boat then shore.

The man climbed with deft motions into the swaying boat, deposited the duffel bag in front of him, and sat down between the oars. His wife walked into the water to hand her husband the lamp and the loaf of bread. He took them, and in that light revealed a face toughened from years at sea, and a large, long healed scar running across his cheek. With little more than a nod to her, he slashed oars into water and pulled away from the shore.

Bay water washed around the woman's ankles and skirts, as she watched the skiff float from view. She stood fixed while the last sound of oars reached her ears, and the dim light from a kerosene lamp disappeared over the horizon. She stood tall as darkness consumed and turned her into yet another shadow by growing moonlight. Minutes passed, hours, and with a slow, deliberate motion, the woman reached to stroke the small bulge in her belly and turned to the great house on the land behind her.

Her steps slowed to a stop. She paused, turned, and fixed Annie with a penetrating stare then nodded.

As if stung by electricity, Annie jolted awake. She blinked at the bright sun-filled room and the man at her kitchen table that held a question in his eyes. Her stomach hurt, and she discovered her hands clenched tight around her belly.

The kettle on the stove moaned and gurgled then shifted into a high-pitched scream. The water was ready.

Water. What was it for?

"Maybe I better take a rain check on that coffee. Are you okay?"

"Yes...no. I don't know." Coffee. She was supposed to make him a cup of coffee. "Raincheck. Yes, I think that would be best."

He stood to leave. "You sure you're all right? I can call the doctor."

"No. Please. I'm fine." She slid into a chair. "Just a little tired is all. I'll be fine."

"All right then," he said with doubt in his voice. "There's nothing I can do?"

"Nothing. Thank you."

Richard pushed open the screen door, walked out, then turned back. "I'll check on you later."

She nodded and waved him away.

"Oh," he said, "I almost forgot. Mr. Mann took Charlie fishing. He hoped it was okay with you."

"Yes. Okay."

The door slapped back and forth against the jamb. She sensed him linger at the door then knew he had gone.

Taking a deep breath, she shored herself up and got busy with the fragments of broken plates and glasses. Then there'd be the laundry, dusting, anything to keep from thinking about the woman in the water and the husband going out to sea with no plans to return.

He was leaving her.

But how could Annie know that? She stared at the letter lying on the kitchen table and decided her imagination was working overtime. Not all men left their wives; plenty of couples stayed married all their lives, and not all divorce intentions were announced by way of a letter.

She crumpled the letter into a tight ball and tossed it in the hearth. Tonight she would build a raging fire and watch David's words turn to smoke and ash. The fire would feel good against the cooling night air, and seeing the paper that represented him go up in flames would feel even better.

It might even help her sleep a night without the dreams.

The past two nights of strange smells, creaking wood, and flights of fancy and imagination without any basis in fact, had a way of distorting perspective.

She knew she had been dreaming if only she could

remember them the next morning so she could figure them out. That's what you were supposed to do, wasn't it, figure them out in the morning then analyze them so they wouldn't repeat themselves night after night after night?

Now, it seemed, the dreams touched her during the day. Strange dreams as if she were a bystander watching an event, like a man leaving on a boat never to come back to his wife. Or a woman holding her stomach, waiting—this time Annie remembered the dream all too clearly.

She grabbed a damp sponge from the sink to wipe scuff marks off wallpaper on the bare back wall. She brushed back a strand of hair from her sweating forehead then turned her attention back to her work.

The woman in the dream *looked* at her, then nodded. Annie closed her eyes against the thought but knew it wouldn't go away.

The woman stared at her. She had desperate, defiant eyes that told Annie the story wasn't over.

She wouldn't think about this anymore. The flights of fancy in her waking state would be held in check, and if she worked hard enough, made herself exhausted enough, restful sleep without dreams would come. There were better things to think about.

Why was the man leaving?

No. she didn't want to know, would not feed the thought.

Why was the woman holding her belly?

It was a stupid daydream, nothing more.

The woman would wait for him. They *would wait for him.*

The sponge fell from her hand to the floor, sending

dirty-gray water drops in a spray around her feet.

They?

The woman in the dream was waiting for her husband to return. Did she expect Annie to wait as well?

If it weren't so ludicrous, Annie would have laughed out loud. Here she was, on a secluded island, slowly going mad via thoughts of a ghostly *ménage a trois*. It was a bizarre kind of madness and one that would make it much easier for a judge to wonder why David hadn't divorced her long before this.

Well, it wouldn't work. Not this time, or any other, for that matter.

She grabbed the sponge and dug it into the dingy wallpaper. Even if he were here, David wouldn't have the satisfaction of seeing her go to pieces. She wouldn't allow it; she was better than that, stronger. Annie would show him, show all of them, that she could handle anything if she wanted to.

An edge of wallpaper rolled off with her angry strokes then another. A small line, a joint of sorts, appeared between plasterboard pieces. She ran a wet finger over the joint until it stopped at the edge of the intact wallpaper. It was a crack of some kind, or maybe it was a groove. Easing a fingernail into the paper, she felt resiliency then give, as her nail popped through.

Something was hidden behind the wallpaper.

Annie stepped back for a better look and ground a piece of a broken plate to dust under her shoe. The plates hit this very place with a dull, hollow sound. She returned to the wall, ran a finger along the edge, and discovered an indentation that ran across and down another side as well.

There *was* something behind the wall, a door by the look and feel of it. She peeled away more of the paper and found the groove did indeed run all the way around. It was a door to somewhere in the house, or maybe to the outside.

But where did it go? More importantly, why did she have to know? It was none of her business. The owner obviously had a reason for hiding the existence of this door. Maybe it was so no one would go in and get hurt or something.

Or maybe it was so no one would go up to the widow's walk.

That was it. Mr. Mann had said there was no door leading up there, that it was just for show. Why would he have told her something that wasn't true, unless he didn't know himself? Or unless something had happened that no one should ever find out.

"Annie?" The voice was shaky, tentative, and it came from upstairs.

Grandma. Probably needing help coming down the steps again.

"In a minute," she yelled.

It wouldn't do to let Grandma or Charlie see the mess she had made. She looked around the room for a large piece of furniture that could be moved in front of the door until she decided what to do next.

"Annie!"

"I said, in a minute. I'm busy."

Annie spotted the antique tile and oak buffet. It would have to do. She pushed the buffet across the floor in small, fishtail movements. The furniture legs scraped across linoleum and left scratches. With a final shove and a groan, she settled the buffet in front of the hidden door, brushed shattered plate dust off it then wiped her hands on her jeans.

"Annie!"

"Coming, Grandma," she said, walking through the dining room to the foyer steps beyond.

She stopped short at the sight of Grandma standing at the top of the stairs. The hair on the back of her neck tickled. The old woman's frail hands, clasped around the wood banister, had become hard knots that turned the knuckles as white as her face.

"Annie," she whispered. "She's here. The woman by the water."

Chapter 9

"Well, Charlie, my boy," Mann said, leaning back onto the weather-beaten wood of the rowboat. "What do you think of fishing?"

He dipped his hand over the side and let it drift in the cool water of the bay.

Charlie yawned, shrugged, and tugged at the rod and reel in his hands. "No fish."

"Yup, and ain't it great." He slapped a mosquito, then lit his pipe and tossed the match overboard into the dark, rolling water. "It's being out in the boat and taking it easy that counts. Catching a fish or two is okay now and then, but me, I like just sittin' around and basking in the sun. It's relaxing, you know."

Charlie peered into the water for any sign of action then reeled in his line.

"Now remember, it's all in the wrist. Pick a place then aim for it with your line. That'll do it."

Charlie spotted a place near a tree stump, then heaved the line with every bit of strength he had. The hook and weight arced overhead and plopped into the water two feet from where he sat.

A whistled sigh of relief escaped Mann's pursed lips. "Not bad. I believe you're getting it. You didn't catch my shirt this time. Good work."

"I'm not good at fishing."

"Of course you are. Throwing in a line is tricky

business. Takes a little practice to be expert at it. Another week or so and you'll be a pro."

"I'll never be as good as you."

"That's it. Reel it in nice and slow. Give the fish a chance to scope out the menu." He sucked on the pipe, puffed out gray clouds of smoke. "You can be as good as you want."

"I want to be as good as you are at fishing."

"You can be better."

"No, I can't."

Mann shifted the pipe from one side of his mouth to the other as if he were pondering this bit of information.

"I can't do anything right." Charlie tossed the pole over the side of the boat.

The little boat pitched steeply to one side. Mann's arm dipped into the murky surface, grappled against the current, then reappeared empty-handed. The pole was gone. His arm dripping, he sat back on the bench and stared at Charlie, the pipe wedged securely between clenched teeth.

"I'm sorry," Charlie said, his voice squeaking. "I didn't mean to. Please don't hate me."

"Charlie." Mann leaned close to the boy. "I don't hate you. I could never hate you. But I have to admit I don't much like what you did."

"I know."

"So why did you do it?"

"I don't know."

"Do you want to go home? Just say the word, and I'll turn the boat around."

Home. The house in Atlanta, or the one here? It was so hard to know where he belonged anymore. He missed his toys, his own room, and school even though the other kids picked on him, and he had no friends. He didn't mean to cause so much trouble, but his father had said "trouble" was Charlie's middle name—he'd always thought it was Wilson—and if his father said it, then it must be true.

He missed his parents being together.

It had been a long time since he had spent any time with his dad, too long. And even though Mom was always there, she wasn't there, not really, kinda like her thoughts took her into a dark place.

Lately, she acted like she didn't see him, but maybe the dark circles under her eyes kept her from seeing good. She said the circles were because she wasn't getting enough good sleep the past couple of nights. Yesterday he had come home to find her sleeping with her eyes open. At least it looked like she was sleeping. He wanted to ask her if he could play spy, or if she had paper he could draw on, but he didn't want to make her angry.

Instead, he had made Uncle Winston angry by throwing the fishing pole over the side of the boat. Only stupid kids did things like that. Stupid, stupid kids. He hit himself on the head, again then over and over and over, faster and faster so that it would never stop, so that he would be punished, so that—

Winston firmly grasped the boy's shoulder. "Charlie? Do you want to go home?"

The hitting stopped. No, he wanted to stay here and learn how to fish like Uncle Winston. "I'm sorry."

"Apology accepted. Promise you won't do it again?"

"I promise. Can we stay?"

Mann smiled, "Sure. And Charlie?" He pointed a finger toward him. "If anyone causes you trouble, or says a mean thing to you, you tell them they'll have to answer to me. You got that?"

"Yes, sir."

"Good. That's what friends are for, right?"

"Um-hmm."

"Right. And I'll come to you if I need some help."

Charlie beamed at the idea someone might need him. "Okay."

"Good. Now, did I ever tell you about the time I caught a fifty-pounder, right here in these waters?"

"Twenty-pounder."

"What's that?"

"Last time it was a twenty-pounder. That's what you said. Twenty pounds."

"Oh. So I did." Mann reached for the lone fishing pole and reeled in the line. "I guess that means I've told you the story before."

"Two times before."

"I see." He handed the pole to Charlie. "The next fishing lesson is called 'Embellishment.'"

"What does that mean?"

"It means lying. Remember to use the wrist."

Charlie flung the line toward the stump again. It dropped neatly on target. Smiling at Mann, he slowly reeled it in to let the fish "scope out the menu." He cast out again, reeled it in, and repeated the move until his arm hurt, and he returned the pole to Mann for a while.

He studied Uncle Winston's gray hair, his tanned face, the crinkled, peaceful smile he wore as he dropped the hook deftly into the water then pulled the line in. Charlie decided he wanted to grow up to be just like

Uncle Winston. Then maybe he'd even have a wife that made gingerbread and lemonade, that is if he ever got married. He scowled at the thought of marrying a girl. Girls were annoying, they hated bugs and turtles and things, and they teased him.

The bay water swirled in small circles around the boat. The current pushed the boat further and further from the shore. Girls probably hated boats and fishing, too. It was settled then, getting married was out. He didn't like to fight anyway, and that's what married people did.

Charlie…

The voice came from…where? He looked to the shore—nothing but trees and dry, dusty shrubs there.

Charlie…

Uncle Winston was intent on untying a knot from the nylon fishing line while muttering a stream of curse words under his breath.

Charlie. Down here.

He looked over the edge of the boat. His breath caught in his throat, his mouth dried to dust.

The face stared at him, just under the surface of the water.

His mother's face.

Charlie, baby. Come to your mother.

Mom? No, it couldn't be even though it looked like her. Even sounded like her.

Leaning over the edge, he saw her beckon. A tight smile formed on her lips. A small wave washed over the face, and it shimmered then faded. Then she was there again, smiling. A warm smile, friendly, but something wasn't right. It was almost as if she held something back, something scary.

Something to surprise him with.

Closer, baby. Come closer.

He leaned further. The boat moved with him. Uncle Winston shouted at him to come back, but he couldn't. Not now, not when his mother was calling.

The face changed then, grew old. Deep creases and pits covered the face and the skull with dark, burning tissue. She smiled again, a bright clear smile. The smile of his mother. And someone else.

Come, there's something I must whisper in your ear.

He bent to listen. And fell overboard.

Cold, deep water surged around him, covered him. The current pulled and twisted. His clothes absorbed the weight and dragged him further under.

Frantically kicking his legs, reaching blindly around with his arms, he searched for anything he might hold on to. There was nothing but the emptiness of the bay and the undercurrent that pulled him away from the boat, away from ever seeing his family again.

His mouth filled with water. He tried blowing it out with the little air he had left in his lungs, but his chest ached with wanting to breathe, needing to breathe, but not daring to. A breath now would be his last.

Something grabbed his legs. He kicked against it, but the grip tightened.

She cackled

He squirmed to the surface, only to be dragged down again.

The laugh heightened, turned gleeful.

Darkness surrounded him, comforted him. He felt its warmth and knew whatever happened to him now would be okay. Dying wouldn't be so bad.

Something batted at his shoulder, moved away.

Another tug on his legs drew him deeper, down into the dark water and the victorious laughing of the female voice.

Tightness in his chest turned to hot burning. He opened his mouth to inhale, to take the final comfort of the dark, when something hit in the shoulder again, hard. Pulled upward by his shirt, his collar caught him tight around the throat.

The laughing stopped. Her shrill voice turned to a moan, then a wail as he was dragged away.

The last yank on his shirt turned cold water warmer. A light breeze caressed the top of his head, his face then his chest. He gasped open-mouthed, and air infiltrated his lungs with searing pain.

Mama?

He gasped again then started to cry.

Chapter 10

Visibly trembling, Grandma stood at the top of the stairs. "She's here, Annie. She's waiting."

Annie crossed her arms as if to protect herself. "I don't know what you mean."

"The woman in the water. She saw her husband off in the boat. She saw you, Annie, and now she's here. In this house. She's back."

Back? From where? From Annie's vivid imagination? She pushed away the mental picture of the woman with cold eyes, staring at her as a dream, a vision of a muddled mind.

"No, Grandma. You're wrong," she said, because she had to. Because thinking anything else led to a madness from which she might never return.

Grandma paled as if she had been bleached. Alertness left her eyes and turned them empty again. She tottered on weak legs, tried to turn away, and loosened her grip on the balcony as her knees wobbled and gave.

"No!" Her feet propelled her up the steps in twos then threes.

The old woman slumped to the landing and slid forward. In seconds she would plummet, to the bottom steps in the foyer and a broken neck.

Grandma's dead weight shifted her body, twisted it in an angle that dropped her down another step. Her necklace broke, scattering bright, luminous pearls that bounced the length of the stairwell in tones like that of a fragile wind chime touched by a light breeze. Some pearls rolled off the edge and fell to the first floor far below.

Annie tried to scream but found no voice as she leaped across the middle landing, scraped her arm against the full-length mirror with the turn, and stumbled over a handful of pearls.

Hold on, sweetheart. Annie's coming. Just another second.

Her legs ached, muscles strained and pulled, her breathing came in painful gasps.

Grandma's shoulders leaned forward, bumped against the banister, and fell back.

Another few steps and Annie would be there.

One more and it would be over.

She dove at the old woman, caught her before the last slide that would have ended on the hard floor below. Threw her back against the stairs. Annie wrapped Grandma in her arms, held her tight then rocked her back and forth. Her ragged breath turned to uncontrolled, relieved sobbing combined with fear of what could have been.

Grandma's soft hand patted her arm reassuringly. "It's all right, Annie. We can make some more pudding. I'll eat it just the way it is. You know I will."

Annie stroked Grandma's hair and cried and laughed at the same time. "Of course you will, darling. I can always count on you."

She caught the two of them in the mirror then, a frazzled young woman, hair slick with sweat, holding a much older, frail woman in her arms. Sometimes she wished it could be the other way around. She kissed Grandma on the head.

"You know I wouldn't give anything for you. Not a thing."

****

Grandma was resting now.

Annie had sat quietly in the big armchair in the master bedroom until Grandma fell asleep, then walked the narrow staircase up to the attic room. The steps creaked and groaned with her weight and matched the cadence of her grumblings. Her legs hurt, but it was nothing compared to what it was bound to be like in the morning, and nothing like what Grandma had been through. The first aid kit, and some elastic bandages would have been nice. Too bad she couldn't remember where they were right now.

She supposed that meant her future as a Good Samaritan candidate was forever in jeopardy. Still, she mumbled a word of thanks that everything turned out okay and offered whatever it took that this would never happen again.

Payback was hell, and so were these narrow steps under the circumstances. She massaged her scraped arm and pulled open the wooden attic door. The old hinge of an empty lock dropped dust sprinkles. She wondered now at her rationalization to put Grandma in the most inaccessible room in the house when navigating steps was her most difficult task.

For her safety, the attic room was in Grandma's best interest. And the master bedroom with its great double bed, antique furnishings, and fireplace was in Annie's selfish interest, but at a cost far greater than she was prepared to pay. Grandma would enjoy the master bedroom now, as she should have in the first place, while Annie absolved herself with anti-inflammatories and hydrogen peroxide. Turnabout was fair play and all that.

She brushed a hand across the bedside table in the little room—no dust yet—tugged at the comforter on the bed, and punched the pillow.

Sniffing the air, she deemed it stale and tried pushing open the lone window to freshen the place. The circular window refused to budge. Obviously more show than function. She pressed her face against it. It was cool against her skin and turned her breath to condensation that she wiped away with her shirtsleeve.

Outside it was a beautiful, early fall day. The sky was a brilliant blue, the clouds rippled and wavy. A hint of a breeze blew small crests on the bay waves. Live oaks swayed with the wind and dropped bits of moss across the lawn. Such a nice day and view.

But it would be even better from the widow's walk. A panoramic view waited for her if only she could get up there.

She could if she wanted to.

But was alienating the Manns' hospitality and angering the owner worth a few moments of solitude and a view of the bay? There might even be an eviction for destruction of private property in it. Right now, she had no place else to go.

She rubbed her chin with the damp shirtsleeve then brushed a loose strand of hair out of her face. No, it wasn't worth it. The view from here, the master bedroom, the verandah, or any place else in the house was plenty. It was by far a better picture than she could get from the grim subdivision in Atlanta. So that was that; she wouldn't jeopardize her right to stay in Manchester Place.

Grandma coughed, shifted in the bed downstairs then quieted.

Annie raised an eyebrow at how easily sound traveled in the house. She stomped. A dullness echoed quietly under the floors, reverberated down the hall, around corners, and far below her. It was the wood floors and framing, or maybe a crawlspace deep under the house that promoted the echoing.

Another cough, another creak from the bed, meant Grandma was sleeping restlessly. Small wonder after what she had just been through.

Annie walked to the door for another listen. There were no more sounds of Grandma stirring. Then she looked down the narrow steps to the hallway and the main stairway beyond. A shiver crept up her spine at the height from this viewpoint. A fall from here was fatal at best, so that only something threatening, frightening beyond words, would prompt her to navigate these steps if she were in Grandma's condition. What could have been bad enough to force Grandma from her room?

The woman in the water.

Annie rubbed away the chill in her arms. Grandma had seen Annie's daydream and tried to warn her. It was a harmless dream, a little unnerving maybe, but hardly worth the risk of a lethal fall.

Most remarkable was that Grandma had seen it without benefit of Annie telling her. She knew some people had this kind of ability to tap into other people's minds, but that didn't make it ominous, dangerous, or true. The vision was a quick dip into mind play, into fantasy, that's all, and Grandma had simply picked up on it with her special talent. That didn't make the woman in the dream real.

Unless the woman was real.

She had to get hold of herself and stop this line of thinking right now. While she was at it, there'd be no more late-night spooky movies to plant additional seeds.

A deep breath later, she felt better and stepped out onto the landing to pull the door closed. It creaked and spilled a small pile of rust from the old lock hinge.

Expecting the hinge would crumble at her touch, she was surprised to find it intact. The flat, rectangular piece connected to the hinge moved freely and held when she tugged on it. It probably only needed a new lock. Then no one could get out of the attic room without assistance and take the chance of falling down the stairs again.

It would be safe, but it wouldn't be right. Grandma was a person after all, not some vicious animal that needed to be caged, even though the two of them had missed disaster by a single step. Maybe, just maybe, this was a way to prevent any further incidents like that occurring, not a permanent situation, but something when she couldn't watch Grandma every minute.

"Annie?"

"Coming." She bolted down the stairs to the master bedroom and threw open the door.

Grandma was curled into a tight ball under the thick comforter. The huge bed dwarfed her.

"I'm sorry. I don't want to be so much trouble. I don't mean to be."

Annie sat on the edge of the bed and reached for

the old woman's hand. "You're no trouble, sweetheart."

"I am. But I'll try to do better." She pulled the cover up under her chin and closed her eyes.

"Grandma?"

"Hmm?"

"Do you remember what you said when I found you on the top of the stairs? Do you remember what you saw?"

Grandma shifted under the cover. Wrinkles appeared on her forehead, followed by a faint smile of embarrassment. "What was it? I don't recall exactly."

Annie sighed heavily, patted Grandma's hand. "It's okay. It doesn't matter anyway."

"I'm sorry."

"Don't be. It's okay. Really." She leaned over and kissed Grandma on the forehead. "Get some rest now. I'll let you know when supper's ready."

"I love you, Annie."

"I love you, too."

"And Charlie loves you. More than you might know. Take some time for him, will you?"

"I will. I promise. Get some rest now."

She padded softly out of the room, closed the door, and leaned against it. Wiping away moistness from her eyes with the back of her hand, she saw the rust stains on her fingertips. There would be no lock on the attic bedroom door. Confusion or not, Grandma just needed a little extra attention, and she'd get it. So would Charlie.

She smiled at the thought of Charlie with his tousled hair, a perpetual smudge on his glasses, and the impish grin when he completed a particularly difficult drawing. Suddenly she missed him more than she knew was possible. The two of them shared the same house, yet sometimes they were miles apart. The Manns with their fishing trips and gingerbread treats had spent more time with him these past days then she did. They had become the mother and father he didn't have right now.

Poor Charlie. He was bound to be having a hard time of it, what with his father rarely around. She closed her eyes against the pain of the letter now crumpled in the fireplace. Charlie would know sooner or later that there were problems if he didn't already know about them.

She would spend more time with him, and not just through his schoolwork. He needed her, and she needed him. They would get through this thing together, the two of them and Grandma.

I promise.

Chapter 11

Annie wedged the straw sun hat harder down on her head and tilted it so the next gust wouldn't try to carry the thing halfway to Bermuda again.

She and Charlie had spent the better part of fifteen minutes chasing the hat until it finally came to a stop against a sparsely grassed dune. Charlie had pounced on the hat like a cat on a mouse, while she cringed at the shape it would be in after his Olympic effort. Holding it like a trophy, he trotted it back with the green ribbon and bow covered in muck then silently returned to work on his sandcastle.

The red, hard-plastic sunglasses slid down her lotion-covered nose. She jabbed at the bridge, felt the glasses slide again then yanked them off. They weren't worth the annoyance on a day such as this, her first day at the beach. And after, finally, her first restful sleep without nightmares.

Leaning on one elbow to make sure all sides of her body had equal time in the afternoon sun, she returned to her book. The review said it was a thriller about people trapped on an island at the mercy of terrorists wielding a contagious virus. She turned the next page, glanced at Charlie scraping out a moat around his castle, and was cheered to be on this island rather than the one in the book.

A peek to the watch in the straw beach bag

reminded her there was little over an hour left to enjoy the beach before heading back over the dunes, through the shaded foot trail, and to her evening chores at Manchester Place. She wished she could stretch the time, but wouldn't abuse Sybil Mann's generous offer of Grandma-sitting services.

What a nice offer it was, too. Completely out of the blue. A chance to get out of the house, be with Charlie, and get a tan was just what she needed. Annie had offered to pay Sybil. But the woman adamantly refused, saying the time she and Winston spent with Charlie was worth more than money could buy. Annie was doing *her* the favor.

A happy couple by the looks of them, the Manns had taken to Charlie like he was their son. Charlie seemed fond of them, even to the point of cultivating new plans with them. It was unlike him to engage with people who were strangers three days ago. But Annie found herself pleased that maybe now he was opening up and trusting people. She found she was a little jealous, too. Charlie, quite frankly, seemed to have a better time with the Manns than with his mother.

She sighed, tried reading again then finally closed the book in favor of a walk down the isolated beach instead. Waving at Charlie to catch his attention, Annie motioned her intent.

He nodded and returned to his project. The wall erected around the moat was fast losing detail with the incoming tide, so he worked quickly to prevent an imminent mudslide—without getting wet. It was quite the dilemma, the waves, the mudslide and his new obsession with staying dry. He dealt with the problem by running like a sandpiper to avoid the water then returning for a quick reinforcement to the castle. This water business was new. He had flatly refused to go swimming today even with the tempting offer of an inner-tube to ride the waves. In the past, her battles were over him getting out of the water. Now he wouldn't even go in.

So today, the battle was different. Tomorrow it would be something else, and no matter how hard she tried, she might never know why any of them were battles in the first place. She had long since learned not to push him too far, or he'd seek solace in the dark place in his mind and never come out again.

Annie had pleaded then cajoled him into coming to the beach knowing he'd have a good time, but she didn't push far. He had conceded finally, but dug in his heels and refused to go into the water when they arrived. It was a trade-off, one of many they negotiated, and it was only the idea of building a sandcastle that kept him here now.

He punched an opening through the moat, maybe for an imaginary arrival of the knights on their horses, and was careful to turn his head away and run with each incoming wave. It was as if he didn't want to look at the water or was afraid of it for some reason, and Annie had no idea why.

During the fishing trip yesterday, Charlie had gone swimming. Mr. Mann had said as much. She was left with what seemed to be forty pounds of drenched clothing as proof of the spontaneous swim. She thought his clothes would never dry out, and decided from now on bathing trunks would accompany him no matter what the original plans were. That, and a case for his glasses wherever he went. She was only glad he had a spare after losing the first pair from an overzealous water fight, Mr. Mann explained. Charlie, of course, offered nothing by way of explanation.

Today Charlie didn't feel like swimming. Everyone was entitled to their moods. One thing was sure, if Charlie didn't want to go swimming now, he wouldn't go any time soon again, and maybe never. He and his obsessions were like that.

"I'll be back in a little while," she shouted. "Are you sure you don't want to go?"

He shook his head and pounded out an opening through the castle wall on the opposite side.

"Okay. I won't go far. You stay here."

Wrapping a towel around her waist, and with her hand firmly on the brim of her hat, she walked south. There was talk of ruins of an old mansion somewhere near this part of the island, and now was as good as any to check it out. Her heels sank in the soft, hot sand as she continued past driftwood, shells emptied of their previous inhabitants, and what was left of a variety of crab bodies.

Out in the water, dolphins rolled with the waves, surfaced, dove then reappeared down the shoreline.

"Look, Charlie," she shouted, but he was clearly more interested in saving the castle.

Further out on the horizon, trolling ships hoisted their great nets and prepared to come in. Other ships headed out into the waters for the start of their day.

They were all so beautiful on the glistening water.

And not one of them was a rowboat with a scarred man, leaving his wife to stand alone on the shore.

****

Sybil scrutinized the drying bowls for any sign of

residual vegetable soup. A rock-hard smudge of tomato marred the bottom of one and offended her sensibilities. Grabbing it up, she then turned the water on full force and scrubbed until the brush dropped bristles into the sink, and the bowl was spotless down to the molecular level.

"Cleanliness is next to godliness," she said over her shoulder to Grandma at the table. "I suppose that saying is just as good for soup bowls as it is for people." She opened the door to the oven for a quick check on the sugar cookies and turned the fire on under the kettle. "How about a nice cup of tea, Mrs. Cameron?"

There was no answer. The old woman looked out the bay window while her thin, arthritic fingers opened and closed, opened and closed, as if keeping time to some tune only she could hear.

Cabinet doors creaked open, one after another, while Sybil searched for tea.

"Instant coffee, instant cocoa, God help us all, instant soup. No sense in trying to keep a family going on something that only needs water added. Now, my soup, there's something to write home about. But then, you hardly touched a drop of it, did you?"

Still no answer.

"Well, I did forget to add the sweet basil to it. Makes all the difference in the world, sweet basil."

Sybil slammed the final cabinet shut, and spat the words out as if keeping them in her mouth would cause a stale taste, "No tea."

Her hands went to her hips while she contemplated this serious infraction. "I suppose instant coffee will have to do as much as I hate it. Mid-afternoon is a time for tea, not coffee, but we do with what's given to us."

She glared at the coffee then found two mugs.

"Richard and Winston will get a serious talking to about their shopping. No tea, instant soup, I suppose the next thing will be cookies in a bag." She shuddered as if the mere thought would turn her to stone. "People can't wait anymore. Everything has to be now, instant, or never."

The kettle rumbled to a boil. She poured hot water over heaping spoonfuls of coffee and stirred. "Cream and sugar?"

The old woman didn't move.

"Both then. You could do with some calories on those bones." She brought the steaming mugs to the table and pulled up a chair next to Grandma. "Here it is. Be careful not to burn yourself." Looking at the woman for a sign of conversation, Sybil saw her eyes were closed, figured it for a quick doze after lunch, but reached out to check her pulse, just in case. It beat a small, slightly irregular rhythm.

Sybil buttoned the woman's sweater then covered her with a bath towel retrieved from the clothes basket in the corner of the kitchen. She cradled the mug between her hands and walked out through the dining room into the living room and foyer.

It had been a long time since she'd been inside this house. There had never been a good enough reason to return. Richard had been kind enough to do most of the work in preparation for the tenants, this time the Camerons, but as of today, he was getting the pink slip. The boy hadn't even bothered to see there was barely a plate or a glass in the place. Renting took its toll on a house and its contents, but no one should pay good money to eat dinner with their fingers.

And when had the buffet table been moved? She didn't recall it ever being against that wall before. Now there was something else to talk to Richard about. If a body wanted something to be done right, well, she'd just have to do it herself. Or not. Until she met Charlie, there really was no need to visit the house again.

Now, it was important she see for herself the lifestyle of Annie and Charlie, especially Charlie. A growing boy like him needed lots of attention and more food than he was sure to be getting. It was no wonder he was as thin as a stick, what with all that instant food mush stashed away in the cabinets and no plates with which to eat it.

She snorted at the thought and made a mental list of fresh fruits and vegetables for the pies and soups she would make, and to look for a sale on dishes and glasses. Oh, and some more gingerbread makings since Charlie seemed to like it so much. That is, until the fishing trip with Winston yesterday.

Charlie had scarcely touched the fresh gingerbread then, and hardly said a word on top of that. Winston had been off his usual appetite and steady stream of conversation as well. Something was up, and she had told them as much, but the two pushed gingerbread around in their plates and stayed quiet as church mice. They wouldn't even look at her, barely looked at each other for that matter, and try as she might, they wouldn't budge an inch on the story behind the silence.

But that was all right, too. Men needed their shared stories and their little secrets. God knew Winston and Phillip had kept plenty of secrets from her. Eventually, the stories surfaced in the form of practical jokes usually, but they came out in the light sooner or later.

She just hoped that whatever it was Winston and Charlie hid was, in fact, a joke and not something else.

****

Annie adjusted the towel around her waist when a sudden gust of wind yanked the hat off her head and sent it flying inward over a dune. She groaned and started what was bound to be a lengthy chase, especially without Charlie helping this time. Leaping over the dune, she scanned the flat landscape near the tree line for a sign of the airborne hat, and stopped short.

The woman from the park bench waited. A light breeze gently swirled the black veil that covered her face and revealed nothing. The inexpensive material that formed her long black dress danced and swayed in the wind, daring only a brief glimpse of painfully thin ankles, and the severe pointed shoes almost buried in the bright white sand. Her hands, covered in gloves, also deep black, reached out as if to summon an embrace.

A knot formed in Annie's throat, her legs shook and threatened a fall if she didn't move away right now. She turned in the thick sand and fought the pull of the beach as if it tried to keep her there. One step away, another, when the voice called out:

"Annie Cameron."

She froze in place, sank deeper into the sand, then slowly turned to the woman. "Who are you?"

The pause was hollow, emotionless, and punctuated only by a wind that moaned softly and rustled the leaves of small underbrush.

"How do you know me?" Annie asked.

"I know myself," came the simple answer. Her

hands dropped to her sides without benefit of any other movement in her body.

Annie took a deep breath, fought the pull of the sand until she was free, and backed away a step while never looking away from the woman in black. "I don't believe I caught your name."

"I never gave it."

"And I never talk to strangers."

"A lesson you've taught the boy?"

"You know Charlie?" Annie asked, brushing away a tickle that brushed across her neck.

"His name is Charlie." It was a statement, colorless, and void of judgment.

"We're staying on the island for a little while."

"Manchester Place."

"Yes. My husband didn't come. He——" She stopped herself as the tickle across her neck traveled up and down her spine and sent a warning signal to her mind.

This woman, this apparition that stood like a dark beacon in a sea of white sand, was a stranger deft at obtaining nervous-induced information that was none of her business. And, until now, Annie found herself all too willing to talk. She backed another step.

"I have nothing more to say to you."

The wind died then, and it was quiet. Annie's steps came faster, easier, and she relished the idea of freeing herself from this strange woman and this uneasy blip in her otherwise peaceful afternoon.

"Wait." The word was soft but urgent.

"I'm going home now," Annie said over her shoulder. "I don't want to talk to you anymore."

"Charlie is in danger."

Annie stopped as if she had been punched in the stomach. Her hands went protectively to her belly.

"How dare you." Fear and anger suddenly surged through her sending her back toward the woman in rapid steps. "How dare you stand there looking like a funeral home poster child and tell me my son is in danger. What gives you the right to say such despicable things? You don't even know me, and I sure as hell don't know you."

The woman's voice was quiet. "I do know you. I know you as I knew myself."

"Well," Annie said sarcastically, "I feel so much better now that you've cleared all this up."

"My name is Eleanor," the woman said, slowly reaching for the black veil covering her face. "Eleanor Trippett. I once stayed at Manchester Place."

She pulled the veil back over the top of her head and looked at Annie with sunken dark eyes surrounded by deep blue-black circles. Her cadaveric face was little more than a skull with pale skin pulled taut over high cheekbones and a pointed chin. The thin line of her mouth held no color. There was not a single hint of what lay beyond the dark eyes.

Annie recoiled inwardly, but held her position and her gaze. "You said my son was in danger."

"Yes. As was mine twenty-five years ago during a storm."

"What happened to him?"

"He was taken from me."

"Taken?"

"By the woman."

"What woman?" Annie asked, trying desperately to understand.

"The woman in the house. She's there now."

"Look, Ms. Trippett, I don't know what you're talking about. And if this is so important, why didn't you tell me before now?"

"I had to wait."

"Wait?" Annie's patience frayed. "Wait for what?"

"For you to leave the house. You never left until today, and I can't go there. She won't let me."

"Who?"

"The woman. She's there now."

Annie rubbed a hand across her forehead and sighed. "We're talking in circles, and I don't mind telling you it's a bit maddening." The thought touched her then. "How did you know I was staying in Manchester Place, and that I hadn't left the house until today?"

"McKenzie's store. I'm staying in a room above it, and I can hear everything. They talk about you, about me."

She didn't doubt for a moment there was talk about the odd Ms. Trippett. That topic alone could probably fuel gossip for weeks, but why would Annie be a source of conversation?

"You're staying at Manchester Place. They know its past."

"And what would that be?"

"A woman alone, her husband gone, and a child. When the storm comes, someone will die."

"That's crazy."

Eleanor shook her head. "It sounds crazy, and maybe it is, but it's the only thing I have left by way of explanation," she said in a monotone. "For twenty-five years, I agonized over what happened and stayed as far away from this place as I could. When my son was taken, I lost everything, but that didn't matter because nothing mattered anymore. I went home, pulled the drapes to block the light, and never opened them again for twenty-five years. It hasn't been long enough."

"Why are you here now, Ms. Trippett?"

"For you. For me. This should never happen again."

"Nothing will happen."

"It will. You must leave while you can."

Annie pitied this strange woman and her illness. That's what it had to be, an unbalanced state as a result of her child being taken. Or maybe Eleanor Trippett's mental status was questioned long before, and led to the child being taken from her. It was hard to say, and their continuous loop of conversation was sure to produce no clear answers. Annie appreciated the woman's concern, and her need to venture from a dark room, but she refused to play along. Manchester Place was now a lifeline while she decided her next move. Grandma seemed happy here, and Charlie had new friends in Winston and Sybil Mann.

Eleanor Trippett seemed to know Annie's answer almost before she did, "She's been watching you, and will use you to get what she wants. That's her way. Keep an eye on your son. She's been watching him, too." Slowly she pulled the veil down over her face. "I've done all I can. It's up to you now."

"Who is in the house?" Annie shouted.

But the woman was gone, a vision of black merging with the dark woods.

A woman in the house? There was no one there right now, but Grandma and Sybil Mann, and neither one of them could hurt a fly.

Keep an eye on your son.

She looked up at the sky and worried at how long she'd been gone, and if he was all right. Her eyes widened at the fear something might have happened. It was a feeling more than any concrete proof, and maybe it was only paranoia set off by a woman clothed in black. But it was enough to touch off guilt and concern for her son's well-being. She should have never left him alone. Never.

Tugging her feet from the thick sand, she walked then ran down the beach as fast as she could.

****

Sybil took a sip of coffee and looked around the living room. Nothing had changed at Manchester Place, yet it felt different, lonely somehow. A house like this needed a family who could bring happiness back to its dark walls and deep shadows.

She had been happy here once, happier than she had ever been before or since. Inheriting this place was the answer to their dreams. The moldy apartment on the mainland was tolerated to make Winston happy while he fought to keep his business going. Then the letter came from England. Winston's uncle, tired of maintaining what he considered to be an albatross from thousands of miles away, finally offered the house and its furnishings free and clear. All Sybil and Winston had to do was say the word.

A smile settled on her lips. It was in this very room where they'd opened the bottle of champagne, an extravagance they could ill afford, and toasted their luck and their love. He told her how much she meant to him, and in the light of a roaring blaze in this huge fireplace, she told him she was expecting their child. Licking her lips, she could almost taste the kiss he gave her that night.

She took another sip of the coffee, frowned at the bitterness, and headed up the stairs. A quick run of her finger across the top of the landing mirror proved Annie Cameron a meticulous housekeeper. That was good; a house should be kept clean and neat. Continuing up, Sybil stopped at the hallway landing to catch her breath. It didn't seem all that long ago when she could take the steps in minutes without so much as a quick gasp, especially if she heard Phillip crying in the nursery.

Sybil trudged up the last few steps, then stopped at the open library door. The shelves Winston had built were still filled with the hundreds of books he had collected over a lifetime, a fraction of what he had stashed away in shelves and boxes at their other house. He had read every one of them, too, but the ones he'd left here were a select group, a choice he hoped would please any tenant who chose Manchester Place for a vacation. The hours he'd spent picking and choosing just the right books would have made a librarian swoon, she had told him. As usual, he ignored her comments and went about his work with the seriousness of an undertaker.

Undertaker.

Why that word of all words? Maybe because this room had been Phillip's room? Try as they might, it would never be anything else. Shelves, books, an easy chair, and a small table might make it look like a library, but she would always know it as the nursery for the son who would never grow up to appreciate the house as an adult—or inherit it from his parents.

She pulled the door shut, and cringed at the latch click in the frame. The room would never be used for little boys again. If it were up to her, it would stay locked forever, sealed if possible, like the door to the widow's walk.

The sound of her feet on the wooden floors mimicked the sudden hollowness she felt. She stopped briefly for a glance into Charlie's room. The bed was a tumble of sheets and blankets. A brief second of narrowed-eyed disapproval turned to a light shrug. Boys always seemed to have more important things to do than make beds and keep their rooms neat. It was to be expected.

Scanning the room with a discerning eye, she stepped back then squinted for a closer look. An ugly, green fuzzy toy with bouncing paper eyes glared at her from the middle of the dresser. The mirror behind it made it look as if there were two of them, instead of the horrible one. Her face wrinkled in disgust at the awful thing. Didn't boys like soldiers and trucks anymore? Maybe things had changed more than she knew, but it certainly wasn't for the better.

Sybil ambled further down the hall to take a look at the master bedroom and smiled at the big bed. She and Winston spent many nights with Phillip snuggled between the two of them. His little feet pushed first him then her until he settled down and slept a contented, peaceful sleep.

A door slammed.

She jumped then tiptoed to the little attic room at the top of a small flight of stairs. The hinge released a delayed squeak, and sprinkled a light rain of rust. Even though the house was a bit drafty, no small breeze could move a door as substantial as that.

Something giggled in Charlie's room.

She cocked her head to listen. There it was again.

It was a tiny squeak of laughter, muffled, growing in pitch, then dropping as if it were catching its breath for the next outburst.

The room was silent, as it was a few minutes ago, and nothing was different.

Except for the toy.

Standing near the base of the door, it looked up at her from the floor where moments ago it sat in the middle of the dresser.

****

Charlie. All alone on the beach.

Nausea welled in Annie's stomach, became a burning in her throat. She ran back over the dune and down the beach to where she had left him, all the while telling herself not to panic. He had to be okay.

He was fine, he'd be working on his castle, his sand masterpiece, and she would laugh herself silly when she saw he was having a good time. But right now she had to see him.

The beating of her heart thundered in her ears. The towel slid down her hips, dropped to her feet; she kicked it out of the way, ran faster.

There was her untouched beach bag, sitting where she left it. She scanned the surf. No Charlie. A sharp pain arced in her chest. Her legs cramped, forcing her to slow to a limping trot.

And then she stopped. The mound of mud and sand at her feet was Charlie's castle, half-washed away by the tide.

Her legs gave way then, and she slumped down in

the mud, gasping for breath and holding her sides with the pain. Another cramp caught her in the stomach. She leaned forward and vomited. Water washed up around her knees, pulled the rest of the castle with it as it rolled out again.

"Charlie." His name came out in a barely audible whisper.

"Mom?"

Standing ten feet behind her on the dry sand was her son.

"Charlie!" She pulled herself up and rushed to grab him with muddied arms. "Thank God you're all right. Thank God."

He squirmed away with the attention. "You're dirty."

She laughed then caressed his face with sandy hands. "You scared me to death, little guy. Did you know that?"

Pushing her hands away, he started walking inland. He was leaving her.

Relief turned to rage. "Where the hell do you think you're going?" She regretted the words as soon as she spoke them. "Charlie?"

He kept walking.

"Charlie, baby. I was worried, that's all. I didn't mean to yell at you. I was just scared. Charlie?"

He hesitated, turned. A split second of hate crossed his eyes, followed almost immediately by wide-eyed fear. Running to her in awkward, floundering steps, he grabbed her around the waist as if he were a much younger child than ten.

"It's okay, baby. We're together now."

"You left me."

"I'm sorry. I'm so sorry." He shivered then held tighter to her waist.

"I shouldn't have left you. Forgive me?"

"She was calling me. She laughed."

Annie knelt in the sand and grabbed Charlie by the shoulders. "Who, Charlie?"

"The lady." His eyes glazed then, and his thumb went to his mouth.

She shook him. "Charlie!" Then shook him harder.

He smiled a simple baby smile as if he had just been fed and burped, and now was ready for sleep. Sucking noisily on his thumb, he had turned inward, gone inside where she couldn't touch him.

There would be no more talking; there would be no more hugs.

"My God." The words were barely a whisper. "Dear God, help me."

She urged him over to the beach bag, wrapped a towel around him and rubbed his shoulders, arms, chest. "Come on, baby."

She picked up the bag, hooked it over her shoulder and steered her son to the tree line. "We'll go home now. I'll make you something really good for supper. What will it be? You tell me."

She guided him over the footpath by her shaking hand on his pliant shoulder. He moved easily at her touch with no will of his own, like a marionette dancing on strings directed by someone else. She kept up a stream of chatter as if stopping would lose him to—what?—a dark hole that swallowed scared little boys? There was no emotional place she could make that was worse than the one Charlie could make for himself. He was his worst enemy, his most heavy-handed disciplinarian, the creator of black holes where he could fall and never climb out of again. Unless he went there willingly, out of fear from things, people.

Her.

Annie shuddered. No, she only had high hopes and high dreams for her son. Dreams were supposed to be fun, fanciful, light-hearted. If she were lucky, really lucky, her dreams would come true. An icy chill crept up her spine, and hair stood up on the back of her neck. But then there were the recent dreams, the ones she couldn't remember, and the waking dreams she wanted to forget.

They walked on as the great house on the bay loomed into view. The big trees, their leaves swaying with the wind and the weight of moss, implied tranquility she didn't feel. There was something very wrong here now, something dangerous. Manchester Place had changed.

She stopped with the sight, tightened the hold on Charlie's shoulder that pulled him to stop as well.

A shadow danced and moved with the wind against the graying light of the horizon, skirted the widow's walk, and reached for the tree overhanging over the walk.

An explosion split the air.

Annie jumped at the sound, screamed, and grabbed Charlie to her.

A large limb from the oak tree snapped, then crashed through smaller branches, plummeting to the edge of the widow's walk where it tottered then came to rest. A tree limb had scared her, nothing else. There were no phantoms that danced across the widow's walk, just evening clouds that loomed large, billowed, and swayed then left as suddenly as they appeared.

Relief flooded through her then was replaced by the new, awful thought; she hated this place and what it did to her. The island, the house, deranged people on the beach, they had all turned her into the frightened child she thought she had long since outgrown. Once a child afraid of the dark, she was now more afraid of sleep and the dreams this place brought her.

Adult or child, she was afraid of losing her family, and in some ways, she had even encouraged the loss by not picking up her toys when her mother told her, or refusing to listen to her father.

And she didn't listen to David when he insisted that having a baby at this point in their lives was a mistake.

She released her grip on Charlie, and moved her hands to her belly.

From the beginning, she knew it was going to be a boy. He would be named Charlie after his great-grandfather, and the three of them would live happily ever after.

If only David could see it that way.

The voice came to her, quiet and calm. *I'll wait for you.*

She looked at the house surrounded and warmed by shades of gray as dusk arrived. A soft breeze blew gently, surrounded her, caressed.

"I'll wait for you," she mouthed.

It spoke again with sound as soft as the wind that enveloped her in warmth and protection while sheltering her from things that would hurt.

She's there. In the house. She will take your son.

The front door to Manchester Place flew open.

Sybil motioned to Grandma to stay in the doorway then bolted down the steps of the porch. She looked up at the huge branch, tottering on the widow's walk then to Annie and Charlie standing among the trees.

"Stay back. There's no telling when that thing is going to give."

Annie's jaw tightened at the sight of Sybil Mann. This was the woman Eleanor Trippett warned of. It had to be.

"Are you okay, Charlie?" Sybil asked. Her voice quavered, her hands trembled, concern in her face.

There, just outside the house, stood Sybil asking not of Annie's welfare, but Charlie's. Sybil and Winston had certainly tried everything they could to wrest Charlie away with their gingerbread, warm clothing, and fishing trips.

And there was Winston's strange behavior at the dock when he caught sight of the woman clad in black. He had turned the boat away from her, refused to explain who she was because—Annie fought with the thought, the memory—perhaps the Manns had taken another child twenty-five years ago. Maybe Eleanor Trippett wasn't crazy after all.

So that was it. There were no specters, no hauntings that could drive people to leave this beautiful house when they had no place to go. Sybil wouldn't interfere with her, or her family again, Annie would see to that.

A warm breeze touched her again and gave peace to the disturbing thoughts. The house wasn't hateful at all. She was wrong to think it was bad, or that it would cause her pain. Instead, the home provided protection and comfort. Her home now.

It was *his* home too and he would be back soon.

Annie would make some bread and wrap it up so that he'd have a little something to eat on the long trip to the mainland. He would like that. And then she would wait. She would stand in the water while the sound of oars dissipated to silence then climb to the widow's walk for the days to months to years to wait for the light from the boat that signaled his return to her.

Manchester Place was where she could stay while she waited for his return.

"Come along, Charlie," she said, propelling him to the house. "There are things to do. Important things."

****

Sybil stared wide-eyed as Annie pushed Charlie's limp, yielding body closer to the door.

"Charlie? It's Auntie Syb."

The child didn't answer; his face was empty, void of any sign of recognition. Uneasiness washed over Sybil. In the back of her mind, something nagged. "I'm telling you, it might be better to wait a bit. See what happens with the tree."

"Nonsense, Sybil." Annie's voice was even, controlled. "We'll be fine. You'll see." She brushed past Sybil without slowing her pace and guided Charlie into the house.

"Wait."

Annie turned. "Everything's fine, Sybil. Couldn't be better."

"I just..." Sybil searched for anything that might buy time while she figured out what was happening. "The cookies. Heavens to Betsy, I forgot all about them. They're probably burned to a crisp by now. I'll get them out of the oven before you know it."

The door closed to little more than a crack. Only a fraction of Annie's face was visible.

"I'll take care of it." Her voice became flat, almost monotone. "Good night, Sybil."

"The tree. Winston and Richard will take a look—"

The door clicked shut, the lock turned in the frame.

Sybil stood in silence then knocked on the door. She pounded, called out, but there was no response, and she knew now there wouldn't be one. Trying to muster anger, she found nothing but unease. Whatever had happened to Annie today would ultimately affect Charlie.

He was an innocent, just a little boy, Phillip's age.

Phillip.

Unease grew to anxiety then an impulse to run.

But running makes you run that much harder until there is nothing left but running—

The bad thoughts came back with a vengeance and refused to budge. Not since Phillip's death had she felt this way, not since the stay in the hospital and the thoughts that kept her there for so long. She rubbed a sweaty palm on her dress.

Sybil stumbled down the front steps.

It wasn't going to happen to her again. They wouldn't lock her up and inject her with tranquilizers and anti-depressants until she didn't know her name or her husband's face.

Whatever was happening, had happened, she could deal with now. Sybil breathed deep, counted then took another breath. Everything would be all right if she took things slow. Anxiety oozed away with each released breath. Edging around the side of the house, she squinted against the coming dusk for the trail that would lead her home. The crawl space door under the house was open. Odd. It had always been locked in the past. Maybe Winston or Richard needed something that was stored there. She'd ask them about it later when she was home.

She shot a look up at the kitchen window then to the widow's walk above it. The tree limb stayed where it had fallen, for now. Winston and Richard would take care of it.

Manchester Place wasn't home anymore. Maybe it had never been her home but belonged to someone else all along, someone that thrived on it. Or someone who thrived by those living in it.

Sybil entered the footpath, looked back over her shoulder at the widow's walk then faced the darkening woods in front of her. The run-down little house she shared with Winston was her home now.

Now, more than ever, she wished she were there.

Chapter 12

Annie peered out from behind the heavy drapes of the living room window and watched Sybil back down the porch steps and turn toward the side of the house. Dropping her hold on the curtains, she went through the dining room to the kitchen where the smell of burning cookies filled the air. With a quick flick of her wrist, she turned off the heat to the oven then went to the small kitchen window in time to see Sybil step into the darkness of the footpath to head home.

Leaning back against the windowsill, she sighed deeply then saw Charlie and Grandma standing in the doorway. "Get your books, Charlie. We'll read a little bit while I figure out what to have for dinner."

He lingered a moment then shuffled away.

She listened to his footsteps on the stairs, glanced out the window one more time, and turned to the refrigerator. "What do you think, Grandma? Meatloaf, or should we keep it simple and go with sandwiches?"

"You made her leave."

"What was that?"

"That nice woman, Sybil. You made her leave. You did it on purpose."

"It's my house. I make the decisions here. Not you, or her, or anyone else for that matter." Annie reached into the meat and cheese bin. "We'll have sandwiches tonight."

"I like her."

"I'm glad for you, Grandma."

"Charlie likes her, too."

Arms piled with sandwich makings, she bumped the refrigerator door closed with her hip, and headed to the counter next to the sink. "We will not discuss this anymore."

"We have to."

"You're tired. How about a quick nap before supper?"

"Annie, I'm not a child. Please don't treat me like one."

A child, not this minute anyway, who knew what age she'd be in an hour, two hours, or tomorrow. Annie turned the faucet on full force, shoved a head of lettuce under the running water, and stole a glance at her mother-in-law, who stared back with clear and determined eyes. Any other time Grandma left the decision-making solely in Annie's lap, had to in fact, but now all of a sudden Grandma had an opinion.

Couldn't Grandma see Sybil was trying to take Charlie away?

The evidence was unmistakable.

Or was it? Confusion nibbled at her.

Sybil was being nice, as was Winston and Richard. Charlie liked them all, so did Grandma. Was Sybil really capable of taking Charlie away from her? Or was it another in a string of hyperactive fantasies prompted this time by a crazy woman in black?

Charlie was her son, a child nurtured and cultivated into what he was and what he could be by her hand. She loved him, and in his way, he loved her, too. No one could break that bond, no one. But somehow, in the course of a few days, she found herself caught in a web of ambivalence, paranoia, and foreign thoughts. It was all so confusing, and not a little disconcerting that there were things she never knew about herself now coming to light—things better left buried.

And if that wasn't enough, she had run off, maybe even alienated, the only people she knew on the island and the only link to the mainland. Her face flushed at her erratic behavior. As of now, she'd watch herself a little more closely, think before she acted then act rationally. An apology was in order, and the sooner, the better—if only she could remember why it all happened in the first place and what prompted it.

She dropped what remained of the lettuce head in the sink. "No, you're not a child, and I should never have implied you were. You're a woman who can still teach this child right from wrong. I treated Sybil badly, and I'm sorry. Tomorrow I'll make a point of telling her the same thing."

"The cookies burned."

"I know. I'd bring her some of my homemade, but Charlie is the only one who eats them, out of pity for me, I think. You've had my cookies. What do you think?"

"They're not very good." A slight grin crossed Grandma's lips.

Annie raised an eyebrow and formed a smile of her own. "You never told me you didn't like my cookies."

"Pity."

"You, too?"

"We can't all be good at everything. I could make a mean cookie when I was younger. Your talent is being a teacher and a mother."

She scrubbed a tomato under the water. "I wish that were true."

"It is true. Charlie needs you now more than ever, but lately, you don't seem to have time for him."

"David's asked for a divorce."

"I know."

"How could you? I haven't told anyone."

"But you have, in a way. Charlie knew before me."

She paused, knife hovering over the ripe tomato. "How is it you know these things, Grandma? Yesterday you saw what I was dreaming."

"Did I?" Her face wrinkled in concern. "I don't remember."

"Yesterday, you called me from the top of the stairs and said...never mind." The memory of what happened to Grandma, and what could have happened if she had fallen was more than Annie could bear right now. "How do you know what people are thinking?"

Grandma shrugged. "It's just a feeling, a picture in my mind's eye that comes to me. Sometimes it turns out to be true. Other times it's just the ramblings of an old woman whose mind is slipping away."

"Don't talk like that."

"I know what's happening to me, Annie. Most of the time. I'm not afraid."

"There's no reason to be afraid. I'll always be there for you."

"Will you, dear? I always hoped so."

"Promise." She sliced the tomato. "Charlie knew about the divorce? How?"

"He knows more than you think."

"I suppose. Frankly, that's a bit of relief since I didn't know how to tell him. David means so much to him."

"David is a shit."

"Grandma!" She dropped the knife and stared at the old woman.

"What's the matter? You don't think I know what David's like?"

"Yes. No. That you would call him that."

"If the shoe fits."

"It does, at least by my calculations. I would have never guessed in a million years you'd call him that, though." She picked up the knife to finish slicing the tomato in thick, meaty pieces and laughed. Grandma was full of surprises. "It makes it easier somehow, you saying that and all. I was afraid I'd made a mistake, missed something that I should have done. I could have been more patient, understanding, tolerant even."

"You have the patience of Job. I'm surprised you stayed this long." Grandma leaned against the doorframe and picked a thread from her dress. "I'm glad you stayed, for selfish reasons, of course. He's my son, and I love him, but honestly, sometimes, I think he should have been left on someone's doorstep." She stifled a yawn. "You know something? I think I will take that nap you were talking about."

"Try the couch in the living room. I'll call you when supper's ready."

"Annie?" There was an edge to her voice. "It's getting worse, isn't it?"

"What do you mean?"

"My forgetting. Not knowing what happened in the past hours or days."

"You'll be fine."

"The doctor lied about how bad it was, but I knew.

It's a horrible feeling, Annie, to know your mind is going and you can't do anything about it, to be an adult one minute and something else, I don't know, the next. But I'm not afraid."

Annie went to her, wrapped her arms around Grandma in a tight hug. "I'll take care of you. Don't you worry."

"There are worse things than dying."

"Please, Grandma, don't say that."

Grandma cleared her throat. "I suppose you should get some clothes on. You'll catch pneumonia in that skimpy bathing suit of yours."

"I forgot I was wearing it. I'll throw on some jeans and a shirt and be right down to finish the sandwiches."

She kissed Grandma on the cheek and ran up the steps. Catching her breath at Charlie's door, she saw him drawing something under the single lit lamp over his desk. His tongue stuck out of the side of his mouth in deep concentration.

"What are you working on, baby?"

There was no response. The pencil in his hand flowed over the paper in rapid, easy strokes. Pushing the paper aside with one hand, he continued the drawing on a new page without a break or pause.

"Charlie?" She stood behind him.

His pencil moved across the paper, creating bold lines, lighter ones then shades of gray. He drew a woman wearing a dark robe that rolled in the wind then shoved the paper aside to start on the next picture.

This one was a lantern tipped on its side. Fire spilled from it and crept across the floor and the walls.

Another page. Rain. A torrential fall of water was interspersed with wind that fueled a battle of fire fighting rain, fire fighting wind.

Next page. A staircase. A menacing woman stood at the top of the stairs, while another woman walked toward her.

"Charlie." Her voice was strained. "Stop it."

The woman, barely a silhouette, loomed over a small boy. His eyes were large with terror.

Annie pried the pencil from his death-grip hold and slammed it on the desk. "Stop it this minute."

His empty hand moved in quick strokes across the paper; his eyes stared straight ahead.

She shook him gently at first, then harder.

Charlie looked at her as if seeing a stranger. Recognition came, followed by stunned silence. His face paled, his eyes glazed.

Then he blacked out.

****

"Thank you for coming, doctor."

The bearded young man hoisted his medical bag under his arm, waved to Annie, and walked down the steps. Winston Mann shook the doctor's hand, pointed in the direction of the bay, and mumbled something about *Errand Two* ready when he was for the trip back to the mainland.

"How about a cup of tea?" Sybil asked. "Might do you some good."

"No thanks, Sybil," Annie said, looking up the stairs. "I'm not in the mood. I think I'll take a peek at Charlie, see how he's doing."

"You were in there five seconds ago, and he was sleeping like a baby. With that shot Dr. Nesheim gave him, he'll be out for the night and halfway into tomorrow. C'mon. Let me fix you something."

Sybil yanked Annie from the couch and propelled her into the kitchen. "Look at that. So Winston did do a little something while we were busy with Charlie. And a nice fire it is. Just right for a night with a touch of edge to it. You sit next to it while I put on a pot to boil. There you go."

"Really, Sybil. You've done enough. More than enough. I can never repay you."

"Who's asking for payment? All I want is some hot tea in that belly of yours. A little brandy wouldn't hurt either." She cocked her head and winked. "I don't suppose you've got any spirits, medicinal, of course?"

"None. Too bad, huh?"

"Well, you do with what you've got. Damn. I forgot you don't have any tea." She fussed around the cabinets then turned down the fire under the pot. "Not to worry. I'll think of something."

"Sybil?"

"Yes?"

"I'm sorry."

"For what?" Sybil's back tightened at the poor lie.

"For the way, I treated you this evening. It was unfair, and I apologize. Will you forgive me?"

"Of course I will, my darling. Sometimes we do things we don't mean. They sort of happen, don't they? I suppose I should apologize myself."

"You? Why?"

"Well, Annie, sometimes I'm a little pushy. Oh, I don't mean to be, but I can't seem to help it. It's the mother in me. I'm always taking care of someone. 'Mothering them to death,' Winston says."

"We have that much in common, at least."

"You might have noticed I've taken a shine to that

little boy of yours. He's a special one, that's for sure."

"Keep an eye on your son," Annie mumbled.

"What's that?"

"Hmm? Did I say something?" Annie rubbed her eyes, massaged her neck. "I don't know what's come over me, what I'm saying anymore."

"Are there thoughts? Different from those you've ever had before?"

"Yes."

"A whisper, a voice that appears in your head?"

"Yes, Sybil. Just like that. I don't always remember what's said, but I know it happened. I think it happened."

Sybil brought two steaming mugs of coffee over to the table. Annie, I want you to listen to me very closely. Just hear me out." Her voice quavered, so she cleared her throat, tried again. "There was a house on this island finished around the turn of the nineteenth century. It was a great house with tabby walls four feet thick and built on a tabby foundation. The ceilings were high, the many rooms spacious and grand and ready to host another of the lavish parties that filled the place. People came from all over the world for the parties, stayed a week or two then went on about their business. Some stayed for months on the graciousness of the all too willing hosts."

"I went looking for the ruins on the south end of the island today," Annie said.

"You didn't find them."

"No, I didn't."

"Because what's left of the house is here, under this one."

"What happened?"

Sybil leaned back in her chair and continued. "Finances became a problem. The upkeep of the house proved expensive and difficult. Materials were hard to come by, and since money was scarce, deterioration started setting in. The owners of the first Manchester Place could find no buyers and were left with an albatross they couldn't get rid of, or restore to its previous state of finery. And then there was the daughter, an only child.

"She was crazy as a beanbag. Word of her mental state had spread everywhere. Many had seen her behavior firsthand at the parties and the lengthy stays and knew all about her. She was of marrying age, past it really, so her parents arranged a marriage. The only man who accepted this arrangement did so after an offer of what money was left, and the house as a wedding present. No one else would consider the woman, even with the dowry. Her parents abandoned her for England immediately after the wedding and were never heard from again."

Sybil sipped the hot coffee, didn't flinch as a splash of it fell to her lap, and saturated her housedress. "He was gone for years at a time, the husband. A whaler from the coast of New England, that meant he had to leave here to reach the northeast coast months before an expedition began. A long time he would be gone, a very long time." She paused, took another sip. "What no one expected happened. She fell in love with the man and tried everything she could to keep him home with her. Nothing worked, not even a son."

Annie stared at the crackling fire, the orange-red flames dancing within the hearth. "What has this got to do with me?"

"She killed the boy, and herself, by burning the whole place down with a kerosene lantern. Eighty years ago, this house was built on that foundation, the only thing left after the fire. Or so Winston thought."

"I still don't see what you're driving at."

"Winston tried to talk to me about it a couple of days ago, but I wouldn't listen. I couldn't bring myself to think it was true. Or to live through it again."

"I'm going to check on Charlie." Annie stood, but Sybil grabbed her arm and pulled her down into the chair.

"I believe Winston may be right, that she's still here since you've heard the whispers, the voice."

"I won't listen to this, Sybil."

"You have to. There's no choice."

Annie yanked her arm away from Sybil. "I don't care about some crazy woman who used to live on this site a long time ago. And I certainly don't buy she's still here."

"It's not a joke, Annie. Winston thinks she took our son."

"And what do you think?"

"I don't know what to think. What I do know is you must leave this place. Leave it now in case it's true, and she tries to take your son, too."

"Or before you do."

Sybil stopped, the mug suspended halfway to her mouth. "What?"

"Eleanor Trippett warned me about you just today."

"Who is Eleanor Trippett?"

"She said a woman took her son, and to keep an eye on Charlie since that same woman had been watching him."

"Annie—"

"You're that woman, aren't you? You've been trying to take Charlie away from me ever since I got here. Don't think I didn't notice."

The mug slid from Sybil's hands to the tabletop. "You're wrong, Annie. Terribly wrong."

"And now you want me to leave. Well, I'll just bet you do. That'll make it a whole lot easier, won't it? I leave, and Charlie stays, is that it?"

"Don't you see what's happening? What she's doing to you?"

"Who? The madwoman who once walked this place? I have news for you, Sybil, I'm looking at her right now."

"I don't know this Eleanor Trippett person or why she said those things. All I know is I'm trying to protect you, Annie, from what I went through. Don't let what happened to Phillip happen to Charlie. You love Charlie, don't you? Well then, take him away before he gets hurt."

There was a knock at the door. Both women jumped at the sound. Sybil looked over Annie's shoulder and waved Richard into the room.

"Good evening, ladies. Mr. Mann sent me here to escort his lovely wife home for the night. That is unless you two are planning a slumber party." Richard winked at Annie, got no response, and found a spot on his tennis shoe to examine.

"No," Annie said, picking up the mugs and carrying them over to the sink. "No slumber party, no party of any kind. In fact, Sybil was just leaving. Isn't that right, Sybil?"

"Speaking of parties," he said, "a real nice one is planned for next week on the mainland. A dressy affair, so I hear. I don't suppose..." He saw Annie's face then found the spot on his shoe again. "No, I suppose not."

"C'mon, Romeo," Sybil said. "I've worn out my welcome."

"It's kinda cool outside," he said. "Unusual for this time of year, and it's started raining. You better wear my jacket, Ms. Mann."

"Thanks, Richard. I'll do that. It wouldn't do for the arthritis to kick in just now." Sybil stopped at the door. "Annie?"

"Yes?" Her voice turned to ice.

"Please think about what I told you. There's no time to waste." She walked out the door then turned back at the last minute. "I mean it. Every word. I'll even give you back your rent money; it's that important."

"I'll keep that in mind, Sybil. Good night."

"Good night."

****

Annie heard Richard's muffled "night" as she closed the door, and an indecipherable comment from Sybil.

So it was true a ghost woman stalked this place for little boys. A ghost woman from two centuries ago clearly had nothing better to do with her time than hang around a vacation house.

She'd just bet.

Sybil wanted Annie to leave the house so she could keep Charlie for herself. It was all clear now. Sybil's own son was gone, and that made Charlie some kind of a replacement. These past days of gingerbread and fishing trips were just a way to win Charlie over with their stability and strength compared to Annie's incompetence as a mother. Taking care of Grandma this afternoon was just a fact-finding mission to get information Sybil could use to take Charlie from her.

It all finally added up. First, it was her husband taken away by another woman, and now Sybil Mann wanted her son.

Eleanor Trippett was right in her warnings. But she had heard other warnings as well, warnings by a voice, a whisper deep in her mind. The voice was nothing but intuition that until now, she had refused to trust.

An inner voice told her she was responsible for breaking up her parents' marriage, but she had buried the thought.

Intuition had told her not to marry David, but she had ignored it. Then it reminded her she was an unfit mother since Charlie had so many problems.

That same intuition now warned her of Sybil Mann's intentions. This time it wouldn't be cast aside. She would listen and do what was necessary.

She will take your son. She will have you leave.

Annie wouldn't leave this place, lose her only son and what was left of her dignity or her independence on Sybil's account, or anyone else's. Charlie was never to see the Manns again.

One decision down, the rest would be easier.

From now on, she would trust only herself and the little voice that spoke to her.

Chapter 13

Bay water swirled in dark circles around her, pulling, caressing, and beckoning her out to sea to follow him. She stood fixed against the current and listened as the sound of an oar to water softened with the distance between them. The light from a kerosene lantern became a pinpoint; a dull glow then disappeared into darkness.

She stood tall, another of many long shadows in the light of the moon, and stroked the small bulge in her belly. The baby, his baby, would be a boy.

And now he was leaving her. He would be gone for months, years. Maybe forever.

Unless she gave him reason to come back, a good reason.

She felt a stirring then, as if the little one knew what she couldn't bear to think.

He had warned her it wouldn't do, had told her to take whatever measures were necessary to prevent it since there could never be a child. Never. A child would not be a part of his life, nor would she if it meant bringing something so unwelcome into this house.

She had tried to obey, tried as hard as she could, but it was so lonely in the big house. Her footsteps echoed through the vast, empty rooms, and her voice fell unanswered in the quiet of the long days and longer nights.

As the cold bay water swirled around her, she caressed the stirring in her belly, loved what grew there, then looked out for one last glimmer of light, a glimmer of hope that he would come back to her.

There was only darkness on the horizon.

Day to week to month to year, if needed, she would pace the widow's walk for the light on the dark horizon that signaled his return.

She walked out of the water, stood on the soft sandy beach, and turned back to the bay. There was nothing but time now, and the stirring within her.

"I'll wait for you. You'll see."

****

Annie bolted awake with a hand to her chest to stop the pounding of her heart. Her flannel nightgown stuck to her in damp, wadded clumps. A chill shook her body with such violence that she pulled the comforter tight around her.

Then she felt it.

A grainy dampness covered her feet. She rubbed them together to rid them of what stuck there as it dug and cut into soft flesh. She turned on the lamp and uncovered her feet. Her eyes widened, and a whimper caught in her throat.

Sand.

The hem of her nightgown was wet from the beach where moments ago, the dream woman stood.

Where she had stood as well.

Chapter 14

Sybil Mann awakened to the cool, gray dawn and stared bleary-eyed at the bedside clock for the hundredth time. Six-thirty winked at her in a red electric glow as she wrangled the bedspread over her goosebump-covered shoulders. The almost obsessively neat tucked edges of the bed had become a tangle of sheets and bedspread as if a war had been waged while she slept. Rubbing away graininess in her dry eyes, she yawned wide and loud to quell the nausea that gripped her stomach from lack of a good rest. It had been a long time since she had a night like this, and only around-the-clock sedatives had stopped the insomnia before. She wished she had one of the little yellow pills now to help her sleep for an extra hour or two.

Another yawn and she stretched an arm to touch her husband. There was only a cool, empty place where he should have been.

"Winston?"

The bedroom door creaked open, revealing first his disheveled hair then his grumpy face. "You rang?"

"Are you okay?"

"I suppose I should be asking you the question."

"What do you mean?"

"The way you were flipping back and forth in bed, a roller coaster should have so much activity. I banished myself to the guest room for a little static shut-eye."

"Sorry. I didn't sleep too well."

"That makes two of us, pumpkin."

"I promise I'll do better if you join me now. I can't sleep without you beside me. Bad habit, I guess."

"There could be worse ones." He winked and rubbed a hand across his unshaven face. "But I'm awake now, so I'll just get on up and do a few chores."

"Mind if I rest a little longer?"

"Good idea." A look of mischief flashed over his face. "And in a couple of hours, I'll bring you some juice. Maybe cactus and lily-pond-water juice. Sound like it would hit the spot?"

She pushed away the nausea that rose in her and forced an amiable grin. "Yeah, and the spot would be about mid-way on that wall over there."

"Turn about is fair play."

"I get the point, you old curmudgeon. Go on with you."

"You're the boss." He pulled the door closed.

A few minutes later, his deep baritone singing voice competed with what she knew would be a steaming torrent of hot shower water. He tried for a waltz then gave it up for a fourth of a barbershop quartet tune. Sinking into the bed, she listened to his singing while trying to identify the thing that nagged, haunted, and disrupted her sleep. It was more than just the failed talk last night with Annie Cameron; there was Charlie to worry about, too.

She hoped Charlie was okay and decided he would probably sleep most of the day with the shot the doctor had given him. That was best since he and Annie had been through quite a shock. The very idea of seeing him draw pictures one after another as if his hand was guided by someone else—well, it was enough to give a body the shivers for a week or more.

If only she could see the pictures, it might tell her something.

Phillip's hand-scrawled message.

If only she had a little yellow pill. Just one.

"You still awake?"

Winston tugged at the towel hanging low over his hips and fumbled around in the chest of drawers, then the closet for his usual flannel shirt and corduroy trousers. He dressed, then sat on the edge of the bed and patted her hand.

"You still worried about the Cameron family?"

"No. Yes. In a way."

"I figured as much. One of my chores this morning is to head over there for a quick check. Will that make you feel better?"

It wasn't enough. The Camerons had to leave. And there was something else that worried her. "Who is Eleanor Trippett?"

He looked at her as if he didn't understand the question and quit patting her hand.

"You know her, don't you?"

"It's not important," he said thinly.

"Then tell me."

"I have things to do."

"Yes, indeed, Winston. And one of them is telling me about Eleanor Trippett."

He hesitated, looked about the room as if carefully formulating a plausible story.

"The truth, Winston. Not one of your tall tales this time."

"She stayed at Manchester Place for a while. That's

all."

"When? I don't remember a tenant by that name."

"It was a long time ago. She only stayed a few days, a week maybe."

"When was that?"

He acted as if he hadn't heard her question.

"C'mon Winston, I know I'm making words because I can hear them, and my mouth is moving. When did Eleanor Trippett stay at Manchester Place?"

"While you were gone."

"Oh."

"We needed the money."

"Yes. I understand now." When she was gone, during the bad times, there had been another tenant. And as bad as things were for Sybil, she would probably never know how awful it was for Winston. Still, she had to ask the question, had to know if her fears were founded. "Did anything happen to her? Anything, you know, out of the ordinary?"

"No."

"You're sure?"

"Positive."

She looked at her husband, his graying hair, the strength in his arms, and thought of the incongruous weakness of his heart. Now was not the time to tell him what she feared most. There would be no further talk about Eleanor Trippett until she was sure there was truth in Annie's words about her, and until all doubt of a ghost woman connection was pushed aside. Sybil rubbed his hand, then squeezed it.

"Yes. It'll make me feel better if you check on the Camerons. Thank-you."

"No problem." He caught a button that popped

loose from his shirt and tucked it into a pocket. "You sure you're okay? I'll be glad to stay and watch over you."

"A nursemaid is the last thing I need right now. Go on. I'll be fine, but don't overdo, you hear me?"

"Aye aye, Captain."

"Enough. Go on."

Mann patted his pocket then searched the top of the dresser. "Hm. I can't seem to find my pipe. In all the excitement last night, I must have dropped it somewhere." He headed for the door. "Well, that's one more chore, find the missing pipe. You didn't hide it, did you?"

"Hide it?"

"Yeah, put it away so I wouldn't smell up the house again."

"You know I like the smell of your pipe. Besides, if I wanted to hide something, I'd put it on the top shelf, very front of the refrigerator. As oblivious as you are to things, you'd never find it."

"Especially not there. Never think to look there. But I'll keep it in mind around Christmas time." He leaned over and kissed her on the forehead. "I'll be back before you know it."

"You do that."

The door closed. He whistled all the way down the stairs and through the kitchen to the creaking screen door that banged shut behind him.

She leaned back, closed her eyes, and knew that any chance of sleep had passed. There was nothing for it but to get up, face the day and whatever it was that bothered her. What was it?

Phillip?

Charlie?

There was a connection between the two, although her role in all this was vague if she played a part at all. And what part did Eleanor Trippett play? She slid out of bed, threw on a robe, and headed down the stairs for a cup of tea. Holding the handrail for support, her head still foggy from the sleepless night, she winced at the ache in her muscles. The stiffness in her body was equal to a disagreeable round with a sumo wrestler. She snickered at the thought. The islands off the Georgia coast might be known for some things—Loggerhead turtles, bird watching, shell collecting—but not sumo wrestling.

Visitors wanted pastime events that made their home routines and their mundane jobs a little more tolerable until the next vacation. They hung on from one year to the next in hope a trip would erase, at least for a week or two, the pain of day in and day out boredom. Even she had some of that, now and then, but boredom gave way to quiet, time to think and to organize thoughts and plans. Eventually, if one were lucky, it gave way to happiness of sorts.

Sybil was happy, happier than she had been in a long time; that is until the Camerons arrived. Now she was filled with worry for Charlie, for old Mrs. Cameron, even for Annie herself, and concerned that events of her past were now turning to them. But the events she had experienced were muddied, vague in recollection, and presented a difficult challenge in putting everything together.

Phillip...Charlie...herself. Phillip and herself. Now Charlie.

And there was a child by Eleanor Trippett, so

Annie claimed.

There was a thread connecting them, a pattern of some sort.

A chill crept up her spine. She shuddered, pulled the robe closer to her, and stumbled across the kitchen to grab the back of a chair.

Mother. Please. Please don't hurt me.

Phillip?

Nausea gripped her stomach, stung her throat. She collapsed in the chair then rested one side of her face on the cool tabletop. A minute passed, another, the thought faded, and she felt a little better.

A little yellow pill would be nice right now, just one to help her relax. "Amnesia makers," Winston had called them, and they had been, but not for near long enough. They worked on her mind while her body was confined within the dark, somber, high-bricked walls of the institution. The pills even worked for a few months after she left, until her natural amnesia could push away, bury and hide forever the truth of what happened at Manchester Place.

It has to be done, Phillip. You know it does.

She had convinced herself they were nightmares that tortured only during sleep, bad dreams that went away when the sun rose, and the body stirred. Now, after all these years, she knew they were more—she knew they were real.

Phillip's death, a house marred by its murderous past, was all at once disinterred from under the shallow mud of a memory-repressed grave.

Where are you, boy? You can't hide from me forever. I'll find you, and it'll be taken care of.

She remembered then, knew it as if it had just

happened. Another hand, another voice deep in her mind called her to do those things. They were things she would never have done before, even with the unchecked anger, loneliness, and fatigue that plagued her. The voice spoke of something else, motivated action by something far more dangerous than the anger and loneliness of a young woman.

The voice spoke of revenge.

The woman had preyed on Sybil, then pushed and cajoled her into becoming one with the dark thoughts and one with the woman who gave them life. Sybil did what she had to do. She turned on her family, her son.

I know you're up there, Phillip. I know you are.

Slowly, so very slowly, she had climbed the steps to his room. It was the room where he and Winston read together, laughed together, the room where the boy lived, and caused a distance between her and her husband.

One more step. There.

The door slammed, the lock was thrown. Behind the door, there was a sound of a book, its pages being rifled.

Sybil fingered the key in her pocket. Phillip was always so predictable. She always knew when he was up to something, and always knew how to correct it.

You've been a bad boy, Phillip. A mean, ruthless child.

She had slipped the key in to open the door, then squinted in the dark.

His shadow skittered across the room, disappeared through the alcove and into the next room.

Bile burned in her throat at the act; power filled her at his fear. She was the strong one, the right one, and now his time had come. Standing still, soundless in the doorway, she waited for his next predictable move. She would wait as long as it took, then do what was necessary, what needed to be done.

A whisper of something sounded behind her. She swung on her heel and grabbed his shirt.

"Mother. Please," he begged. "Please don't hurt me."

Confusion crossed her eyes. A second of pain, a moment of distraction from the task at hand, allowed her to see the face of her son, the child born to her, a child she loved more than anything in this world.

He ducked her grasp and bolted down the stairs.

The thing within her screamed with rage and pushed her to continue, to do what needed to be done.

You can't run from me, boy. I'll find you. I'll stop you.

She ran, came close to him, lunged, and missed.

He jumped the last few steps and twisted the front doorknob. It was locked. Glancing over his shoulder, he turned the lock, threw open the door, and was gone.

Into the dark. Into the storm.

The ghost woman had joined Sybil Mann to go after Phillip.

Now, after all these years, the woman was cultivating a liaison with Annie, then she'd go after Charlie.

A soft moan escaped Sybil. She slumped forward on the kitchen table.

A knock sounded on the door.

Phillip was forced out into the storm and the roiling ocean because of her. *Errand One* had crashed against the jagged rocks that killed him instantly—the only thing that saved him from dying at her hand.

And now it was Charlie's turn. With Annie's help, the ghost woman would have it no other way.

Sybil moaned then wailed at the pain that gnawed within her. There was nothing she could do, nothing.

Another knock. It was louder, insistent.

She couldn't stop this event that ended years before in tragedy but moved relentlessly ahead unfinished now when Annie refused to listen. Sybil remembered what it was like first-hand, the nightmares, the dream-like movements that propelled her up the stairs to the widow's walk to look out, to wait.

The widow's walk.

Winston had boarded it up, secured it, and covered it with wallpaper to hide its existence so that no one else would be hurt. It had started there, all of it, and if Annie didn't get to the widow's walk, there might still be time to figure something out, to plan against what would otherwise be inevitable if it wasn't too late.

No, she couldn't think it, couldn't bear the thought she had waited a day, a minute, too long.

There was work to do, lots of it. Papers, books, the old family Bible to look through, anything she could find that might put the missing pieces of the puzzle together. Then, perhaps, she would see the answer, and God willing, be able to act on it.

If only she could be sure Annie hadn't discovered the widow's walk.

The door opened with a high-pitched wail.

Sybil raised her head from the table and stared open-mouthed at the woman standing in the doorway.

"I'm Eleanor Trippett."

Chapter 15

Winston pulled up the collar of his jacket against the cooling wind and sprinkle of rain then looked back over his shoulder to check the distance between himself and the house. It was okay. He was safe. Sybil wouldn't be able to see him even from their bedroom on the second floor. There was nothing between his secret and her, but the quiet solitude of great trees, damp moss, and the distant slap of bay water. He couldn't ask for a better place to live and a more appropriate place to die. But death wasn't on his agenda today. There were too many things to do.

He rubbed the tight pain in his chest as if it were a pulled muscle that could be coaxed into relaxed submission by a firm kneading of his palm, and sensed the pain deepen. Still, he was glad to be away from Sybil and the fear and sadness his pain left in her eyes. She would never see him like this again if he could help it. He would do whatever it took to guarantee that quiet promise to himself.

God, his chest hurt. It hurt worse than it had ever before.

Closing his eyes for a second, he mumbled a silent prayer then looked around. The ground rolled and swayed as if he were viewing it from the bow of a storm-riddled ship. Dizziness threw him off balance, and he stumbled. With trembling fingers, he reached into his shirt pocket to search frantically for the little bottle of pills and realized they weren't there. A pat at the other pocket produced the same result. Digging deep into his pants pocket, he felt the tiny bottle escape his grasp then caught it. Another spasm of pain, deeper this time and searing, seemed to grab his heart and squeeze. He cried out. The pill bottle slipped from his fingers and spilled its contents to the ground.

Falling to his knees, he fought blurring vision to focus on the scatter of white pills spread out before him. One pill, covered in sand and grit, stuck to his finger. He forced it under his tongue and tasted the bitterness of Mico Island mixed with medication.

Mann staggered toward the sturdy bulk of an oak, leaned against it, and tried to catch his breath, to will away the pain that permeated every muscle of his chest. Better now, it was better, easing some. A little. Another few minutes of rest, and he'd be okay.

The pain dissipated in slow layers. He took a deep breath, felt it catch then loosen. Another found pill dissolved under his tongue, leaving only thickened mucus tinged with salty sand. Rubbing a moist hand across his lips, he leaned heavily against the tree to think the situation out.

The heart problem was getting worse. No doubt about it now. And wouldn't Doc Nesheim get that gleam in his eye when he said everything but "told you so." Doctors were paid for that kind of nonsense to suggest this test and that—and for what? To tell a body what they already knew, while his heart was in the right place, it wasn't working quite up to par.

Good money, hard-won, was used to more thoroughly diagnose what he didn't want to know anyway. It was as if being in good health all his life hadn't counted for anything. At one time, he could ignore away any annoying malady, head colds, broken bones; it didn't matter. This time it was different, frightening. Even more, it was unfair.

Sybil needed him. He needed her. Damn it; they needed each other. Shouldn't that be the way it worked?

If only he could tell her, be honest about the entire situation, maybe even face up to his mortality, but that wasn't the real issue, was it? Death was just a phase— something you went through, like puberty and pimples, on the way to something else. Leaving her alone to fend for herself was the worst part.

She was better now, better than she had been in years. A hopeful recovery the shrink had said, but a shrink was just a doctor without a scalpel. Shrinks didn't cause the open wounds in the first place; they just sometimes forgot about the thickened layer of skin that covered the wounds and hid them from view. It was a layer separating sanity from...questions, from pain.

The pain lingered, hidden deep in his wife's eyes. He had seen it surface once in a while, had tried to talk to her about that night, and Phillip, then saw the dullness come back to her face. The conversation fell on deaf ears. She closed her mind and pushed whatever tried to surface further and further in until she could almost forget, and the wound was once again covered.

But she was better; he reminded himself.

The lack of any emotion in her face had suddenly erupted as anger in her voice, a sign she was better, and better left not knowing about his latest problem.

Or the story of Eleanor Trippett.

He took a deep breath. The fading dot of pain left his chest.

These would be his secrets. Maybe, if he found the time, he'd let the doctor in on the latest heart problem to see the gleam in his medical eye. But never, never, under any circumstances, would he let Sybil know about this or the woman in black. She had enough on her mind without bother of his petty, nagging heart mess, or knowing about Eleanor Trippett's loss two years after he and Sybil lost Phillip. The similarities were uncanny, and a rare night went by that he didn't blame himself for the tragedy. To this day, his mind rolled around and around the problem and how he could have solved it, but there was nothing he could do.

What he would give to solve the Cameron problem, too. If it were in his bag of tricks, he would erase Sybil's worry over Charlie, Annie, and the mother-in-law like a dusty blackboard and fix the fractured family.

It was a broken home, all right. No doubt about it, that is if you could take Richard's word in the letter, and Charlie's stubborn refusal to talk about anything to do with his father and mother being together. Then there was odd behavior of Mr. Cameron at the dock, and his conspicuous absence since. This was not a man who took kindly to his family. Worst of all, he bet Charlie thought he was responsible for his parent's marital problems.

Mann shook his head and wished he could say something, or do something that would make it better for the boy. Charlie had become almost a son to him, a picking up where things were so abruptly left off many years ago. Not that Charlie was a substitute for the love he still felt for his son, but he was transference of sorts, a salve on empty, ragged emotions. Charlie was different from Phillip in a whole list of ways, but the same in one way: he was a boy who cried out for attention that Winston was all too ready to give, as was Sybil. He smiled to himself, wondered who was crying out for attention, the boy, or him and his wife. But that was okay, too.

Sybil's curt talk after his collapse had been persuasive all right, but the facts stayed the same; Phillip's handwritten message found in their favorite book then the mysterious disappearance of both. Or maybe it wasn't so mysterious after all—he could almost see Sybil's protective hand in the whole thing. Had she tossed the note into the garbage, or hidden it? Whatever happened, it was Sybil's doing, of that much he was sure. More important now was figuring out what the message meant and why it was written. What prompted Phillip to run, to get away, to get killed?

Phillip was young, but he wasn't stupid. The bay and the workings of *Errand One* was almost instinct for him. There was no reason to crash on the rocks, storm, or not. Phillip had said himself what a dangerous place that particular stretch was had made a point to avoid it, in fact.

Yet there he had been, his thin body, washed pale with the rain and wedged tightly among the jagged rocks. His mouth gaped open as if in protest at a sight too horrible to comprehend.

Something, or someone, had chased his son to his death.

Ghosts of the past lived in the mind, deep in the heart, or showed themselves as someone trusting and loving, like a parent, and no amount of running could escape her.

Her?

His forehead wrinkled in thought. He stroked his chest, absently then stopped.

It was *her*, this hand from the grave, his however many great-greats aunt ago, who went after Phillip; it was Lady Manchester herself. What better place to isolate a deranged woman than on an island prison of live oaks and tabby mansion walls with nothing to do and no one to talk to. And then eventually there was a son.

Until she killed him, then stood among the flames on the widow's walk and allowed herself to die.

The house, much later rebuilt as an investment, stood empty, its fate sealed by reputation until he and Sybil acquired it. A dab of paint here, a two by four there, the original family name christened the place and Sybil, and he had a home free and clear. Then things changed. A child died, his mother was locked away, and the Manns would never return to the house again. The history of Manchester Place had returned to haunt them. Only the tourists were fooled.

The natives knew the story and passed it from one generation to the next. Try as he might to forget, he remembered it, too.

And somehow, over almost two centuries, Lady Manchester remembered and reached out for his son. But how, why, and more importantly, would it happen again?

He shook his head to clear it of the subtle euphoria that comes when pain gives way to comfort, and gathered up the bottle with the few remaining pills. With a groan, he hoisted himself to a standing position and stretched. He paused for a moment, let his body adjust to the residual light-headedness from the pill when something jabbed him from inside his jacket pocket. The hornpipe.

He pulled the clarinet-like instrument from his pocket, blew a puff of air through it, and listened to a dull note drift away with the wind. Another try, stronger this time, produced a shadow of the resonance it would have had in its prime. Mann stroked the scratched wood, fingered the holes, and hoped that Charlie would like this old family heirloom. Finding it tucked away among the clothes, tools, and boxes accumulated over decades of garage storage only served to remind how unimportant it was to him, but maybe pushing out an occasional tune would provide some joy to Charlie. Playing with the hornpipe would at least kill a little time between fishing trips.

He shuddered at the thought and knew this past fishing trip was the last. Mann wiped sweat from his forehead then patted his shirt to draw away the moisture that covered his chest and clung to his back.

No more fishing trips unless they stood firmly on the bank, but most assuredly no more trips on a boat. The incident had taken a bigger chunk from the few remaining years of his life than he wanted to think about. Maybe the hornpipe would be a consolation of sorts.

He tucked the instrument into his pocket, took a deep breath, and walked to Manchester Place on shaky legs. Another breath and he felt stronger. That was the key, let things go and put them all behind you. There was no point in dwelling on things that were best left forgotten.

The great house loomed into view. He hesitated briefly, wondered why he did so then continued until he saw it.

The huge, broken branch of an old oak hung precariously off the edge of the widow's walk, as Sybil had said. He would have to hire a professional for this job, someone from the mainland, and at a premium price, no doubt. Richard would surely volunteer, but it was too dangerous. Besides, there was no telling what kind of shape the walk itself would be in, much less the unkempt steps leading up to it. So he'd need a ladder and a hired professional when he would have preferred to do it himself.

But that was out of the question for many reasons. The most important reason being Sybil, who would stand on solid ground shouting a nonstop stream of warnings up the length of the ladder while wringing her hands into a knot. That is if she ever agreed to the proposition in the first place. And much as he admired Richard, the boy would probably stop at every window for a hopeful glance at Mrs. Cameron, assuming he didn't insist she stand at the bottom and wring her hands right along with Sybil. Annie wasn't the type; if he judged right, the woman had too much on her mind without dealing with Richard's juvenile attempts at flirtation. Poor boy. He wore the most effective blinders when it came to romance.

The tree would be number one priority when he got home; in the meantime, he had another mission to complete. Deliver the hornpipe, check on the family to see they had everything they needed, and move on to the rest of his chores.

A cool wind blew up from the bayside. He zipped

up his jacket, pulled the collar tighter around his neck, and looked up into the darkening skies.

Storm weather.

And by the looks and feel of this particularly cool September day, the storm might be a maritime high. This was a rare event, and if his guess was right, the cool weather and smidgen of rain were just a hint of things to come.

Now there were more things to add to his chore list: a call to the National Weather Service for confirmation, with follow-ups on the radio reports. If he was right about the storm, and he was almost sure he was, the list of chores would grow in a hurry.

The oak branch hanging overhead would have to wait for now. No one in their right mind would come across the bay in a maritime high. Not for a tree, not for anything.

And no one would be leaving the island.

He sighed, climbed the front porch steps, and knocked on the front door.

Chapter 16

Charlie pressed his face against the staircase landing window until the frame of his glasses left an imprint around his eyes, and the view of Winston Mann coming up the steps became a blur.

Hearing the knock, he toyed with the thought of bolting downstairs to fling open the door and escape his newly imposed "grounding." Only an hour or so old, just since he woke up from the shot the doctor had given him the night before, the grounding had already become a total bore. Having done nothing, at least nothing he could remember, the anger and fear were as clear on his mother's face as the glasses pressing on his nose were now.

Uncle Winston's knock, louder this time and more insistent, buzzed in his head like a nest of hornets. Charlie took a tentative step down the stairs, hesitated then scurried up the steps with the sound of his mother's approaching footsteps. He dove into a shadow trying to make himself thinner still, until he believed he could hide behind a balcony strut. She wouldn't see him here, not unless she knew where to look, and since he was almost invisibly thin like a superhero, she wouldn't be able to see him if she wanted to. He would watch carefully, see what Mr. Mann had to say; then maybe she would change her mind and unground him.

Brushing a stray strand of unkempt hair out of her

face, she tucked it into her ponytail with a deep sigh, and hesitantly opened the door as if her hands hurt somehow at the simple act. Mann's foot poked over the jamb, but the fixed stance on his mother's part made it clear he wouldn't be allowed in.

Charlie leaned forward to catch the forced pleasantries and grown-up small talk. Mann's jacket-clad arm crossed the boundary from porch to foyer and laid a horn of some sort in his mother's hands. It was a recorder kind of like the ones they played in school when the music teacher came, only it was different.

"For Charlie." Mann pointed at the instrument.

He squirmed in place behind the balcony, strut for a better look. At least now, there'd be something to do while he was grounded, thanks to Uncle Winston. He could pretend he was the leader of a band and maybe play little songs for Grandma.

Another short exchange, something about a storm, and his mother closed the door and threw the lock with a *click*. She paused, glanced briefly upwards as he ducked further into the shadow then turned back to her work in the kitchen. The present from Mr. Mann went with her.

Charlie stood to call out, then remembering her mood, caught himself, and slumped back into the shadow. It wasn't fair. The present for him was gone almost as fast as the big plans he had for today, the hero plans. First, he would pretend he was a hunter. He'd wait for an animal to show up, look at them through his sights, then *wham,* got it.

Not really, but it would be fun to watch all the animals that hung around the island. The deer were pretty, but the skunks smelled bad if you gave them half a chance. He'd stay far away from the skunks.

Then later, there would have been a quick game of spy. Underneath the house would be a cool place for spy headquarters. That is unless the crawl space was a hideout for the criminals Uncle Winston had talked about. It would be dark in the crawl space for sure, so dark that no one would ever be found.

He blew a particularly wet raspberry as loud and long as he could. It didn't matter what his plans were now, not while his mother was upset. He stopped with the thought; it was his reading again, wasn't it, that's why she was angry. As hard as he tried, he couldn't make the words work. It was if they got all jumbled up just to confuse him, and even with deep concentration, the words refused to make sense.

At home, Mom worked with him every night, but since their arrival on the island, there'd been no time for lessons. That was good news as far as he was concerned, but his mother wouldn't care for that one bit. She wanted him to do better, to be more like the other kids, and she was unhappy with the lack of progress in his reading. No wonder she was upset, angry even, but it didn't seem bad enough to cause a grounding.

His stomach growled. He pressed a hand to his belly to stop the noise. The piece of burned toast she offered him this morning had long since gone. Rising from behind the balcony strut, he took a step down.

Scrape, scrape, scrape. The sound came from the kitchen.

He paused and decided to wait until she called him for lunch. There'd be no sense in making her more upset by bothering her when she was busy. Rubbing away the rumbling in his stomach, he took a last hopeful look out the window for Uncle Winston, but saw he had disappeared into the woods. Now there was nothing left to do, absolutely nothing.

Looking up the stairs, he considered visiting Grandma again. She wasn't talking much lately and had slept through most of his earlier visit, but that was okay. This time he'd talk enough for the both of them with his stories, or sing her a song. She'd like that.

He held his breath and tried closing his eyes as he passed his room, but had to see. Cocking one eye open for a split-second glance at the mirrored dresser, he saw the green Mr. Giggles there, and let out his held breath in disgust. He would have thrown the toy out if he thought his mother wouldn't know, or if he could bear the thought of touching it, but he couldn't touch it, not ever. And he never wanted to hear that horrible laughing sound again, not in a million, zillion years. A quick run down the hall brought him to the door of the master bedroom.

"Come in, Charlie. I hoped you'd be back before too long."

He pushed open the door. Grandma sat upright in a bed that looked perfectly made all around her.

"You had a busy night last night." It was a statement rather than a question. She patted the bed for him to sit.

"I guess. I don't know. I don't remember much about it." He sat on the edge of her bed then squirmed to lean against the wall with his legs stretched out the width. "I didn't want the shot, it hurt, but the doctor said it would help me." He ran a finger over his smudged glasses and squinted. "I don't need no help."

"*Any* help."

"Any help."

"Can't say as I blame you. Sometimes doctors do things we don't want, but they mean well." She pulled her nightgown tighter around her and shivered against a coolness he didn't feel. "You slept like a log. I didn't know when you'd get up."

"Me neither. How does a log sleep?"

"Quiet and still."

"Oh." He wiggled his toes in sneakers that draped untied shoelaces. "Did you sleep like a log?"

"On and off. Mostly dreamed, though."

"Did you dream scary stuff?" he asked, reaching over to tie his shoes.

"What kind of scary stuff?"

"You know…stuff."

"I'm not sure," she hedged. "I do know that you drew some pictures last night. I could see you do that in my dreams. I know the pictures scared you, and your mother. I think they scared me a little, too."

"How come?"

"They weren't fun pictures like you usually draw, were they? Not cats or horses, or little crabs that change their shells. It was something…more."

"Yeah. I mean, I guess. I don't remember." He stretched the length of the bed to lie alongside her and popped a thumb into his mouth.

"You're scared, I know you. But don't you worry, little one, I'll take care of you. You know I will."

He barely nodded then squeezed tight against her.

****

She wrapped an arm around his shoulder, rubbed his back, then pulled the nightgown as close as it would go around her. It was cold, so cold in this house. The cold wasn't because of the wind that blew fitfully around the attic eaves, or the chill the September air was suddenly taking that tickled the back of her neck when she saw in her mind's eye the pictures Charlie had drawn the night before.

Pictures.

The drawings had called Grandma within herself as they did again now, deep inside where she could see. She closed her eyes.

They were dark, ominous, pictures of things to come.

And there was a portrait of a woman. She was young but aged with madness. She was Annie; she was someone else then Annie again.

There was Charlie, standing frozen with fear as the woman's steps approached. Who was she? What did she want?

Stairs now, they were so tall, so high. Grandma stood at the top of the stairs and silently mouthed the words: "Stop her." Legs already so weakened started to shake. "Stop her. Stop her now before—"

Grandma jolted in bed. Her eyes widened with a sight that went beyond the shadows of the room. The dim light from a single lit lamp faded and dulled in the room's periphery, but she didn't notice as something else had captured her attention.

In a matter of days now, it would happen. Or was it just a few hours? Whenever it was, she had to stop what his drawings and her dreams told her was inevitable.

But there were no more mind's eye images forthcoming.

And then it was cold again.

Like the winter when she was five and visiting relatives in the north, it was cold then, too. She loved her bright pink coat and the matching mittens and earmuffs, and the way the snow fell on the pink and made it all polka dotty. It was the only time she went sledding. The rush of cold air stung her face, the rhythm of the sled gliding across packed snow. Her breath caught. Nothing had been more fun or more exhilarating in her whole life.

And then the mittens that matched her coat and earmuffs were gone, lost somewhere in the thrill of the moment. She looked everywhere for them, had to find them before Father found out. He would be mad if she lost them since there was no money for another pair. There had been barely enough money for these.

"Where are they?"

Charlie stirred beside her. "Grandma?"

"My mittens. They were here just a minute ago. Help me find them, will you?"

Chapter 17

It was tedious. More than tedious, it was painstakingly slow.

Annie winced as a wood splinter jabbed into her already bleeding fingertips then returned to pulling yet another thin, amber strand of wallpaper away. One shred after another joined the growing, sticky pile at her feet. A second sliver caught the edge of her fingernail. She gasped at the pain then popped the hurt finger into her mouth. After a moment, she lowered her hand and shuddered at the ache that coursed from her fingers to her hand to her arm. Teeth clenched, she reached for another uneven pull at the wallpaper.

Layer covered layer that covered yet another. She dug a broken nail into a teal blue edge and pulled. Her finger went numb. That was good; maybe the pain would be a little more bearable now. Another edge, this time it was a rectangular piece of olive green wallpaper.

Behind all the wallpaper would be the door to the widow's walk. That is unless her pain and drop-by-drop spilling of blood proved there was no door, but a crack in an otherwise impenetrable wall.

She leaned back to survey the puzzle pieces of wallpaper. Behind all this, there had to be a door to the widow's walk. By the layout of the house, the walk would be just about over her head. A little curve to the steps from here, around the back end of the kitchen and the dining room, then outside to the bay view. The widow's walk.

It had to be here. And if it was, that meant Winston Mann had been wrong in telling her there was no way up. It would mean he had lied to her. What else would he keep from her?

Stroking her bloodied fingers absently across her jeans, she stopped at the sudden thought. Winston Mann had just now dropped in unexpectedly. Before this one, he had always made a point of planning visits, either his or those of his young cohort, Richard. This time it was different. He just appeared, with no warning. Richard seemed an impulsive sort, in a nice kind of way. He even smelled nice, definitely male, and natural, not covered up in expensive cologne and a strange woman's perfume like David always was. Bits of paper stuck to her clothes and her tennis shoes. She rubbed a sore hand through her uncombed hair. Better it was Winston Mann showing up instead of Richard. The young man would undoubtedly question her strange state, but Winston Mann wasn't the type to pry.

Here she was, pulling paper off a wall like some kind of a madwoman, but since the voice told her it was okay, that was all she needed to hear. A flicker of confusion stopped her train of thought.

Unless scraping wallpaper piece by puzzle piece was a crazy, stupid thing to do.

What if someone figured out what she was up to? A growing panic gnawed at her insides. Her stomach twisted.

Winston Mann had to have noticed, and he would want her to stop. He might even evict her back to the depressing house in Atlanta, and to her more depressing life with David. No. She wouldn't leave now. She couldn't leave.

But if he saw, if he knew…

She pulled a piece of wallpaper from her clothes. "I'm crazy." Another piece. "I'm crazy, not."

Maybe Winston didn't know.

The knot in her stomach loosened a notch. That was a possibility, too. He might have thought she was deep into some kind of a hobby or something.

Sure, that was it, a hobby.

She kicked the wall as hard as she could. A cracking sound split the air. A flake of plaster floated effortlessly to the floor, followed by a strip of wallpaper. The door creaked open ever so slightly. Her eyes widened, a gasp caught in her throat.

The door to the widow's walk opened.

She reached out to nudge it a little more.

"Mom?"

His voice stung. She turned, fell against the open door to cover it, and glared at her son. There was a question in his eyes.

"Mom?" His voice was unsure, tentative. His thumb went to his mouth.

Thumb-sucking was for babies, not fifth graders. Didn't she have enough on her mind without thumb-sucking as an additional trial?

"What is it, Charlie?" She was sure her voice translated a calm and patience she didn't feel.

He looked away, the thumb firmly in his mouth.

"Charlie? You came here for a reason. What is it?"

He shrugged ever so slightly.

She forced her voice to soften. "Baby, Mommy's busy. What do you need?"

Another shrug.

Anger welled in her. She closed her eyes against the surge and tried counting, taking deep breaths, and all the other things that worked in the past. But he was testing her patience on purpose, trying to make her blow up at him. It was malicious on his part and a premeditated attempt to make her lose what little sanity she had left. Couldn't he see she was busy? Of all the hours in the day, why right now did he have to nag her and bother her with some petty little problem?

"I'm hungry, Mommy." His words were quiet, simple, and barely audible.

She contemplated his statement as if it were a foreign language that needed translation then glanced out the bay window for a hint at the time. Dusk. Where had the day gone?

She studied her son, his eyes downcast, standing a safe distance away. He had gone as long as he could without bothering her, longer than he ever should have. It was his right, by birth, if nothing else, to come to her when he needed something.

Her mandate was to provide for him, yet he waited until a gnawing pain of hunger in his little stomach finally forced him to do the unspeakable—interrupt his mother in the act of peeling away a house.

Annie would have found this strange scenario amusing if it wasn't so tragic, so heart-wrenching to see the fear in his eyes.

It was there, clear as the pile of wallpaper lying before her. Hiding in the shadows behind the balcony struts was a symptom of his fear.

She had felt him there, lurking at the top of the stairs, watching, waiting, and almost gave in to him until the voice spoke and she listened.

Two could play that game.

He toed the floor with a foot covered in a too-big sock, shifted the thumb in his mouth then peered up at her. A single tear crept down his face, lingered at his chin then fell away. He stood still, prepared for whatever she had in mind for him.

She tried to stand, but the numbing weakness from squatting for hours held her back, so she opened her arms to him from the floor.

"Come to me, Charlie. Give me a hug. Charlie…"

He hesitated, withdrew into the darkness of the adjoining room then tentatively reappeared. He was checking her sincerity to see if she meant it. And she did mean it.

Didn't she?

He was just a little boy, one that warranted a watchful eye, perhaps, but still a little boy. She crawled a step, tried to stand again and cried out with pain.

"Please, forgive me," she said, her words flat and emotionless, but it was enough.

Suddenly he was in her arms crying until there was nothing left but dry sobs followed by a silence broken only with an occasional hiccup. Annie waited patiently for him to stop.

"Would you like a little something to eat? You'll be happy again, and Mommy can get back to work?"

She felt him nod against her shoulder.

"Good." Annie squeezed him tight, tighter than she meant to. "Okay, then."

She stroked his hair harder then caught sight of the door leading up and out.

The widow's walk.

She smiled.

Two could play that game.

"It'll be better, Charlie. You'll see."

Chapter 18

Eleanor Trippett braced herself against the growing wind and chill that cut through the thin black material of her long dress as she navigated the dirt road that would bring her back to Kenzie's store. A sudden gust caught the black veil covering her face and yanked it back over her head. She captured it then held it tight under her chin for these last steps.

The storefront loomed into view. Worn and battered, the frame building was named after Gerald Kenzie, the wiry and bearded entrepreneur who ran the place, distributed the mail, and price-gouged his customers. Kenzie and his store hadn't changed in twenty-five years, but the place had at one time been something else.

Old when Kenzie bought it, the building had originally been used as a community post for trading goods, services, and information. Trading in the traditional sense was replaced with the exchange of money for goods that might still be safely within their expiration dates. Information, or more likely gossip, was always free and highly encouraged. Kenzie's store was a hotbed of gossip.

The business of sharing suspect information, in which facts rarely stood in the way, was cultivated by Kenzie himself, and perpetuated by the usual congregation of male natives who made the visit to the store a daily routine. Many stayed for hours. Frequently gossip turned to stories that turned to weathered island folklore embellished for the sake of the natives and the rarely accepted "regular" to the island and the store. This was a dubious honor and one that would never be awarded to her since she was far more suited for speculation and story fodder.

The screen door to the building slammed open and closed in its frame then finally settled down. Over the door, the hand-painted sign, faded and dulled with years of harsh conditions, now read "zie's Stor." No one noticed, and it didn't matter anyway since this was the only business on the island.

Her pointed heels clicked a staccato beat across the wooden ramp that led to the entrance. An orange cat appeared from one side of the building, stared at Eleanor with yellow eyes, then slithered away, its belly close to the ground, its ears folded back over its narrow head.

She crossed the threshold of the store to the high-pitched wail of hinges that needing oiling, and the sudden silence from the men gathered around the cash register. Their gaze followed her while she perused the sagging shelves for canned food with a minimum of dust and an acceptable amount of rust around the rim. They turned in unison to watch as she slid open the cooler covered in caked dirt and cobwebs, and reached past packaged bait for a soft drink that might still have a little carbonation. The drinks appeared viable, but they were lukewarm, and the little appetite she thought she had now waned. Without so much as a nod on either side, she took the narrow steps to her rented room at the back of the store.

The silence that met her when she dared enter the sanctity of this male domain of scratched walls punctuated by stale smoke and calendars of scantily clad young women resumed when she closed the door to her windowless room. What they didn't know was how thin the walls were, or that their voices carried their secret information to her quite clearly.

Perched on the small cot, the only piece of furniture in the room, she carefully removed her gloves then the pin that held the veil on her head. The clothing was carefully folded and stacked while she listened to their wild and blatantly wrong theories of her. There was no need to correct them. They wouldn't listen, she didn't care, and her time on the island was coming to a close anyway. Besides, the thin walls gave her an advantage.

It was in this very room where she heard the legend of Manchester Place without having to ask. The story had been recounted and vastly adorned depending on who held the story-telling center of attention that moment, but the basic thread never changed. A crazy woman, lonely and abandoned by the man she loved, burned the house down and killed her son and herself. Sybil Mann had even said this much when she finally started talking, but the islanders in the store had taken the story further. They claimed the man, her husband, never came back, and so didn't know he caused the entire disaster. If, indeed, he was the cause. Thus the controversy raged.

One theory disputed the husband as the cause by saying Chief Mico, the island's namesake, cursed the entire place for want of something better to do. This story was met with cuffing, derision, and a warning of potential anti-tourism then was dismissed with a round of beer.

Other men believed that once mad, always mad and Lady Manchester would have killed her son and burned down the house anyway, or something equally as appalling, regardless of what happened to her husband. The men at Kenzie's store would have given weight to this thought with a moment of quiet contemplation, then another round of beer and a shared bag of fried pork rinds.

But the most chilling story offered around the cash register was the child as a bone of contention between the parents. The men in the store had tried to nip the story before the fiction had a chance to evolve into fact as bar tales were wont to do, and they were almost successful until Sybil Mann ended up in a psychiatric hospital after her son's death. Word was that Sybil refused outright discussion of her mental incarceration. Eleanor couldn't have agreed more.

Some demons were better buried deep in sallow institutional walls and colorless days. Others like herself, however, tamed their demons by closing the curtains for twenty-five years and covering their eyes with a black veil. Then when that wasn't enough, she covered her hands, feet, her whole body in a uniform of black. It had to be black since all color in her world had twisted and merged, melted one into the other until the only thing left was a deep, moonless, lifeless, black.

Sybil Mann would be spared knowledge of Eleanor's tragedy since it would make no difference. There was no need.

In the dark room of twenty-five years, with the curtains pulled tight so no light would ever enter again, and the black veil blocking painful sight, she had turned her attention inward. Nothing would bring back her son; nothing would fill the space where he belonged, or appease the pain that burned and lingered. But maybe there was something she could do. She returned to Mico Island and Manchester Place to break the chain of events that killed children and diminished the lives of their mothers.

But it hadn't been that simple. After twenty-five years, the sun stung her eyes and illuminated thoughts she had long since forgotten. Bright light revealed the tremble in her hands and the fear that bubbled below the surface. She was on her way home when she saw them. Annie Cameron and her son and mother-in-law settled on Winston Mann's boat, headed into the eye of a storm.

So Eleanor stayed then pursued them to the island.

Leaving her little room in the back of Kenzie's store, she walked the dirt road to Manchester Place, and even attempted the deer paths through the woods to get there. No matter the route, the house, and the presence within, stopped her as if by an impenetrable wall. She tried pushing past it then reeled back with the agonizing painful effort. Air was pulled from her lungs, her stomach lurched as if prodded, then punched, and a searing pain ran through her head with every approach to the house. No voice spoke to her this time, but its will was as strong as ever.

There was no way to get to Annie except to wait, watch, and hope an opportunity presented itself in another way. Annie's visit to the beach was the one chance to convince the young woman she must leave before it was too late. Manchester Place had seduced

Annie to stay, and now another child was in danger.

This tragedy had repeated itself through Sybil and herself, and she finally saw the pattern for what it was; the ghost of Manchester Place had things to do and would stop at nothing until the grim task was complete. Now it was Annie who would do the ghost's bidding and Charlie, who would suffer the consequences. But there might be something else as well.

If the child of unhappy parents was a catalyst for tragedy nearly two hundred years ago then twenty-seven and twenty-five years ago, there might be a last chance Eleanor could do something. The key was family.

A child had more than just a mother.

Time was slipping away as if an hourglass had been turned, and the sand was down to the last meniscus. It was a clock ticking like the final beats of a heart before death came to silence it.

Not this time, not on her watch.

Eleanor would find the man Sybil spoke of and convince him of her plan. He would do as she directed and then she would leave. There'd be no point in staying.

There was no need.

Chapter 19

Annie held Charlie tight, stroked his hair, and perceived a soft whimper from him.

Two could play this game, the voice told her.

His glasses pressed into the soft flesh of her shoulder with her hug. He tried to pull away. She pulled back. A grateful son would do what she wanted.

She eyed the door to the widow's walk, wondering what it would be like if she were at the top looking out instead of sitting here at the bottom. Always at the bottom, it seemed she was constantly trying to claw her way to the light, where it was quiet, and she could be left alone, just for a little while.

It wasn't possible that he'd leave her alone, not while his stomach craved something to fill it. Funny, she wasn't hungry in the least. She was barely tired. It was if finding the door held more for her than just a dark hallway and stale air, and if she went to it right now...

Charlie shifted again then stilled as if afraid any movement would disengage her from her thoughts.

He's afraid of you.

The voice was there then. What it said was appalling in a way. Scary. Powerful.

Her pulse quickened. She loosened her grip, and he slid away if his body housed no skeleton. A tight smile formed on her lips.

"Yes, you want some dinner. Of course. A little something to stop the belly-growl."

She opened a drawer and randomly grabbed at utensils. The carving knife came first. A small reflection of light sparkled from the base of the knife and rode to the pointed end. She paused, then quickly thrust it back into the drawer, slammed it shut, and looked over her shoulder to see if her son had noticed.

He had. His widened eyes filled the lenses of his glasses; his face paled to wax.

She faltered at the sight of him. Fear filled her.

"I...don't much feel...like cooking. Is that okay?"

There was no response.

Annie grabbed an overripe banana from the counter and held it out to him. "This'll tide you over for a while."

Taking his hand, she saw the palm streaked with pencil marks and crayon smudges and clenched her jaw at the sight. He wasn't to draw anymore, never again, not after last night. Hadn't she made that clear? She placed the fruit in his palm then curled his fingers around it and patted his hand.

"There now. You eat that, and everything will be fine."

He stared at her, stared through her.

She hated when he did that. The only thing worse was when he purposely disobeyed her.

But he never disobeyed, not really. Charlie almost always listened and did as he was told. He was a good boy, a quiet boy. He was her flesh and blood, and she loved him. Didn't she?

Charlie was all hers, and nobody would have him, not David or Sybil and Winston Mann, not even

Grandma. He was her son, he belonged to her to do as she wished, and that was final.

He will betray you.

He was a child, and no child of hers would do anything to hurt her, to betray her. She wouldn't allow it.

"You're a good boy, Charlie. Aren't you? A fine boy."

His gaze shifted to a dark corner of the room. A flicker of interest crossed his face.

Annie followed his look and spotted the hornpipe tossed carelessly to the floor. She picked up the old instrument, then dangled it in front of him.

"You want this, don't you?"

There was no answer. He even refused to look at her.

"It's for you, from Mr. Mann. I know you want it."

Tentatively he opened his hand.

She snatched the hornpipe back to her chest. "And you can have it, but I want you to promise me something first. Is that a deal?"

His gaze narrowed on the hornpipe.

"I want you to promise me you'll never see Sybil or Winston Mann again."

Bewilderment settled on his face. He looked from the hornpipe to her then back again.

"They are mean people just pretending to be nice. You will never see them again. You have me, and I'm all you need. Just the two of us together. Promise and this old thing is yours. Come on, boy."

He hesitated then turned away from her.

Fury raged in her. She clenched her teeth and turned her hands to tight fists. It was too late, after all.

The Manns had sunk their claws in and held tight. But this wasn't finished, not if she had anything to do with it. She stalked over to the table, slammed the hornpipe down and reached for the heavy vase centerpiece of silk flowers. She hoisted the vase high behind her shoulder and threw with every bit of strength she owned.

Silk flowers scattered across the floor. The ceramic vase soared across the room toward the middle pane of the bay window. The glass exploded with the impact and rained razor-edged shards outside the house.

A cold, sharp wind from the edge of the storm filled the kitchen. The tablecloth billowed then caught the wind and blew across the room. Framed pictures fell from the walls. The screen door slammed back and forth and tore free from one hinge. Countertop knick-knacks fell crashing to the floor.

Within seconds the temperature dropped.

She snatched up the hornpipe that had rolled to her feet and turned to Charlie. "One last chance, boy. Promise me."

He stood with his back to her and said nothing.

"Okay then," she said, and casually tossed the instrument out the window.

The electricity went out. They were in total darkness.

The wind howled through the kitchen.

The screen door battered against its frame, splintered, then squealed as if it had been thrown open.

"Charlie?" She groped in the darkness for him. "Call out, honey, so I know where you are."

The dull overhead light flickered on then off again. The quick light gave her a second to look around the room. He was gone, probably hiding in the living room.

"Charlie? Where are you?"

She flung open random drawers to fish blindly around for a flashlight or candles.

The screen door crashed in its frame then slowed to a brief staccato as the gust of wind died. Light crept into the room from the overhead fixture, dimly at first, then with increasing intensity until it filled the kitchen.

"Charlie?" She walked to the doorway leading to the dining room and called again.

The screen door reverberated in its frame then became silent.

Deep terror filled her then.

"Charlie? Please, honey. Tell me where you are. That wind was scary, wasn't it? Real scary. Are you okay? Charlie?"

She spotted the quiet screen door and knew what happened. Ice crept up her spine and tickled the hair on the back of her neck. She knew what happened, and it was all her fault.

She ran screaming to the door, flung it open then ran down the steps. Pain ripped through her ankle as something within tore and gave, and dropped her into a crumpled heap at the bottom of the stairs. Tears stung her eyes. She gasped at the pain and at the horrible realization of what she had done.

Charlie had fled into the storm to escape her.

Annie looked up at the sky turning blacker. Clouds billowed like steam from a teapot. The wind picked up again and threw icy barbs that cut through clothing like a razor blade. Charlie was out there with nothing but a pair of tattered blue jeans, a T-shirt, and the too-big socks.

Shuddering at the cold, and the stinging pain in her

ankle, she knew he was going through something much worse. She pulled herself partway up, cringed at the throbbing, and knew she couldn't run after him now even if she could guess in what direction he had gone.

The edge of the roof caught her gaze.

The edge of the widow's walk.

From up there, she could see in every direction. If she could make it up there, she'd be able to see him and call out to him before he went too far, before he was lost.

She hoisted herself upright by the railing, then forced herself to take one step, another then another until she crossed the threshold into the kitchen.

She limped to the door, shrouded in torn wallpaper strips, and pulled it open. Dank, salty air filled her nostrils, but there was something else, a burned smell, ages-old. There with one breath, the smell was gone with the next. A small collection of candle stubs stood in a pyramid at the base of the wooden steps. No matches were readily available to fight back the dark of the stairwell, and there was no time to look for any. Not if she was going to find Charlie.

The first step tested her weight on the damp wood. She cringed with pain, then the wood beneath her foot shifted and groaned.

Climbing further, she pressed her hands against the inside of the narrow walls and caught a splinter in her palm. Ignoring the jab, she followed the stairs as they turned off to the right and rose yet higher over the kitchen and toward the bay.

Step over step, one after another, they stopped suddenly at a narrow landing. The door in front of her was rough and weathered and low, and it refused to budge when she pushed it. A roar of wind on the other side crept around the edge to touch her with sharp cold. She ran her hand along the wood until she felt the cool metal of a hook and eye latch and inched it open. A powerful gust of wind threw the door open. It crashed against an outside wall. The strong chilled air pushed her back into the dark stairwell. She leaned into the wind, then stepped up and out onto the widow's walk.

The door slammed shut behind her.

A groan then a sharp crack sounded to her left. She whirled on her heel. A small branch from the giant oak hanging over the widow's walk fell soundlessly away. Large sheets of bark sheared from the tree by the viciousness of the wind took flight then fell across the walk.

The remaining bulk of the heavy oak branch hung half on and half off the edge of the walk. Swaying ever so slightly, the wood was poised for a lethal fall at any time.

She eased carefully around the branch, ducked her head into the wind, and approached the bayside of the walk. She shuddered, held herself tightly, and peered out over the back lawn to the steep slope that led to the bay. A black cloud rolled over the dim haze of a moon and threw her into darkness. Panic picked at the corner of her mind. She had to find Charlie soon. The weather had turned dangerous, and would not wait for anyone by the looks of it.

The cold had come so fast. This was an island for god's sake, September to boot. This kind of weather wasn't supposed to happen. It didn't make sense. Nothing made sense anymore.

Maybe she was crazy as a loon and deserving of

every bit of misery coming to her. Her throat tightened at the turn of events in her life; a tear oozed down her face. She meant well, but something horrible was happening to her. If only she knew what it was and could stop it. She'd even go back to her boring little subdivision in Atlanta with David if that would make things right again.

The cloud passed. A flicker of light from the moon cast an eerie glow on the trees, shrubbery, bay. The wind howled. In the distance, a tree crashed to the ground. She jumped at the sound and backed into the wall of the attic room.

A sudden draft propelled her to the edge of the walk. Instinctively she fought for balance. Another step and the two-foot-high decorative wall would have fallen with her. She backed up and peered at the latticework, the crack running top to bottom, the splintering across the top. It had been broken before and then repaired.

She glanced out over the edge and imagined her mangled body intertwined with latticework wood.

She inched closer to the edge.

See what he would do to you?

Annie spun on her heel at the sound. It was different this time, louder, all around her. The wind itself gave energy to the words in a clear, unfaltering voice.

The boy. There. Hiding. Waiting. He has disobeyed.

She called out into the woods beside the house. "Charlie?" There, a small movement in the dense pines and underbrush to the left of the house. "Charlie."

His name died in the wind.

He ran for cover under another clump of underbrush.

See how he turns away from you? See how he disobeys?

Fear turned to panic then to anger.

"Charlie, come back this minute. Do you hear me? Come back." Annie side-stepped the fallen oak branch and limped to the other side. Hot pain ran from her swelling ankle into her calf.

She wouldn't have hurt her ankle if it wasn't for him. They'd all be fine and happy as they deserved to be. That's all anyone asked for, wasn't it? Of course, it was.

It was true. Charlie had disobeyed her at every chance. First, it was the drawings. The crayon and pencil smudges on his hands when she gave him the banana was irrefutable proof that he had gone against her wishes. Now here he was out in the storm when he knew he wasn't allowed to go out after dark.

And if that wasn't enough, he was clearly disobeying her order never to see the Manns again. Sybil would ply him with her damned sugar cookies, and it would be all over but the singing.

If only David were here. David would straighten him out in a hurry. That was the only thing he was good for, doling out punishment. He'd spent years developing his punishment expertise through incessant comments that she wasn't any good at anything. Now it was time to punish Charlie, and her husband wasn't here to do it.

Why did he leave so suddenly that night?

She had scarcely enough time to throw together a little food for his long trip. A loaf of bread was all she had, but it was his. There was barely enough kerosene in the lantern to show them the way to the small boat, let alone his way to the sea, but that, too, was his. She would give him anything he wanted, do anything he wanted if only he would stay. Her loneliness had become unbearable. She had become nothing without him.

It was so dark, so cold. She had stood in water that pulled and tugged her down into its murky depths while he pushed the oars into the shore then sliced them into cold bay water. Further and further, he went away from her until the lantern became a speck on the horizon, and her choked cry fell limp on the water's glassy surface.

She stood fixed for minutes, hours, until there was nothing left on the horizon but hope of his return. Hope turned to despair, to hope again, and a clearer vantage point from the widow's walk. From here, she would see the first flicker of light, the signal of his return.

There were mistakes, but she had taken care of them. The child would trouble them no more.

She would wait for him, she would walk for him, and when the child was taken care of, he would come back to her.

Annie looked up into the sky, where dark clouds boiled overhead. Tomorrow night then, when the storm would be at its height.

Then, and only then, would she see a light out in the bay.

Chapter 20

Sybil yawned, stretched, and sipped tea that had grown as cold as the night. Her lips curled in disgust at the bitter taste, but she drank again and brushed an ink-smudged hand across her robe. Touching fingertip to tongue, she turned the next page of the family record.

It was a stroke of luck the account was found at all. The sudden move from Manchester Place to this little house down the road those many years ago could have resulted in a loss of everything they owned. The move was quick, disorganized, and clouded in raw emotion, for Winston anyway.

The clouding for her came later as a result of medication. A lot of things from the move were missing to this day, but as of this evening, the family record was no longer one of them. It was only at the urging of Eleanor Trippett that the record was found.

An odd woman, that Eleanor Trippett. Once Sybil got past the woman's notable attire and wraith-like demeanor, she found herself comfortably back in the role of hostess and was grateful for the excuse to change her mood.

Eleanor had even accepted a cup of tea and a cookie. Not that she finished either, but it was a start. Scarcely more than a shadow, the woman was thin enough that Sybil imagined she could see the sip of tea and the cookie nibble travel the length of Eleanor's throat. It gave one pause to consider what the outside of her stomach looked like when the food arrived.

Eleanor was uncanny in her ability to pull out information from a reluctant hostess who minutes before barely had the strength to raise her head from the table. Sybil was equal to the task of information gathering—at least she thought she was.

In hindsight, she realized Eleanor had revealed very little. Her attire of black was a result of mourning, and she conceded a short stay at Manchester Place a quarter-century past, and that was pretty much that. There was something both women shared though. More than just the common ground of a Formica table between them, they shared concern for Annie Cameron and Charlie.

Eleanor had urged her to look for anything that might reveal family history, and Sybil had obliged without question. That resulted in finding the family record in a water-stained box in the back of the garage. Before today the boxes held nothing for her but a chore that she would get around to someday. Now all she had to figure out was what to do with the information the family record might offer.

She took another sip of cold tea and decided there were a few more things to figure out, like why Eleanor asked that her visit not be mentioned to Winston, or how she knew Annie Cameron. Funny, but they never did get around to those particular bits of conversation.

Instead, Eleanor was gone as quickly as she had appeared and left Sybil the day and most of the evening to tear into boxes until she found an assortment of memories and the written verification of the Mann family chronicles.

Leaning forward in the hardback chair, she rubbed her lower back and bottom, and groaned when numbness turned to pinpricks of discomfort. The chairs, although a good buy when she first saw them, were no good for duration sitting. Her arthritis was bound to scream in protest tomorrow—she looked at the plastic clock on the wall—make that today

Time was ticking away, but she wouldn't know for sure how fast things were moving until she saw the Camerons again. Annie had already revealed confusion, pain, and anger, but it was Charlie who would show her how much time was left.

Sybil would see it in his eyes, in his actions toward his mother, and if she were lucky, she'd know what to do. Whatever she could dredge up from this book might help decide the next action. At least she hoped it would.

The light in the kitchen dimmed, surged, then went out completely.

The storm. Winston said it would be a big one, a mean one by anyone's standards, certainly by the island's. A maritime high he had called it, marked by sudden winds, rain, ominous clouds, and temperatures as cold as Lucifer's rumpus room. The weather event would be quite a shock for those used to a balmy coastal September.

She struck a match, paused as the flame caught and leveled, then touched it to the wick of a stout candle anchored by its wax to a salad plate. The candle sputtered and hissed then bathed the kitchen table in a soft glow while leaving the room's periphery in shadow. Squinting at the leather-bound book, she ran her finger down the yellowed paper to find her place. Old paper crackled under her touch.

The script was small and difficult to read, but she recognized Winston's grandfather in the style. His anecdotal approach to the stories, and his liberties in the interpretation of events, were all duly recorded with color and enthusiasm only he could bring. The entries were vibrant, alive. All except one.

Winston's grandfather wasn't around when the incident took place, so once again, the story was third, maybe fourth hand, from the truth. But it had been written down, and that somehow made it a little more credible.

It was certainly more information than she had found anywhere else. The family Bible had simply stated the dates of death, but this record had a little more to offer, including a note on the events leading up to the deaths of Lady Manchester and her son.

It was just speculation, she reminded herself, and there was room for doubt and further questioning. Unless she could tie what she knew on a personal basis with what was written in the dusty book she had exhumed a few hours ago, the entry could only stay rumor. Otherwise, it was worth little more than the moth-eaten hats and dresses that filled the boxes to brimming and shrouded the book in the first place. The dresses didn't fit, the hats weren't worth the material they were made out of anymore, and perhaps it was the same with the information she had uncovered.

The lights blinked on and stayed. She cupped her hand behind the candle flame and blew it out. Another storm meant another on-again, off-again with lights and candles.

Glancing over her shoulder to the pile of supplies on the counter, she assumed there were enough candles to last the duration. There was plenty to be had at Manchester Place. Hopefully Annie had discovered them and would use them so Charlie wouldn't be scared. The child needed a hot meal now and then, light when it was pitch black outside, and some comforting when things got a bit out of hand. Comforting was something Sybil could give in spades. Could Annie do the same thing?

She shifted in the hard chair, and worry bubbled in her stomach. Winston would go to the house first thing in the morning to see that Annie, old Mrs. Cameron, and Charlie were okay, and prepare them for the violence of the storm.

His offer came without her asking him since he cared for the little scamp of a boy as much as she did, maybe more. So he would check on them again then report back his findings as he always did.

Now that she thought of it, Winston never mentioned whether or not Charlie liked the hornpipe. In fact, he didn't report anything at all about the entire visit of the day. He had been unusually quiet all the way through dinner, sat still and thoughtful during the evening, and suddenly disappeared to the depths of the house with a mumbled "good night."

Granted, she was preoccupied with the found book, and he was deep in plans for the storm, not to mention the dinner casserole was rather unremarkable, but the lack of conversation tonight suddenly stuck out almost as much as her varicose veins.

Something had happened.

Sybil closed her eyes at the thought and deliberated if she wanted to know. She toyed with the idea of stirring him from his sleep and finding out, then decided against it. If he wanted her to know, he would tell her. It hadn't always been easy between them. The horror of Manchester Place, Phillip's death, and her locked room behind cold institutional walls, all could have dissolved their marriage, but they didn't. Instead, the two of them worked the rusted metal of a marriage until it became a polished, eighteen-carat shine partnership.

If only Phillip were there to share the happy times. Their son only saw fighting, yelling, the rusted metal times, and then death.

The voice had come to her that night like so many other nights before and whispered her son's intentions to drive his parents apart. It wasn't Winston's wandering eye that hurt her, the voice said, it wasn't her fault she couldn't keep her husband at home. Phillip caused the trouble.

Sybil had chosen not to hear, but the voice was persistent, relentless. It called to her, beckoned her to the first narrow step, then the second, through the small door at the top, then out on the widow's walk.

The voice was there, too, soothing, warm, comforting. It was a comfort she desperately needed and formed words that surrounded her, came from within her, and explained in quiet tones what she had to do.

She listened then, and she believed.

Phillip ran from the safety of the house to take his chances. Screaming, he left the house and disappeared into the cold arms of the storm and death.

Sybil knew when he was taken. The sound of laughing exploded around the widow's walk. Her heart skipped then beat a hollow staccato with the sudden knowledge he would never come back.

She stared as a wisp of smoke from the extinguished candle on the salad plate twirled and danced to the ceiling.

A truth buried almost thirty years ago had finally come to the surface. The voice brought Sybil to the widow's walk to look out over the bay for a light that never came.

There was only darkness. The darkness on her son's face as the casket lid closed; the black of drug-induced amnesia within the walls of a state building that blotted out the sun and kept her locked away; and the truth that she had tried so hard to deny. She had killed Phillip, killed him with her hand guided by another.

A lone tear trickled down her cheek, hung on the edge of her chin, and dropped softly to the open page in the old leather-bound book. This volume unlocked the door to her hidden horror and forced her to see the pattern she didn't dare see before: a failing marriage, a child, the ghost of Manchester Place, and a storm.

Phillip was dead, and unless she did something to stop the nightmare, another little boy would die as well.

Rubbing a dry hand across red, swollen eyes, she bit her lip until her teeth drew blood. Nothing could pay back the damage she had done to her family, and no amount of personal pain would equal what she had done to her son. If only she could know Phillip forgave her and that he understood what had happened.

Here was a second chance for Charlie, and maybe for herself. She had to go to the house and thwart what she knew was inevitable without the intervention. Only she could do it, and do it alone. She would go out in the storm and right the wrong of twenty-seven years ago.

Winston would never believe her. How could he after she rode him so hard about the ghost of Lady Manchester? This was Sybil's battle anyway. It was her revenge. Besides, she didn't dare jeopardize Winston's health. His heart couldn't take it, and she wouldn't take the chance of losing him, too. The clock read 5:38. She looked out the window and saw the heavy gray of the storm around the house. It would get little lighter today.

Standing on weak legs, she prepared a mental list of what was needed: warm clothes, sturdy shoes, thick gloves. She pulled open a kitchen drawer and reached past an assortment of candles for a piece of scratch paper to leave a note for Winston. A small container tucked in the dark back corner rolled forward and stopped at her fingertips, label up.

Pills. To help her relax.

She would have never put a bottle of pills there. Someone else had done that. Winston had chided her for her "addiction," then encouraged, cajoled, and finally ranted that she needed to stop taking them. So, he had helped things along a little faster than it would have happened anyway by hiding the pills in a drawer.

After twisting off the pill bottle top, she poured the contents into her hand for a quick examination. They were intact, solid. She sniffed for any sign of deterioration, detected none, then looked over her shoulder. Winston was still asleep. If there was ever a time she needed a pill to relax, it was now.

She popped one of the pills into her mouth, swallowed, then capped the container and slid it into her pocket in case she needed another one later.

A quick check in the hall closet produced the shoes

she needed. Now all she had to do was throw on a few warm things and she'd be off and back before Winston knew she was gone. Later she'd think of a story explaining why Charlie was having breakfast with them, then together the three of them would figure out how to help Annie.

****

Static from the portable radio hissed and sputtered. Mann stirred at the sound then groggily recognized he had dozed off for a few minutes. A glance and a tap at the cracked face of his watch surprised him with the time: 5:52. It had been hours rather than the few minutes of sleep he would have bet on.

He blinked, looked around his library lit only by the lone lamp over his armchair, and fiddled with the radio dial to raise a clear station. There was nothing but static. So he was on his own now. Last night's report on wind speeds and tides would have to do.

He'd hoped for a more restful sleep before the storm preparations went into full gear, but now there were too many things to do. A day wasn't enough if it were all to be done, and done right. He coughed. The tightness in his chest ebbed and flowed like the waters of the sound was bound to be doing about now. He decided that things would be done right regardless of the amount of time he had. There wasn't any other way.

If wishes were effective in hindsight, he'd wish for Richard's arrival earlier than the time they agreed on. The young esquire should have spent the night in fact. No matter, Richard would stay this time, maybe even the next few nights.

With the choppiness of the water and the high winds, nobody in their right mind would chance a crossing to the mainland later in the day. Hopefully, not even a risk-taker like Richard. Mann would simply have to put his foot down and tell Richard no, nada, no way in hell. Sometimes it took the force of a father-figure to knock some sense into the young man. If that didn't work, he'd take a bat to Richard. Now that *always* worked. It should anyway.

Perhaps this time, it wouldn't take a bat or a threat. The motivation to keep Richard away from the mainland was already here on the island in the form of Annie Cameron. Love worked in mysterious ways and made a man do things he wouldn't normally do, like go all sap-faced and weak at the thought of the woman he admired. Richard had that look. Winston could spot it a mile away and always felt a grin come on when he saw it.

Too bad, the woman of Richard's dreams didn't see it. From what he saw in Annie Cameron yesterday, there was only hardness and cold in her. The two of them right now were a poor combination to expect happy results.

Cold and sap-face. The only cold Richard would benefit from right now was that from a shower, and there were probably plenty of those taken lately. Winston could feel the water table drop right out from under his feet if he tried hard enough. And if the poor kid got the shoulder from her much longer, everybody on the island would feel the shift. They might even have to go screaming into the streets from the sudden cave-ins.

Winston smiled at the thought and shifted in his chair. The story of Huck Finn slid off his lap and slapped the floor. His lost enthusiasm for the works of

Twain when Phillip died had changed tonight, became renewed. The dark, the wind, the isolation of an island, the feel of the night—it all seemed a good chance to recoup his loss of special literature. Then sleep claimed him, forced his eyes to close, and he dreamed of the work that lay ahead.

If only he could read Twain to a little boy again, to show a child the magic of the Mississippi through the eyes of a character much the same age. What a wondrous experience it would be for someone like Charlie. The words would be music to his ears.

He wondered if Charlie ever got the hornpipe, and decided he hadn't. No reason for the opinion necessarily, just an inside nudge and something he saw in Annie. She was hiding something, something big, that much he was sure of, but what it was, was anyone's guess. Or maybe not.

He squirmed uneasily in the chair. Annie Cameron had changed almost before his eyes. It was as if something on the island had caught her eye and held her attention then forced her to settle something. Or maybe the something had settled for her.

He rose with a deep, resonant groan and stretched. There were windows to cover, a boat to secure, and things to tie down. Then he would have to check on the supplies for his family and that of his tenants. So the first order of business would be to send Richard off to Kenzie's Store. The selection was limited, but no doubt, the splintering shack of a store would be open. Old Kenzie wouldn't miss a chance to shoot the breeze with the islanders and make a buck on a regular day. On a day like this, premium talk and prices would make it all the more worthwhile.

When Richard got back from the store, they would pull *Errand Two* up on the shore, cover her, and tie her down. It wouldn't do for a wild lick of a wave to come up and pull the boat out into the water, wouldn't do at all. Some folks got a bit mad when a storm came up all of a sudden, especially an odd one like a maritime high. Those folks would decide it was safer to be heading back to the mainland than to wait it out on an island even if the storm was upon them.

Some folks were stupid, but that was their decision. He would be safely tucked away in his house eating food out of a tin while *Errand Two* was temporarily, and safely, dry-docked. The water could be dangerous enough in the best of times. In a storm like this, Neptune himself would check into an inland cement block motel and feast on tuna sandwiches and sweet ice tea.

He turned to the bookcase where the leather-bound *Tom Sawyer* had once been. A neighbor book tilted inward, half filling the space as if the book had never been there occupying the same place on the shelf for over thirty years. To a stranger, the space would never be noticed; to him, it was as obvious as his face in a mirror and represented events equally as clear. Phillip and Charlie.

Phillip's hand-scrawled message asked for help, and hours later, his body was found crashed against a rock. The storm, the boat, his attempt at escape, all of it ended in death.

Then there was Charlie's near-drowning in the water during the fishing trip.

The two events were independent of one another, yet they were too similar to ignore. Maybe it was the fact he knew both boys and loved them both that brought the picture under microscopic scrutiny. Or maybe there was an underlying thread that held the pictures together and brought attention to detail.

The two of them had been on a boat, different boats, but boats owned by him and used by him. This didn't account for the blood-red message in the Twain book unless someone had scared Phillip and made him think the boat was the only safe place for him.

Sybil could belittle his theory as much as she wanted, but there was no doubt left in his mind at what happened. The ghost of Manchester Place had reached a hand out from the past to take Phillip then tried for Charlie but missed. Both efforts had used the bay to lure them into her arms, to take them away from people they loved, and who loved them, but for what gain, and why? He shook his head, rubbed a callused hand over his temple. All that mattered now was the boat dry-docked and inaccessible to little boys who might see the bay as a safe way out of the storm.

He rubbed his temples harder this time. A headache stretched across his forehead like a tight headband. It was all too crazy, too unbelievable, and incredible that he would even consider the matter of a ghost. At the same time, there was no room for doubt.

Leave it to the parapsychologists to figure out the details, and to the exorcists to cleanse the water of the beckoning hand that called little boys to a watery death. He had things to do today. For beginners, there was a boat to yank as far out onto the shore as he and Richard could pull.

Damn it. Where was Richard anyway?

He stretched a kink out of his back, ambled to the

kitchen for a quick cup of coffee, and blinked at the bright kitchen lights so early in a dark morning. He sniffed, missed the smell of breakfast cooking, and caught sight of the open book lying on the kitchen table. A single drop of moisture blurred the dates of Lady Manchester and her son's deaths. Sybil had been up all night reading the journal, contemplating the meaning, and speculating on the situation at Manchester Place. His stomach twisted at the implication.

"Sybil?"

The empty house groaned with a wind that whipped around its eaves.

"Sybil, please. Answer me."

She was gone. He touched the frail paper of the book as if it were a map of her whereabouts. Worry curled around him. She would be at the house trying to stop what they both knew would happen but were afraid to speak.

Wind pounded at the screen door, and a garbage can rattled across the yard to slam into the overturned patio furniture.

Sybil was out in the storm to fight the even greater one that raged within her.

A tree scraped dying branches across the window.

Fear coursed through his spine at the sound, at the reminder. His headache turned to an insistent explosion with every heartbeat; his hands trembled with the thought.

The branch lay on the widow's walk and waited for the right wind, the right time, the right person. Sybil would walk under that branch to get to the door and complete her mission.

There was a knock on the door. He bolted for it,

stopped as it was flung open. Richard flipped back the hood to his jacket and stomped on the doormat. Clumps of wet sand fell around his boots.

"Jeez, it's getting bad out there. Almost didn't make it over to the island. Mr. Jasper's ferry was wheezing and coughing like an asthmatic. He said it was the last round of the day as far as he was concerned, but the beginning of many rounds of hot toddies. Had a few already if you ask me. This early in the day too. Jeez." He paused. "What's wrong?"

"Sybil's gone."

"Gone? Nah, she's probably upstairs doing whatever women do to fix themselves up."

"She's gone, boy. Didn't you hear me the first time?"

Richard raised an eyebrow. "You two having problems?"

"What?" Mann scowled. "We're not two teenagers playing back seat shenanigans. She's stepped out for a task of some sort."

"She'll be back."

"You certainly sound sure enough. You seen her or something?"

"No, but she's bound to be right back. She knows storms as well as you and I do. And she knows the island backward and forwards."

"I wish she were here."

"Want me to go find her? I'll be glad to."

"Would you?" He stopped. "Wait. What am I saying? You're right. She's a grown woman, and she'd be mad as a hatter if I went after her and was wrong about the situation. Maybe I'm just overreacting. But damn it, where is she? It's not like her to run off with no reason." He eyed the open book suspiciously. "Or even with a good reason. I can't wait. I'm going after her."

"No. I'll go. I'll start with Kenzie's Store. Everybody goes to Kenzie's when there's a storm. She's bound to be there picking up a few things. If I'd thought about it, I could have picked up some stuff on the mainland. Who knew this storm would come up so quick? She's probably picking up an extra can of something and a few other odds and ends. Bread and milk excepted. People hear they may be homebound for a day or two, and wham, the stores are emptied of bread and milk like no tomorrow. You stay here in case she comes back. No sense in everybody wandering around."

"I suppose. Okay, I'll stay here, do a few chores, and keep my eyes peeled. But if you or Syb aren't back soon—"

"Don't worry; we'll come back. Let's see, nails I bet, a couple of candles, anything else?"

"Yes to the nails, no to the candles. Maybe some bread and milk. Canned milk, and anything else you think we might need."

"See," Richard mumbled, pulling the hood up over his head. "Just like on the mainland."

"And be quick about it. We've got a boat to take care of."

"Got it, boss. Back before you know it."

"See that you do. And Richard?"

The young man turned in the doorway.

"Be careful, okay? We need you."

Richard grinned, gave a thumbs up, then bent into the rising wind.

Winston stroked the page to the open book and

tried to force the picture of the fallen branch out of his mind.

"Just come on home, sweetheart. I'll take care of it. Come home."

Chapter 21

It was so cold, colder than it had ever been before, and she couldn't find the pretty pink mittens her father had given her.

Grandma shivered under the thin sheet and comforter, pulled them tight around her, and worried about her punishment.

Father had found out about the mittens and had locked her in this attic room. She didn't mean to lose the mittens; it just happened. If she could get out to look, she'd find them before he knew she was even gone. Then everyone would be happy again, and safe. And warm.

Under the comforter, she rubbed her feet and smiled when she could barely feel them. It was best not to feel discomfort when one didn't have to.

Charlie's feet hurt, her dreams told her. He was cold enough that soon, he wouldn't feel pain anymore either. The pain in his shoeless feet from running in the woods and the hurt in his mind from something that scared him would welcome a cold that numbed and helped him forget.

She squinted in the dark of the attic room and thought of this little boy Charlie. He was a cute thing, smart, but his relationship to her was suddenly unclear.

Her eyes narrowed with the sudden realization. Charlie had stolen her mittens. He was the one who tricked her into taking them off then told her to close her eyes and count to a hundred. When the count was up, she opened her eyes and saw he and the mittens were gone. She had looked everywhere. Behind trees, under snow-laden bushes, she had even looked behind the leaning snowman she had so carefully built that day.

She had come close to finding them, so very close. His laughter told her that much. Loud laughter rounded corners just ahead of her, glee sounded behind her and all around her, until finally there was nothing left but silence and a dark, empty street far away from home.

Her hands hurt from the cold; a lone tear froze solid on her cheek. He had tricked her by making a game of stealing her mittens with no intention of ever giving them back, and now she was lost.

She shivered at swaying shadows in the darkened street and tucked her hands under her arms for warmth. If only her father would find her and bring her home to the small house and the roaring fire, she would willingly accept any punishment he saw fit.

Street signs made unfamiliar letters form words she couldn't yet read. A dull half-moon grinned at her then hid behind thick clouds that turned a gray night to black. The moon was mean. It tried to trick her like that boy, Charlie.

That was his name, wasn't it? It seemed right, yet wrong at the same time. Charlie. She would have to think about that.

Her stomach growled for food, but it was dark in the little attic room, and the stairs were empty of footsteps that would help alleviate the hunger.

She had been sent to bed in the tiny attic room without supper as punishment for the mittens. Severe discipline like this didn't happen very often because she was a good girl, but any time was too often, her father had said. She rubbed the ache in her stomach and wished for a cracker and maybe a little water to take away the edge.

Milk would be nice, she loved milk, but milk was a special treat when Father brought in a little extra money. Money was scarce; you work hard for money then treat it with respect. She tried to understand what he meant, and tried to respect his money, but she had lost the mittens anyway. The pretty, pink mittens.

Her hands would stay cold for another winter now. And her feet.

She rubbed one foot against the other under the comforter. Numbness crept to her lower leg and tickled her knees. A fire would be nice now, then she and Charlie could be safe.

She searched the dark room for Charlie and worried where he was. A sharp pain burned in her foot. She cringed at it and tried to understand what it meant.

Charlie was Annie's son. She was Charlie's Grandma. They were living in a house on an island.

The wind howled around the corner of the house and carried with it a low, guttural laugh. A woman's laugh.

Footsteps tapped across the ledge outside the attic bedroom wall and stopped. The woman looked over the bay, waited, watched for someone to come, then resumed her pacing. Watching. Waiting.

For Charlie.

The woman on the widow's walk waited for Charlie's return. And he would return, Grandma knew, to the woman's waiting arms that tightened and squeezed until there was nothing left. Charlie would return because he had no choice.

Grandma pulled herself up in the bed, whipped back the comforter, and shivered as the cold in the room touched her bare legs. Sudden dizziness sent her mind spinning. She reached out to the bedside table, wobbled when she stood, then pushed herself toward the door to yank the handle. It stuck tight. She tried again, and fell back into the room, to the hard bare floor with a solid thump. Pain arced through her hip and ran down to her foot.

The woman's laughter pounded her head.

There's no place for you, old woman. No place.

That's not true. They love me. They need me.

You're an empty box. An old, discarded box.

Charlie...

A troublemaker. He will be punished.

Cold surrounded her and lured her to sleep. Her eyes closed, opened, closed again. Charlie's a good boy, a gentle boy. He doesn't deserve to be punished. Losing the mittens was my fault, not his.

Her head nodded forward; her chin touched her chest. *Charlie shouldn't have tricked me. He took my mittens, and that was wrong.*

Cool air covered her like a shroud, numbed and deadened. Her breathing slowed. The pain in her hip and leg faded. Sleep drew her in and claimed her in its shadows.

It was cold. So very cold.

Chapter 22

Charlie hid behind a small palm and tried to make himself as thin as the leaves that jutted out from the narrow stems. He crouched down, received a slap in the face from a wayward branch, and stepped on a dry twig as sharp as a needle. He gasped, caught the sound before it traveled the wind toward the widow's walk, and squeezed back a tear of pain. A trickle of blood stained his sock and cooled almost immediately from the frigid wind. He shivered more from fear than from cold, and peered out between the branches.

She paced the widow's walk, stopping now and then to call his name half-heartedly. "Charlie. Charlie, baby. Charlieeee."

The hair rose across his arms at the insincerity in her voice. She didn't want him in that house.

"Charlieee?" She stopped in mid-stride and stared directly at him. "Come home, baby. I'm waiting for you." Her voice melted with the wind and became a quiet ripple in the current. "Now, Charlie. Now."

He ducked down, staying frozen in place until he guessed she had looked away. A quick check proved him wrong. She hadn't moved.

The small palm was no longer safe. He held his breath and ran. Refuge came behind an oak a few yards away. He collapsed at the base of the tree and leaned heavily against it, and took breaths in deep gulps. The tree moaned, creaked then exploded with sound as a leaf-laden branch dropped in a solid heap at his feet.

Laughter filled the air around him.

He leaped to his feet then stole a glance over his shoulder at the woman on the widow's walk. Her teeth were bared in a smile as if a puppeteer pulled a string on either side of her mouth.

Charlie ran as fast as he could make his legs go, deeper into the darkness of the woods. Adrenaline coursed through his body. His heart pounded and ached. His lungs strained with the effort as if they would burst through his chest.

He dodged a bush here, a stump there, turned left then right then left again.

He wished his daddy was here.

He wished his mommy was here. Not the lady on the walk, but his real mommy. The mommy who loved him and helped him learn how to read and gave him something to eat when he was hungry.

His legs cramped and stung with overexertion and the cutting wind.

It began to rain.

Running slowed to a lope then a walk. He turned his face up to the rain, allowing the coolness on his skin mingle with the flow of tears. He stuck out his tongue to catch a few stray drops of rain, swallowed dryly then gave in to a spasm of coughing. The cough turned into dry sobs.

He pressed his face against the rock's side and leaned into its sturdiness and strength, and its lack of warmth. He wished he was in his bed tonight, even if it meant keeping one eye open as long as he could to check for any movement from the fuzzy green, laughing toy. But he could never go back now. Never.

He was cold. So cold.

His bed would be warm.

The rock was out in the storm.

The house would be safe.

He pressed hard against the rock and cringed at the thing that gouged his chest. The hornpipe. Running his hand over the length of the instrument, he was glad he had spotted it when he did. The electricity had come on just as he ran from the house. It was a risk to stop and pick it up outside the broken window, but one he couldn't resist when he saw it lying in the sand.

His mother was wrong to keep Mr. Mann's present from him, and she was wrong to make him promise things he couldn't keep. He twisted in the hard sand for a more comfortable position. His mother had never been wrong before, she always knew what was best for him, but now things had changed. Now it was he who knew the difference between right and wrong.

Holding tight to the rock, he decided he was too little to be making grown-up decisions and be out in the cold and dark alone.

This island trip wasn't a real vacation, no matter what his parents said. If he had any say in a vacation, he would have picked something else. He wouldn't pick a place that separated his parents from each other, or a place where he ended up in the woods at night in a storm, alone.

Before tonight, his mother would never allow him to be by himself. If they were back home in Atlanta, she would have paid that pimply-faced baby-sitter, Ramona, to come by. He looked around the shadows of the woods and decided Ramona would be better than this. Even if she made him watch gushy love shows on TV instead of cartoons, and spent the better part of the night talking to her boyfriend on the phone while keeping a tight vigil on TV in case he changed the channel. She was better than being out in the rain. It was Ramona who once showed him a hickey on her neck and waited patiently for awe that never came. Who wanted a bruise on their neck? He had splotchy places on his legs from playing spy, and no one seemed to care, especially Ramona. If her bruise were in the shape of an animal or something, now *that* would be impressive.

Ramona and her hickey. He'd settle for both of them right now.

He ran his hand over the surface of the hornpipe, brought it tentatively to his lips, and blew. A tight, shrill sound crept out from the end and blended with the wind. Taking a deep breath, he covered some of the holes and blew harder this time. The sound deepened, became full and melodious. He stopped, examined the instrument, and noticed a louder sound independent of the hornpipe shift to a higher octave.

Peering into the woods for the source, he dismissed the sound as a quirk of the wind and hoped one day he could play the hornpipe for Grandma. She deserved a little something fun, too. Then when he was a famous hornpipe player, he would save up his allowance and buy her some pink mittens so she wouldn't worry anymore, even though he never remembered seeing her with any.

The rain picked up. He pulled some fallen leaves and a small branch over himself in a makeshift sleeping bag. Cold water soaked through his clothes and stuck to his skin. He tucked his feet up under him and wished he had on shoes or had a blanket. Even pink mittens.

Pink was a girl color, not for an almost-man like himself. Pink could be for grandmothers, too, like clothes and stuff. Why did Grandma talk so much about the mittens all of a sudden? It was as if she couldn't think of anything else.

Maybe her mind was wired different like his, and it made her think about mittens and talk about things that didn't make any sense. Suppose her wires got messed up, and she forgot about him? Worry surrounded him like a shroud, and then fear stole its place. If she didn't know who he was anymore, it would mean he was all alone. In the dark, in the cold, he'd be by himself with no place to go.

Grandma was alone, so was his mother and father in their way, but secluded just the same. So if growing up meant he'd be isolated, he'd stay a kid forever and ever and hope that someone would always be there for him.

A pang of guilt nagged him. He should be there for Grandma, taking care of her. Without him, she had no one to talk to and no one to listen to her stories.

He would have to go back.

He couldn't go back.

The wind whipped around him so that he could almost hear the laughter and the pacing from the widow's walk. But he had to know Grandma was okay and see for himself she was safe. He would tell her he was sorry for leaving her in the first place; then he would make her something to eat.

His stomach rumbled then fell silent. Wind and rain stung his skin like burning needle pricks. The smallest of morning light filtered through the trees and underbrush. Maybe that meant the storm was going away. He looked up at the dark clouds and doubted it, but was at a loss of what to do next, or where to go.

Scanning the unfamiliar surroundings, he wondered if he could find his way to Uncle Winston and Auntie Sybil's house. Suppose he got even more lost and went so deep into the woods that no one could ever find him again, then what? He leaned against the rock and tried to stretch his stiff muscles, but they cramped in protest.

He dug his hands into his pockets for warmth, and felt the coin he'd found in the sand. It was different enough from his piggy bank money and might be from a place far away, like one of the yellow states on his map puzzle at home. Or maybe the coin came from a green state.

Running his thumb over the surface of the coin, he wondered if he could use it to buy a candy bar or gum. On second thought, he would keep it to bring to Grandma as a present. She would like it, and might even be able to tell him where it came from. The candy bar could wait. Grandma would have the coin as a present from him.

The rain came harder, stung more. It was time to take his chances in the woods. A quick brush over his clothes moved the leaves and small branch aside. He stood on legs tight with cold and damp and turned to the rock he had leaned against. His eyes widened, his jaw slackened.

There was a name carved in the rock.

His name.

Next to his name was today's date.

He licked his dry lips and stared unseeing at a far off point. Darkness tugged at the back of his mind. It turned him inward and beckoned to a safe place where he was more than willing to go now. His eyes rolled up into his head; the eyelids fluttered with myriad thoughts. There was nothing left to do and nowhere else to go but inward.

Inside the dark, he would be safe from the laughter on the wind and from rocks that held his name. It promised him safety from anything that could hurt him.

The darkness opened its arms to him.

He went to it.

Chapter 23

Light from the bare bulb in Kenzie's store glowed under the door of Eleanor Trippett's room like a flashlight in a deserted campground. The cash register rang almost non-stop and added to the din of excited conversation. She knew they were all islanders by the now familiar voices, and they were all men. It seemed the women had better things to do before a storm than last-minute gossip in a drafty building tainted with the smell of old bait, spilled beer, and stale tobacco smoke.

Slowly and methodically, she pulled the black veil over her face, pinned it in place then slid the gloves over her hands.

Kenzie's warnings last night finally superseded his quest for additional pocket change when he suggested she leave the island immediately. She had acknowledged his advice with a nod then refused. Concern for her safety in this rickety building during a storm, or outside in the harsh elements, was dismissed as unimportant sometime before Kenzie even approached her.

The storm, eventually, would pass, the damage totaled, and the repairs began. But some things could never be repaired so she would stay and do what she could to prevent it.

Taking a deep breath, she stood tall, opened the door to her room, and stepped over the threshold.

Conversation ceased. The myriad acts of loading canned goods into boxes halted. All eyes turned to her and waited.

She met their gazes. "I'm looking for a man."

They looked at each other as if collectively agreeing on the topic of conversation after her departure. No doubt, the subject would be Eleanor Trippett.

A grizzled man wearing faded coveralls wheezed, coughed then spat a stream of brown tobacco juice in the direction of a bucket in the corner of the room. He ran a hand across his mouth and smiled at her with his few broken teeth, and took a deep swig from a beer.

"Well, you ain't gonna find a man dressed up like that, I can tell you."

A ripple of guarded amusement traveled through the men congregated around the cash register.

"That's God's truth. 'Course with a little fixing up, you might be worth a second look."

"But what's she gotta look at, Gabe?" The man in a rain parka smiled broadly. "A woman's gotta be blind, and stupid to boot, to take up with the likes of you."

Gabe snarled then slowly recognized the joke. "Maybe so. Maybe so. I've had my fair share of the ladies, and can't no one tell you otherwise."

The man in the parka winked. "Stockpiling centerfold pictures doesn't count."

"C'mon boys, enough already." Kenzie leaned his beer-induced girth against the cracked wood counter, stroked his beard with a fleshy hand decorated by a horseshoe-shaped diamond ring, and cleared his throat. "What can I do for you, little lady? You say you're looking for someone?"

"That's right."

"Has he got a name?"

"Richard. He works for Sybil and Winston Mann. Where might I find him?"

Gabe stumbled toward her, stopped short, then tried to check his sway while peering closely through her black veil. "Who are you with such high and mighty talk?"

"Back off, Gabe," Kenzie ordered.

"Won't do it, Kenzie, and you can't make me." He leaned toward Eleanor. "And what business have you got asking for folks that have better things to do with their time, when you won't even show us what you look like? What are you anyway? A ghost?" His laugh turned to a wheeze and a rattling cough.

She closed her eyes at the stench of alcohol from him, but never moved. "Do you know where I might find this Richard person, Mr. Kenzie?"

"I'd be more than happy to give a call over to Winston and find out, Mrs. Trippett, but I'm afraid the phones are out. Could be days before they come back on."

"Trippett?" Gabe dipped precariously to one side then caught himself with a step back. "I know that name."

"It's getting kinda dangerous out there." Kenzie nodded at the window. "But I suppose you might still have a chance at making it to their house if you've a mind to do that. I wouldn't advise it, though. Wind could knock a little thing like yourself clear out to the next island."

"I'll take my chances, Mr. Kenzie." She skirted the drunken Gabe and walked to the door.

Gabe reeled after her. "I know who you are now. Yes, I do."

"C'mon, Gabe," Kenzie said. "Don't do this."

"It was a long time ago, but I remember it as if it were yesterday. You were at Manchester Place, weren't you?"

Kenzie came out from behind the cash register. "You're cut off, Gabe, no more beer. And I think you better head on home now."

"I ain't going nowhere." Gabe pointed his finger in Eleanor's general direction. "You killed that boy sure as I'm standing here. Weren't no effen proof, but I know it had to be you since no one else was there."

Eleanor Trippett turned to him and stood frozen in place.

He hesitated, eyes widened, then took two steps back. "You don't scare me."

"Don't I?"

Gabe spit, wiped his hand across his mouth, then backed to the counter and the cash register with the other men. "Damn women. Aw, hell with it."

"Don't I scare you?" She slowly walked to him. "I should. If someone's killed once it's easier the second time, you've heard that, haven't you? The second time is much easier because there's nothing left to lose. And there needn't even be a good reason for killing again. In fact, there needn't be a reason at all, but you've given me plenty of reasons. Should I list them, or will you figure that out all by your drunken self?"

Gabe's face paled. He slid down the front of the counter and turned away from her. "I didn't mean nothing by it," he whimpered.

"Hell with it?" She bent over him. "You don't

know what hell is."

Smoothing the black dress and the veil across her face, she turned on the heel of her pointed black shoes and walked out of the store.

"Get up, Gabe, you old fool. As if a storm outside wasn't enough, you had to go and get one started in here. Damn fool."

She paced the wooden planks outside the store. Damn fool was right, but Gabe was just one of many. Maybe she was, too. Sybil's passing mention of this Richard fellow yesterday, and his growing romantic interest in Annie Cameron, had planted the seed in Eleanor's mind. If she could talk to him, convince him of her theory, then maybe Annie and her son would have a chance. It was worth a try, however absurd it sounded. So maybe Gabe was not the only fool in the store this day.

The disagreeable drunkard had done something right, though, something she never thought possible anymore. He had made her angry. After two-and-a-half decades of feeling nothing, any emotion would have been progress. The first to show itself after so long was anger, and it felt good. It felt great. And there was a lot more where that came from.

"This is pretty bad weather for taking a walk, don't you think?"

He was wearing blue jeans tucked into brown boots. A flannel shirt poked out from under a heavy jacket. He smiled at her from a handsome face covered in two days worth of beard and crowned by a mass of dark, curly hair.

"Are you a friend of Annie Cameron?"

His face a blank mask one second, reddened the

next. "In a way, I guess. Maybe. In a way."

"I've been trying to find you."

"My name's Richard."

"Yes. I know."

"I don't think I know who you are."

"Annie's in trouble and needs your help."

"Trouble? What kind of trouble?"

Eleanor sat down on the bench by the door to Kenzie's store and patted the place next to her.

"Sit. I don't expect you to believe what I'm going to say, but I hope you'll hear me out anyway. You're the only one who can help."

Chapter 24

The rain stung her cheek then clung to her like a second skin. Sybil wiped a bare hand across her forehead, pushed away tentacles of wet hair, and squinted in the overcast gray dawn. By her calculations, it was a little after six.

Fallen leaves stuck to her booted feet. A pile of twigs, damp from the rain, bent then snapped with her weight. She jumped at the sound. It was sharp compared to the almost hypnotic one of rolling wind, and rain rhythmically dropping through trees and shrubbery to ground. The harsh sound seemed almost out of place in the quiet the storm had brought.

Maybe it was the sedative she had taken that brought the contrast so harshly to her ear. The little pills were still as potent as she remembered, and as effective in bringing about a much-deserved calm. She could cope with anything now.

Her feet moved at a pace separate from her will. She would have them take their time, but they were on a mission of their own. It was a task of goodwill if she remembered correctly.

Yes, goodwill. That's right. She would see that Charlie was okay then smuggle him back to her house for a hot meal, a warm bath, and a comfortable bed with a kiss on the forehead before his eyes closed to sleep. He deserved a little calm, too.

A twinge of anxiety penetrated the drug then dissipated as quickly. She smiled at the thought her plans would be realized then hoped she would know what to do for Annie. Annie was just as much a victim as Charlie, more so in a way, but Annie was an adult. By virtue of age and experience, adults weren't supposed to be as vulnerable.

She stopped suddenly. If that idea were true, what was the defense for her deeds at Manchester Place? Taking a deep breath, she claimed the calm again by refusing the bad thought and patted her pocket to make sure the pills were where they had been a few seconds ago. They were. Sighing deeply, she allowed her feet to carry her farther into the woods.

It was a circuitous route to the big house on the bay, but a way to keep out of sight of the windows. A squirrel scurried in front of her and disappeared into the underbrush. Her feet were moving, the animal ran off, yet things were suddenly slowed, as if someone had shifted a record from seventy-eight to thirty-three. The time wasn't right. It was all too slow; there was too much time.

She patted the cylindrical bottle in her pocket, just to make sure.

If she had the little pills at Manchester Place, maybe things would have been okay. Phillip would be here, Winston would read to him every night, she would make tea and sugar cookies, and everything would be just the way it should. They would be a family again, they would be happy, and Phillip would always be their little boy.

She leaned into the wind, ignored the rain stinging her face, and traced the edges of the pill bottle in her pocket.

She missed Phillip more than she thought she could after so many years. Winston was right. It never got better. Memories were pushed away, crowded out with the urgency of things that needed doing here and now, but they never went away. Like a flower or the fragile shoot of a tree in a broken sidewalk, memories pushed up and out when they should have been buried under cement.

Or under earth.

Sybil missed Phillip's pranks, his puns, his crooked smile when he had been caught doing some minor infraction. If only she had just one more time to touch his face, tell him how she loved him, tell him she was sorry.

She stroked her pocket, pushed the bottle back and forth, back and forth. If she listened close enough, even over the wind that surrounded her, she could almost hear the few pills left rattle around in the bottle. This was the first time she had been here since it happened. She knelt, then pushed away a pile of damp leaves, and ran a finger over the carved letters.

Phillip Mann.

His name was engraved in cold marble. There was nothing else: no date, no inscription, no age. There was only a simple name unless one was lucky enough to know the person behind the name or underneath the marble.

Marble, like memories, decayed with time, withered away in the elements if it were given long enough. How long was enough? She brushed a leaf from the top of the stone as if brushing a strand of hair from the boy's forehead.

Phillip had been feverish that night, trembling from the chill of pneumonia. She brushed sweat-damp hair out of his eyes and felt his high temperature on her lips with the kiss. He smiled at her through his illness and turned to his father for the next chapter of Twain's *The Adventures of Tom Sawyer*. Sybil had taken care of him, bathed away his chills, fed him when he was hungry, and still he looked to Winston for answers, for consolation with a scraped knee or a homework problem. He was the son, and she was the mother, and always there were responsibilities.

Winston departed after Phillip's eyes closed, and the last word of the last chapter ended the book for the tenth, maybe even fifteenth, time. He left his son to finish the chores before the cold, windy rain could cause any more damage.

It was dark that night, darker than it had ever been before on the widow's walk. She had barely been able to make out the shadows of the big oak that grew near the walk, and squinted in the dark until she felt the low railing press against her. Any other night and the moon would have cast a warm tunnel-like glow across the bay. That night it was different.

The voice told her what she must do if she would see the light come across the bay. She wanted that light, wanted it more than anything. So every night, she had walked and waited, and every night ended in confusion, disappointment, and finally, anger that ate away at her until it found a small crack where it could escape.

Phillip.

Leaning against the cool of the marble headstone, she wished she could produce a tear. There were none left. Years of weeping had left her dry. Still, she wished things could have been different.

And maybe they would be now. She had one chance left, no more. Too many things were riding on her actions: Charlie, herself, and in hindsight, Phillip.

She pulled back from the marble, caressed it one more time, and promised him she'd be back. He wouldn't wait twenty-seven years to see her again. Sybil rose slowly, fingered the bottle in her pocket then gasped. "Charlie?"

Fear held her feet solidly in place unwilling to propel her forward just as minutes ago they would barely stop.

He was pale, and still in a wind that should have knocked him over. His gaze stared past her. They were colorless eyes, dead eyes.

She stared at the wet shirt, and trousers plastered to his frail body. He was so little, so vulnerable. Father in Heaven, he had no *shoes.*

Sybil went to him. He tottered then fell into her arms like a piece of wood. "Boy, boy, boy. My little boy."

She pulled Charlie to her, rubbed his arms, his chest, anything she could touch as if the act of stroking would warm him. Without ever losing a physical connection to him, she slid her coat down her shoulders, over her arms, and around him like a blanket. She yanked the scarf off her head and pulled it over his with a quick tie under his neck and a kiss to his forehead. God, he was cold. She lifted his chin with her hand and looked deep in his eyes.

"Charlie, talk to me. Are you okay?"

He stared past her with an expression she remembered seeing in old Mrs. Cameron. The look turned inward, away from the pain, away from things that were happening against her own will. Now that same expression was etched across Charlie's face.

Sybil wrapped her arms around him, but it wasn't enough. If she didn't get him indoors and warmed up, he would die. She glanced back from where she came, scrutinized the other way, and knew there was no choice. Manchester Place was by far the closer.

What the hell was he doing out here in the first place? She shuddered at the thought, and knew the answer. It had already started in the house. They couldn't risk going to Manchester Place, not now. Not ever. Closing her eyes, she wished for another pill from the small bottle but was afraid to let Charlie go. They'd have to make it back to her own house somehow.

He whimpered and blinked as if trying to orient himself. Uncontrollable shivering racked his body. He clung to her, dug his fingers into her flesh. She patted his head, brushed her hand across his cheek, and pulled back at the touch. Cold skin had turned hot. There was no way around it. He had to get to a house before he caught his death. Manchester Place would have to do.

Under her breath, she said words of hope, of help, then bundled him up in her clothes as tight as she could and propelled him across the debris-laden ground as fast as she dared. He went easily as if the wind dispersed any will he had left. She talked about a recent magazine article she had read on losing ten pounds in ten minutes, discussed the merits of wood stoves versus fireplaces, explained the difference between detergents, and spouted off the ingredients used in gingerbread.

Manchester Place loomed into view.

Holding him tight, she stopped the recipe recitation

at the point the cake entered the oven. It was a mistake to bring him here; it was wrong. She should have taken him to her house, even if she had to carry him every step of the way.

Charlie faltered, stumbled. His knees buckled but finally caught. A deep, loose cough rattled in his chest.

The front door to the house opened. Backlit by the glow from the light within, her silhouette filled the entrance to the house. Her hand reached out as if to beckon then stopped. Annie stood still, waited.

Sybil's arms involuntarily tightened as Charlie shifted.

"I've been worried about you, Charlie." Carried on the wind, Annie's voice was calm, emotionless. "You've been gone a long time. Too long. All night in fact. Come in now."

Sybil tightened her grip and caught the boy before he fell limp..

"Now, Charlie. I've waited long enough."

He stiffened, slipped from under Sybil's arms then moved toward his mother as if dragged by an invisible rope.

Sybil grabbed his arm. It slid from her grasp; then, he was free. She followed, tried to pull him back, but he was too fast for her. His pace quickened with every step, a few inches, a foot, two feet just out of her grasp.

"Come back! Come back to me!"

"I've waited long enough, Charlie."

"Don't go in there!." Sybil lunged for him and fell.

"Now, boy," Annie said.

He staggered from one woman to the other, back and forth until his gaze settled on his mother. He climbed the steps, hesitated again.

"That's right, boy. Come in now. I've waited long enough."

"No, Charlie." Sybil tried to stand, But something stronger, more powerful, tried to hold her back. Fighting the thing that would stop her from getting Charlie, she crawled to the steps.

"Don't go."

Charlie's shoulders sagged as he walked slowly to the doorway.

Annie stepped aside to let him pass. A flicker of a grin crossed her face. She backed into the house behind her son, closed the door, and threw the lock.

"No. You won't have him." Sybil crawled up the last few steps. Inch by inch, she crossed the porch and pounded on the door. The sound was weak, ineffectual.

"Charlie." She took a deep breath in preparation for a bellow, a yell that would wake the dead, but the air became trapped in her lungs. The door stayed closed.

No sound came from the house. It was ominous in its lack of stirring.

She scratched the door weakly. "I'm not giving up, Annie. I won't go away."

Reaching overhead, she rattled the doorknob. It stayed firm.

"Two can play this game."

Sybil crawled back down the stairs, one at a time. She didn't trust the fogginess that had settled in her head or the shakiness in her legs, but she wouldn't give up. Not now, not when she was this close. Pulling herself up by the banister, she then turned to the side of the house and stumbled toward the kitchen door.

He would die here.

It was her fault.

The screen door to the kitchen hung from one hinge, then broke free and sailed across the side lawn. She tried the solid interior door; it wouldn't budge. Then pressed her face to the glass. The partially opened refrigerator sent a thin line of light across the room. Dishes were piled haphazardly in the sink, dirty water spilled into a small puddle on the floor, and cabinets stood ajar, but no one was in the room. Then she saw it.

"No, no, no, no, no!" Pounding the door, the glass, until her gloves split at the seams from the impact, she wailed then fell exhausted to the doorstep.

The door to the widow's walk was open. Annie had been up there.

It was happening again. Sybil had killed one boy and pushed Charlie toward the same end.

"Dear God, please. Please help me help him."

She looked out across the woods and imagined Winston well into his day of chores with Richard by his side. Once she found the two of them, and anyone else they could recruit, together they would get into the house, break down the door if they had to, and take Charlie away.

When it was all over, she would burn the house down herself. Burn it as Lady Manchester had done, but this time no one would be hurt. She would take a match to it and smile as every piece of wood charred and fell to the earth to become ash. She would laugh aloud as nature claimed its rightful place and covered the blackened area with green life.

She headed down the steps, with a glance over her shoulder at the locked door and its dark window. In another hour or so, they'd be back, everyone she could get, and her nightmares, finally, would be over.

"Auntie Sybil?"

She froze at the sound. A tickle crept up the back of her neck.

"Auntie Sybil?" The voice came from the back of the house, the bayside.

"Charlie?"

There was no answer. She looked at the window then walked around to the back, looking under hedges as she went.

"Charlie? Is that you?"

"I'm scared."

"I know you are, darling. And I'm going to help you. Where are you, Charlie?" She hurried past the opened door to the crawl space and nudged it closed with her elbow. "Charlie?"

"In here, Auntie Sybil. I'm scared."

She stared at the low door to the crawlspace under the house. It was dark in there, dirty, and there was no telling what creatures might be sharing the same place with odds and ends long forgotten. Unless he'd managed a minute away from his mother and ran for it, he couldn't possibly be in there. Wouldn't Annie be out here looking for him? Maybe she didn't know he was gone yet, in which case there was no time to waste. Sybil cracked open the door ever so slightly.

"Charlie? Are you in here?"

No answer.

She pried it open a little further and ducked down. "Charlie? It's me, Auntie Sybil. You're safe now. Just come to me, okay?

A whimper was barely discernible.

She got down on her hands and knees and crept just inside the door. "Charlie? It's okay now. See? It's me. I'm going to take you home now. Just tell me where you are, and I'll come to you."

A cough came from the back corner of the space. But how far back did it go? She'd always thought it too creepy to go in this place, so she never had. That dirty work was left for Winston to handle.

Crawling another two feet into the dark, she brushed against something with her knee. It fell in a hollow, metallic clang on the ground in front of her. She gasped and tasted rust in the air then gingerly reached out to identify the fallen object. A rake.

"It's all right, Charlie. Just a rake. I'm okay. How about you?"

The air under the house was still. She could hear no movement in the house above either. That seemed odd. She would have expected at least the sound of the refrigerator humming or footsteps. She crept further into the space.

"Charlie? Can you see me, honey? Come to me, and we'll go home and forget this whole mess." Something touched her hand; a bristle-soft warmth followed by a leathery whip of a tail against her other hand. She jumped up with a shriek, hit her head on a strut, and shivered from disgust and fear.

"Oh god, oh god, oh, god!" She tried to calm her voice. "Charlie? I'm going out now. Come with me to my house. Come on, Charlie."

She turned toward the scant outside light. The door swayed with the wind then slammed shut. A metal hook rattled.

She crawled over and pushed. The door bowed and creaked but stayed. She kicked it with both legs as hard as she could. It wouldn't budge. She kicked again.

Pounded on the door with her fists until the gloves shredded. Then remembered the small boy in the dark corner of the crawl space.

"Charlie? Come help me. We'll get out of here together."

Without a clue how that would happen, she figured it sounded good. Maybe Charlie would buy it, too. He was bound to be frightened out of his wits. A low, guttural giggle echoed from the corner of the space and rode the sudden drafty air current to the locked door.

The teases, full of mirth and cunning, now hovered outside the door. Then the sound became a woman's laugh, one that Sybil knew intimately, and had heard uttered from her own throat.

Charlie wasn't in the crawl space, had never been.

She was trapped, and no one knew where she was, except one.

And that one would never tell.

Chapter 25

Winston pounded the last nail into the plywood that covered the kitchen window and looked over his shoulder for any sign of Sybil or Richard. The hammer missed its mark and collided with his thumb. He grabbed his thumb with his other hand, hopped about on one foot to distract himself from the pain, and swore loudly. Damn the hammer and his swelling thumb, and damn Sybil and Richard for making him worry about them. Where were they anyway?

It had been hours since Richard left for Kenzie's store. Winston had filled the time with fixing this and making that and compiling a list of the things that would need fixing and making yet. The chores on his list had barely been touched thanks to his worry over missing-in-action Richard. He'd skin him alive if the boy had been jawing with the islanders instead of preparing for the storm. Damn it. Everyone else seemed to be in a hurry except Richard.

And where was Sybil?

An occasional quick wave by an islander was all most had time for on their way to the ferry or their boats in the escape to the mainland. A few managed a hurried conversation, and not one had seen Sybil.

"You staying?" Peter Burke had asked earlier that morning. "Not me. We'll let this storm happen without us this time. Yup," he said, glancing at his mirthless wife beside him. "A visit with the in-laws is long overdue. Figured this was as good a time as any. See you."

That conversation was a good two hours old, and still no Sybil or Richard. Winston tapped his watch, listened for the whir that proved it was still working, and looked down the road. There was no one in sight. Hell, if Peter Burke was leaving, maybe the storm was worse than he had thought. Or maybe the Burkes were just stupid, which was more likely the truth. Anybody who jumped in a boat during a storm didn't have the sense God gave a donut, which pretty well summed up Mrs. Burke's personality.

He stacked up aging boxes marked storm supplies and carted them into the house for later use. The open family journal on the dining table caught his attention. He lowered the boxes in a corner of the room and went to it. A glance at the page and something clicked in his mind. He slammed the book shut, then tossed it carelessly onto the countertop and just missed the sink when it landed open.

Wasn't there enough to worry about without ghosts and the less than golden past of the Manchester history? He hadn't modified his name for lack of something better to do, but now Sybil had been caught up with his family's past, too. Obsessed with it, she had stayed up all night reading then disappeared into the morning without a note or a hint of what she was about.

He eyed the journal splayed out on the counter. It was a hint of her whereabouts, wasn't it? Or more likely a slap in the face. She was out on a mission related to the house, and if he guessed right, something that had to do with Charlie. She should have been back by now, they both should have. He'd go look for them, but if he missed them, they'd all be out wandering around in the storm.

Mann looked at his watch again, tapped it, and paced the room. Damn it, where were they? He had things to do, things that couldn't be done by one man. He needed Richard's help, and he needed Sybil safely home. If she was home now, and *Errand Two* was up on the shore, he'd pour himself a drink and sit out the storm with his feet propped up on the table edge. Sybil would chastise him for the drink, and all would be right with the world.

But she wasn't here, the boat was bobbing in the water like an apple in a Halloween barrel, and that tree branch was still hanging over the edge of the walk at Manchester Place.

Damn, damn, damn. How could he have forgotten the huge oak? There was one more thing that needed to be done. He'd give them one more minute to show up; then he'd be out the door to Manchester Place. One minute.

Or maybe five. Just in case they showed up.

He hated waiting more than anything. If he had a choice between not knowing and a hot stick in the eye, the hot stick would win hands down.

A knock on the door rocketed him to his feet.

"Sybil? Richard?"

The face in the glass was pale, and began to talk before Winston could open the door.

"…looks broken to me. Can you come?"

"Wait just a minute, Stretch. Back up. What are you talking about?"

Stretch bowed his head under the doorframe and

spewed out words between labored breaths as if he had run a marathon.

"Peggy. An accident. The wind." He caught his breath, swallowed dryly, and continued. "The tree. Just fell over. Caught her, made her fall. I think her leg is broken. I pulled her out, but she started screaming." His voice cracked. "She's out there, in the cold and the rain. Help me. Please."

Winston grabbed a jacket off the coat tree by the door, scratched a brief message on the refrigerator notepad, and tossed the chore list on the table.

"Sure, I'll help. Let's go."

Maybe he'd see Sybil and Richard on the way.

****

"She'll sleep now, Stretch."

"Thanks to you, Winston. Hey, I owe you one. A big one."

Winston patted the tall, lanky man on the shoulder, and was cheered to see a hint of color come back to his face. On the other hand, it was possible the change of mood came from the four shots Stretch had shared with his wife than from anything else.

"She ought to be okay until after the storm. Then we'll get the doctor over here."

"Does it look broken to you?"

"Hard to tell, but I don't think so. The doctor'll know for sure."

Winston pulled on his jacket, headed for the door, and peeked out the window. The storm had worsened. Trees swayed and groaned with the wind. Rain pelted the earth in dark sheets.

"Looks bad out there. Real bad." He glanced at his watch. "And it's getting late."

"Stay and have some supper. I can make a mean omelet when I have to." Stretch stared out the window as a lawn chair sailed by. "Maybe later. When things aren't so hectic."

"Thanks, Stretch, I'll keep it in mind. You haven't, by any chance, seen Sybil or Richard anywhere around?"

"Not a one. Been busy around the house, then this thing happened."

"Just thought I'd ask."

"They're okay, aren't they?"

"I hope so, Stretch. I hope so."

Stretch shrugged. "I wish I could help you out." He nodded to the bedroom where his wife slept then shrugged again.

"I understand. No problem. See you later."

"Take care. And hey, thanks again."

Winston waved and stepped outside. He leaned into the wind and headed home. The storm was getting worse, heading to its peak, then in a few hours, it would start on the downside.

He reviewed the list of the things left to do. Less than half were possible now, and those would have to be done according to priority. *Errand Two* was at the top of the list after he had checked the house for Sybil and Richard's arrival. If luck were with him, Richard would have handled most everything by now, and Sybil would be baking something. She always baked when she was bored or nervous.

At least the Camerons were in a warm, safe house. Manchester Place had weathered plenty of storms and always managed to stand its ground. A little dampness in the crawl space, a few cracked or fallen boards was all that would happen, and it'd be ready for the next storm. He looked up into the sky, getting darker with every minute, shivered as the hard rain soaked through to his skin, and decided this storm would last him a while, a long while. If he never saw another one, it would be too soon.

Charlie would be safe, a little frightened maybe, but safe. Mann would have liked to see the boy before the island took the brunt of the storm. As soon as it edged up a bit, he'd be over there to check on him and his family, maybe even have the boy over to the house for a read from the leather-bound collection. That would be nice. A warm house, a few of Syb's treats, and a good read. Life just didn't get much better.

Unless it included the tree branch hanging over the widow's walk taken down and dismantled into stacked firewood.

If time had been kinder to him, he would have had the chance to cut the thing into kindling and get it off the walk once and for all. But Annie wasn't stupid. She'd see the danger of the branch and steer clear of it. Still, it would have been a load off his mind if he'd gotten rid of the branch before now.

He pulled his jacket tighter and wished he had a heavier coat on instead of the thin windbreaker that Sybil said he looked "dashing" in. He didn't feel dashing right now, just tired, wet, hungry, and anxious. Being prepared for potential problems, storms especially was something in which he took great pride. Today was a weak example of what he could do if he had the time. But who would have guessed that Sybil and Richard would disappear and that Stretch's emergency would pop up?

There was bound to be more problems. He could feel it. Sybil would call his prediction cynicism, but he called it simple observation. One problem always seemed to lead to another. It was in the cards, it was in the storm, and the result was bound to be a long evening, maybe even an all-nighter. For someone who was no longer a spring chicken, bad storms didn't bode well.

Rain fell in cold, hard walls of water that bounced off the ground and cut visibility down to a few feet in front of him. Water pounded his bare head, rolled down his face, neck, and back. He snorted at the joke in calling his jacket a windbreaker and knew that even an honest raincoat would be no match for this weather.

Maybe it was time for a move. Just pack up and leave. He rolled his eyes and knew he wasn't kidding anyone with that thought. Mico Island was his home. Aside from any familial connection, he loved the place, thrived on it needing him as much as he needed it. He couldn't imagine living anywhere else or working anywhere else, and he needed work as much as he needed Sybil. Without one or the other, he'd wither up and die or sink into the role of cardiac cripple. Self-pity or a day without a chore list would dig a six-foot deep hole for him quicker than any undertaker, so he'd keep things the way they were.

With Charlie around, there was renewed interest in the other things he loved as well. The child had been a blessing to him, a breath of fresh air in a sometimes stale day-to-day routine. He knew the Camerons would leave someday, probably not long from now, although Annie hadn't mentioned any particular date, but when Charlie did go, it would be with the Manns' phone number safely tucked in a small pocket and a promise of a visit every summer.

Any other nighttime in a storm meant sitting back and listening to the wind and the rain as if it were a great symphony and enjoying the warmth of being inside and dry. He would empty his glass, slap Richard on the back for a job well done, and slip off to bed with Sybil at his side.

Right now, though, the symphony was just chaos of unstructured sound and threats that reached right down to the bone with chilling rain. He knew that it would be a while before he felt dry again, really dry, and since he was already drenched to the skin, there was little reason to change at the house and go out into the elements again to check on *Errand Two.*

If Richard hadn't already beaten him to the punch, he'd pull the boat as far inland as he could and secure the anchor. Better to do a little something than nothing at all.

Turning toward the bayside, he leaned into the wind. The air cut through his clothes as if they were made of paper. At least he could see a little ahead by walking the shore of the bay. If there were any problems with the boat, he had an extra few minutes to formulate a plan. Hopefully, the worst that could happen was maybe a slow drift of the boat out into the bay. Tying additional ropes to the small floating dock should prevent that kind of problem and would hold the boat upward from the wind for the most part as well.

If the boat were capsized by waves kicking up or by the wind, then at least it wouldn't go anywhere, and when the storm passed, he'd get a few folks together, and they'd turn her back over. This kind of thing had happened enough to other islanders that they all knew the routine.

Heading down the steep embankment leading to the water's edge, he slipped in the wet muck and running water that drained the island and fed the bay. He landed on the soft beach and sank into the damp sand. The water was agitated and higher than he had ever seen it before, which was even more reason for not going out into the bay as a means of escaping the storm. He pitied the people who might still be trying their luck by counting on it being calm and seductive on their way to the mainland, and bet the general store on the dock over in the mainland was doing a booming seasickness business. The bay travelers got what they deserved.

He raised a hand to cover his eyes as a new, more violent wall of rain fell around him and obstructed the view. He quickened his pace to reach *Errand Two* and be done with it so that he could get home to Sybil. This weather wasn't doing any good for his health, and getting sick meant more of Sybil's liquid cures.

A last bend in the shoreline, and he'd be there. A few more steps and he'd see for himself what the next few minutes or hour would hold. He stumbled over some driftwood in the sand, caught himself, and looked up to see the whereabouts of his boat. His mouth dropped open in shock.

Errand Two was gone.

He blinked in the rain, brushed torrents of water from his eyes, his mouth, and looked around for confirmation on his location. *Errand Two* would be around the next curve of the island, around the next bend. But there was the small dock saturated in wave after wave. He recognized the dock as his but refused to consider the implications.

Maybe the storm had torn away the ropes and pulled the boat out. That was possible. The wind was strong, high gusts, strong enough to break a rope and tow a boat away. He reached the dock, grabbed the nearest rope, pulled it hand over hand to check the frayed end for himself.

The wind towed the boat and caused the rope to break. That was it had to be. He pulled the rope harder. No problem then, just a simple call to the insurance company. That's what they were there for.

Another pull.

No one took the boat, not a little boy, not anyone. It was the wind, the storm. Not a little boy who had been scared by a storm, or something else, and then left a note for him to find years later.

The rope slid through his hands. He retrieved it and found the end neatly cut and sealed just as he had left it. The rope had been carefully untied, not broken from the wind, or torn. It had been untied by someone who had taken her out into the bay, maybe into the ocean itself, untied by someone who didn't know how dangerous it was to try storm waters: someone who had to get away for whatever reason.

Like Phillip, twenty-seven years before.
Like Charlie. Today.

No. His mind refused the thought. It wasn't happening again; he wouldn't allow it. The boy was safe and warm and dry in the old house overlooking the bay.

But he hadn't checked.

The boy was there. He had to be there.

Suppose he wasn't. Suppose...

A sharp, burning pain arced through his chest and brought him to his knees. His mind's eye showed him Phillip's body, blue, bloated, clinging to the rock outcropping, a rigid grin fixed permanently on his face.

You should have seen the note, Dad. Why didn't you see it? You let me die. It was your fault.

Help me, Uncle Winston. Help me, or I'll die, too. And it'll be your fault. All your fault.

The body against the rocks shifted with the current, turned upward. His smile widened, revealed shattered teeth and a small stream of blood running from the corner of the mouth. His eyes fixed him in their stare, then winked.

It was Charlie's face, smiling. Staring.

Chapter 26

"Grandma?" Charlie tapped on the wooden door to the attic with his free hand. The other held a stack of paper, pencils, pens, and a large box of crayons securely against his chest. "It's me." Another tap. "Grandma?"

It had been a long time since he walked back into the house. Hours at the very least, he guessed, but time was hard to know for sure. He'd never been much good with watches, and a look out the window showed only a dark, unfriendly sky.

His mom had escorted him to his room, wordlessly, with the same frozen smile on her lips, and closed the door: no explanation, chastisement, punishment, or even a hug of concern.

He'd sat still on the edge of the bed and hid in the darkness of his mind while his mother pulled off his wet clothes and replaced them with dry. Statue still, he dared not move when she left with Auntie Sybil's coat and scarf and closed the door behind her. His darkness held him in its warmth and quiet until Grandma's call pulled him away and sent him up the narrow stairs to the attic room. She had been in the big bedroom before, but now she was in the tiny one.

She loosed a deep, rattling cough that hurt his chest. He knocked, again and again, got no answer. Suppose she, too, had run out in the rain and the cold?

"Grandma?"

She had to be in the room since even if she wanted to run away getting down the stairs was something she could barely do. The "pain in her bones" as she called it, made it hard for her to get around.

Charlie turned the knob and pressed his face against the barely cracked open door so that one eye looked in on her.

She lay in bed; the covers pulled up to her chin.

He looked to see the rise and fall of the comforter with her breath, released a sigh of relief, and padded in.

Her hand rolled out from under the edge of the blanket and hung there palm up.

Papers and crayons dropped to the floor, then he grabbed her hand and held it. The slightest of stirrings made him think she knew he was there.

"Grandma? It's me. Charlie. I came home." He squeezed her hand then rubbed it between his palms. "I'm scared, Grandma. Are you okay?"

He squeezed again, waited for a response that never came then spotted a small tray in the corner with a sandwich on a flowery-green plate and a mug. Letting her go, he went to examine the contents of the tray. Peanut butter and jelly by the looks of it, and there was something dark in the cup. He stuck a finger into the stone-cold liquid then grimaced at the bitter taste.

He brought the tray to the bedside and raised the mug to her lips. The black liquid rolled down the corner of her mouth and soaked the comforter. He bunched up the material around her neck and tried again. This time it splashed on her cheek, sprayed drops across her forehead, and rolled in a wet wave across the bottom of her chin. She didn't move.

Hot soup was more to her liking, but maybe she'd eat peanut butter and jelly. He rubbed the edge of the sandwich across her damp lips and pried open the corner of her mouth with the crust. A few crumbs hung tenuously to her lips, but she wouldn't eat.

"Please, Grandma. It'll make you feel better. It'll put hair on your chest." That may not have been exactly the right thing to say, but he figured it was worth a try.

Pressing the sandwich to her mouth again, he remembered those arguments didn't work for him either, and gave up by tossing the sandwich back on the tray and shoving it aside with his feet.

If only she would talk to him, even if it were about pink mittens.

He closed his eyes, tried to hear her in his thoughts, tried to talk to her. There was only silence. Opening his eyes, he spotted the stack of paper carelessly dropped when he entered her room and decided to draw a picture for her. She always liked that. This time he would draw a horse for her, a funny one wearing a hat and holding a pipe between his teeth. She'd like that a lot, and might even laugh.

He reached for a blank sheet of paper, deliberated over pen or pencil, settled on a pencil then began to draw. He started with the eyes and drew the elongated face next. Too short. He erased it and drew again. This time the face was too long, way too long. Marking a big "x" through it, he started again on the other side. His tongue popped out from between his teeth.

"Fire."

He stopped, looked up at her.

"Fire. Burning. Run." Her voice rose in pitch, strained with the effort.

Her hand hanging out from under the comforter clenched open and closed, open and closed.

"Grandma?"

The drawing dropped from his grasp and fell to the floor. He jumped up to stand over her.

"Candlelanterncandle." She panted. "Stairs."

"Stop, Grandma." He trembled.

"Coming. Stairs. Coming. Help him. Stop."

He shook her gently at first. "Stop it, Grandma."

Tears fell from his eyes; sudden coughing hurt his chest. He shook her harder.

"Grandma. Stop it. Stop it."

Her eyes opened. She stared as if she'd never seen him before.

Charlie recognized the look immediately and turned away from it. It hurt too much to see that she didn't know him anymore. He reached for her hand, afraid to meet her empty gaze.

"Now there's a good boy. Just leave them here, and I'll show Father they're back. That's a good boy. A good, fine boy." She pulled away from him and rolled over on her side to face the wall.

Charlie waited a few minutes until her breathing settled into a rhythmic pattern, and knew that she was asleep. He gathered his materials, and slowly headed for the door then stopped. Fishing around in his jeans pocket, he realized the coin was missing and bolted down the hall to his room. There, rolled under the bed when his mother removed his wet clothes, was the coin. He held it tight and returned to her room.

Reaching under the comforter, he found her hand, pressed the lucky coin into it, and closed her fingers into a fist. He kissed her, then walked quietly out of the room and pulled the door closed.

She had escaped to her darkness, a darkness that was far away from him, and one where she didn't know him anymore. He brushed away a tear and scowled at himself for the weakness. Only girls cried, not almost-men, but he couldn't help it. He kicked the door to his room, welcomed the sound of it slamming shut, and fell on his bed amid paper and pens and pencils and crayons, and cried until he couldn't cry anymore. His darkness loomed near, one that would never let him go if he went this time, and one that would forever separate him from Grandma.

Rolling to one side, he saw an untouched tray of food on the dresser next to the laughing toy. Soup and milk. Plain milk. His mother only half-remembered what he and his grandmother liked to eat. She had placed the tray in his room next to the laughing toy without a word to him, just the smile that was part her own and part someone else's. He wasn't even hungry anymore.

A shiver traveled through his body. He pulled the sheet around him, coughed then stuck his thumb in his mouth. Maybe the lucky coin would help Grandma get better; then, he wouldn't be alone anymore.

Even Auntie Sybil left him. She had tried calling out to him from the porch steps, he knew, but it wasn't enough. His mother's voice spoke to him inside his head and told him to go into the house, or no one would love him. His daddy, his mommy, Grandma, Auntie Sybil, Uncle Winston, no one would love him if he didn't do as she said. He didn't want that to happen.

Maybe Auntie Sybil and Uncle Winston didn't like him as his mother said. They didn't care about him, were mean people in fact just playing mean games. Try as he might believe his mother, he couldn't. The Manns did like him, and he liked them.

So why did Auntie Sybil leave him here?

Things didn't make sense anymore. He hit the side of his head as if that would clarify things, then hit harder, faster. The only thing he knew for sure was he was scared and didn't know why. It was just a feeling deep in his mind that something was very, very wrong. Using both hands, he hit the sides of his head over and over and over until there was nothing left to think about then stopped.

He spotted the hornpipe lying just behind the laughing toy on the dresser. A quick retrieval wouldn't disrupt the quiet of the toy, so he eased over to the hornpipe, snatched it away, and carried it back to bed for a closer inspection. The wood was worn, but solid. Fingering the holes, he started to blow into it then hesitated in case his mother heard him.

Why had she left it here for him? She didn't want him to have it earlier today, and just a while ago, she'd taken it out it of his wet clothes and could have taken it away if she wanted to. Maybe she changed her mind, and it was okay now.

Or maybe it was a trick of some kind, like suddenly putting Grandma in the attic room. He dropped the hornpipe by his side and leaned back into his pillow, not feeling so good all of a sudden.

Weak, hot, and cold at the same time, his clean, dry clothes turned damp with sweat, and his chest hurt. He coughed, holding his arms across his chest as if it would ease the pain, and decided not to call his mother. Whatever she was doing was more important than taking care of him.

He was scared of her, scared of what she would do if he disrupted her in any way, and scared of just being in the same house with her. She would leave him alone if he stayed in his room. There was no way of getting out again, even if she wasn't watching him like a hawk, and there was no place to go if he did get out.

Charlie coughed, cringed at the discomfort, and rubbed a corner of the sheet across his face.

He missed Uncle Winston and Auntie Sybil already and wished things could be different. Picking up the pencil at his side, he began to scribble on the paper.

A boy his age to play spy with and hide out under the bushes until one or the other was captured would be great.

A drawing of an engraved, marble headstone appeared on the paper below his hand. He pushed it aside and started on the next page.

Later on, he and his new friend could go out on *Errand Two* for a fishing trip, but only if they wore life jackets.

A drawing of a boat appeared and spilled light from a single beam.

Another page.

He'd introduce his friend to Grandma. She'd like him a lot and would tell him stories about when she was a kid, and she'd be all better.

Stairs. Tall stairs. There stood a woman at the top, holding on, barely holding on.

Another page.

Maybe his mother would like him, and the two of them could play together as best friends. But now he was lonely, and so very, very scared.

The face in the picture smiled. The woman in the picture stood on the widow's walk.

Candlelanterncandle.

It was time.

Chapter 27

The storm raged around Manchester Place.

A heavy, blue blanket, nailed to the frame around the shattered kitchen window, billowed and popped like a sail suspended from a large mast.

Annie sipped coffee from the mug before her, propped her feet on the edge of the table, and stared into the crackling orange-red flames of the hearth fire. Tonight the light across the bay would come. It was a light she had waited years to see, the light from a lantern.

She sipped steaming coffee. Its warmth settled in her middle and spread outward, encompassing her—she caught sight of the covered window—like a warm blanket. With an iron poker, she sent glowing red cinders dancing in the air. They sputtered, floated on heated air currents, then settled down to join the hot, steady glow of the burning wood. The source of the bright-hot oak was probably the result of a fallen branch from a year or two ago.

She smiled, sipped her coffee, and glanced around the sparkling clean kitchen. It was cleaner than it had ever been before. Remnants of stray, peeled wallpaper had been gathered and disposed of. All the dishes were washed, patiently dried until not a drop of moisture remained on them, then put carefully in their place on the shelves.

Many things would be put in their place tonight.

The floor had been swept then mopped free of all dirt and stain. What part of the linoleum that wouldn't cooperate was merely cut away in pieces with the help of the big butcher knife.

Many things would be excised tonight.

She jammed the poker into the coat that lay next to her tightly taped ankle, prodded it this way and that until a wet pool of water crept out from under it and collected at the edge of her chair. The fire was almost ready for Sybil's coat, almost. Another few minutes and it would be hot enough to engulf the rain-wet material in a maw of flame. Sybil's scarf had already become black ash.

Many things would turn to ash tonight.

Sipping her coffee, she settled deep into the chair. He would soon be coming for her, very, very soon. She would know him by the light.

Only one thing remained, one thing that had stood in her way for years, decades, multiple decades. A mistake that needed correction in the past would be corrected tonight. That was only right. She had created the problem, so she would be the one to destroy it. The boy would not stand between her and the light across the bay ever again.

She poked at the wet coat that had covered him, and sneered. The sneer slowly vanished and became a smile again. She sipped her coffee.

The Mann woman had almost ruined it. Sybil tried her best to prevent what had to happen, but her concern for the boy's health caused a misjudgment she would live to regret. She had gotten away with one mistake already. Her son had died his death and not by her hand as it should have been. The light would have come that night if his death had been by her hand, but she had failed.

Annie jabbed the poker into the coat and watched each puncture inflict a wound on the damp material.

Tonight there would be no mistakes. When the time was right, she would correct the problem that had haunted her.

Underneath where she sat in a hardback chair facing a roaring fire, a woman trembled in the damp, cold crawl space and moaned when furry things brushed against her.

And upstairs, her two wards lay in anticipation of the night. There was a boy, drawing pictures that held no meaning, and a sad, old woman who had lost her reason to live. Tonight they would get what they deserved.

She lifted the coat on the edge of the poker and tossed it into the flame. It sizzled, released a cloud of steam, and caught fire.

Just what they deserved, and that's what they'd get.

All of them.

Then she would see the light from across the bay.

Chapter 28

There was a tentative knock on the door. "Ms. Trippett?"

"Yes, Mr. Kenzie." She didn't move from her spot on the narrow bed.

"Uh, I'll be locking up now."

"Goodnight, Mr. Kenzie."

"Well, then." His shadow under the door wavered slightly then stayed. "I guess I'll be locking up."

"Yes. I believe you said that."

"Yeah, I guess I did." The shadow stayed in place. "Are you going to be all right?"

It was a question she had asked herself many times in the past twenty-five years. Now, in the throes of a violent storm, sitting in a closet of a room in the back of a store on an island she never expected to visit again, the question had passed into the category of ludicrous.

"I'm counting on it, Mr. Kenzie." And she was. At least she was counting on being all right until her mission was complete. After that, all bets were off.

Something dropped to the floor with a tinny sound outside her door.

"It's not much," Kenzie said, "but I kept back a couple of cans for you in case you need them. Could of sold them eight times over, but it's better you have them, being here by yourself and all."

"Thank you, Mr. Kenzie."

"There's not a whole lot, but help yourself to anything else that might be left on the shelves."

"That's very kind."

"Just write down what you get in the notepad by the cash register, and we'll settle up later." His shadow under the door swayed. "Did you hear what I said?"

"I heard, Mr. Kenzie."

"Well, I guess I'll lock up then. Good night."

If all things went as planned, it would be a good night, if not... She refused to entertain the alternative. Richard had been justifiably skeptical, even with his apparent strong motivation to do whatever it took to keep Annie safe.

When the details of the plan were revealed, she almost lost him completely. Her calculated manipulation by mentioning Annie's name at every opportunity, and playing to his sense of adventure finally won him over. And it probably didn't hurt that she hedged the truth. Better a lie than the real story, especially when she saw his skepticism.

Their roles were clear. He would wait for her signal of three shorts, three longs, and three shorts. When the time was right, she'd send the message to Richard, and he'd take it from there.

She yanked the thin wool blanket off the bed, rolled it tightly, and tucked it under her arm. The black veil and gloves were folded neatly in the corner and would stay just where she placed them. Her hands needed to be free tonight, and the black veil would obstruct vision that only recently became clear. Tonight she would see things as they were, and act accordingly as planned.

She turned the small latch on the door, walked out

to the abandoned store, and flipped on the light switch. The sound of her heels tap-tapping across the wooden floor echoed a hollow tone. A glance out the windows showed a night, darker than she could remember for this time of day in September. The wind howled around the walls of the store and carried with it branches and debris. Rain pelted the roof above her, and sheets of water rolled off the gutterless eaves.

It was a night, she knew, few would ever forget.

She didn't bother scanning the sparse shelves but instead went directly behind the counter in which the cash register sat. After digging past half-empty water bottles, an opened potato chip bag, a stained dishtowel, and a sheathed hunting knife, she found the large flashlight Kenzie had used earlier that day.

Pushing the tab to *on* for the expected light produced nothing. She clicked the tab *off* then *on* again and got a dim, brown-yellow light that leaked out the front of the flashlight and disappeared into the room a foot away.

Foraging further under the counter, she was not surprised to find there were no batteries, and there wouldn't be any in the store after the big business Kenzie did today. But there was a box of wooden matches that she pocketed.

She knocked the flashlight against the countertop. It surged to life, sending a brilliant stream of light across the room and squarely onto a lone can of corned beef hash. If her eyes were better, she could have read the ingredients label, but for the matter at hand, having a light that worked was enough.

Tucking the flashlight deep into the roll of the wool blanket, she took one last glance out the window before joining the elements that raged there.

She hoped Richard was true to his word and hadn't forgotten the code. It was all up to him now.

She could do no more.

Chapter 29

Cold, wet sand matted his hair. Winston stirred, tasted salt, spat on the ground beside him, then coughed. His chest hurt. He rolled over on the bay beach, groaned with the effort, and looked to the black sky. The searing pain in his chest was responsible for his unconscious state—how long had he been out this time? He couldn't remember what compelled him to this place to begin with. A sticky line of saliva rolled from the corner of his mouth. His hand clenched around something rough and worn. The rope to *Errand Two*.

Charlie was on the boat. Winston knew that had to be true more than he knew his name.

"Get up," he said aloud.

The words sounded as if they came from a feeble old man straining in the last days of a life that had long since ceased to be useful. He had become a pitiful man who could barely feel the rope that lay sprawled across his hand, a rope that had once held *Errand Two* on the shore, and away from the prying hands of a young boy. A rope that at one time held *Errand One* as well.

He moaned, tried to sit up, and slumped back with the pain that snatched his breath and pulled queasiness into his stomach. A roll to the side and an attempt at sitting up forced his stomach into revolt. He vomited bile until he was left with dry heaves, and heavy sweat on his forehead, under his arms, and down his back.

Night air turned the moisture into cold goosebumps that covered his body like a shroud. He trembled. His chest tightened and ached all the way through to his back.

Mann knew what would have to be done, and that he would be the one to do it since there was no time to find help. If he got there in time and could wade the frigid, strong undercurrent, maybe, just maybe, he could stop the boat before it hit the rocks.

The ghost woman in the water would try again, but on another boy and in another time. This time he would see that she missed at least one young life.

It would be easier if Richard were here to help him, and even better if he could be sure Sybil was all right. But the icing on the cake, the gravy on the biscuit, would be knowing Charlie was safe on the boat and that this was all some little boy prank. He could forgive a prank, overlook the nonsense of a ten-year-old boy, and could even forget any damage to the boat, but never again could he live through the heavy lid of a casket throwing the face of a child into final darkness.

His hand twitched around the rope. Better the deep wood of a coffin shadowed his face than that of a child who had his whole life before him.

Pain poured through him. It was the pain in his chest, the pain of a son taken from him, and a deeper pain of fear for a second child that worried him. Deeper still, was the pain of his ineffectiveness in a task yet accomplished. With every passing second, the task held odds against it being completed successfully.

"No."

Gathering up every ounce of strength that held him together, he allowed the energy to build on itself.

"No. Not now. Not ever. You'll not take him!"

He pushed himself up on his knees. Another push and he was standing, leaning into the wind, and holding his chest as if it would open up and spill on the ground if he let go. He staggered the first few steps until his legs could steady themselves, and headed down the shoreline to the rock outcropping far away from Manchester Place.

He wished he had the little pills to curb the pain.

It didn't matter. He would live without them.

A little pill. Just one.

He wrapped his arms around his chest, caught breath in shallow gasps, and walked down the shore.

****

Warm fur brushed against her hand.

Gasping, Sybil jerked away from it.

A nudge to her leg then one to her foot, was followed by a whisper of motion at her side. A squeal sent little legs scrambling around her, running, circling. They were on the rafters above her, in the walls, in the corner, outside the door, just inside the door. They were next to her. *Touching her.*

She opened her mouth in a scream that would not come. Frantically, she waved her arms in an arc, hit something solid, warm. Furry. It fell, recovered with a shriek, and scurried off.

Her muscles shuddered then spasmed inward as if they would crack. Sybil closed her eyes and talked to herself. Be calm. Stay calm. Willing her heartbeat to slow, to somehow reflect a steady even beat she didn't feel, it pounded relentlessly in her chest and her temples. She rubbed her head and worried about the tenuous thread that held her between sanity and the other side.

It was all too much to think about.

She was trapped in a tiny dirt cell with furry things nibbling at her fingers and toying with her sanity, while overhead a drama played out that only she could stop. Death would happen again if it hadn't already, and she was trapped.

How long had she been here, minutes, days, or a lifetime? It was hard to know.

She crawled over to the locked door yet again, kicked it, pounded at it. A crack and screech of splintering wood echoed back to her, but the door stayed firm.

They were behind her now. Filthy creatures the size of small cats that watched and waited. They smelled her blood, her fear, and knew they would have her in time.

She reached into her pocket to fondle the small bottle. The last pill that could block out the nightmare rattled around in a small, almost tinny sound. After it was gone, there'd be nothing left but the dark, the furry things, and the wait until she died alone.

The ghost woman had waited as well. Her game was almost won twenty-seven years ago, but the light never came. Tonight she would try again. Annie would stand at the widow's walk and turn toward the bay. And if everything had been set right, all matters neatly handled, and in their place, the light would blaze a tunnel across the water.

Sybil threw her full weight against the door. Searing pain crossed her shoulder, numbness shot down her arm and burned in her hand. Something was broken, fractured into useless pieces. Her shoulder and neck swelled almost immediately. She folded her arm intuitively across her chest and dared not move it again.

A small, curved shadow loomed before her. She kicked out, and it squealed in pain as it scurried off to the back corner. It and others would be back.

She pried open the top of the bottle with her good hand, then grappled with the pill and swallowed before it touched her tongue. Maybe it would help with the pain. Maybe it would calm the seething terror that gripped her spine and knotted her muscles. Maybe.

A breeze crept around the door. It was stronger from the side of the lock. Kicking again, she moaned in pain, and confirmed what she hoped was true: the door had budged ever so slightly. But there was little strength left in her to keep up the battering, and not near enough to outlast the solid door.

Rain pummeled the ground outside. Small rivulets of water trickled in under the door and pooled at her feet. She backed up a few inches, looked over her shoulder at the blackness, and knew the furry things waited for her there. She couldn't go back any further.

The pool of water widened, lapped at her feet. A single tendril of water rolled away from the pool to start its accumulation beside her.

Wind gusts beat the door and sent more water under the groaning wood to surround her in cold dampness. She inched back slowly, ever so slowly, and checked the dark behind her. Tiny feet and squeaking chatter sent hurried messages of the move.

Her body trembled, the hair on her arms and neck stood on end. Cold from the dampness enhanced the chill from within her. No will or little yellow pills could stop any of this from happening. It would only stop when the ghost woman decided it was over.

She wanted to see Winston just one more time to tell him how much she loved him and how she would miss him. She wanted to see Richard again, too, and little Charlie.

But if it were meant to be, she'd see Phillip first. There was so much to tell him, so much to say.

Water poured in from under the door, saturated her clothes, touched her skin.

Little feet scurried then settled.

****

Eleanor fought for balance every step of the way.

A strong wind pushed her thin frame forward in rapid, awkward steps then just as easily knocked her back and to one side. Reeling in the wind like a foundering kite on a frayed line, she tried to anticipate the random gusts but was wrong far more often than she was right.

She held tight the wool blanket with the flashlight within. The blanket was a small attempt at cold-weather gear if she found need of it, but it was no match for the rain that assaulted her from all sides.

Her black dress clung one minute then whipped around with loud cracking sounds the next. Like a wounded sail on a mast, the dress caught the next gust and pushed her toward a particularly vicious looking mass of underbrush. She fought the wind, stepped out of one shoe, and tried to hold on to the blanket that was sliding from her grasp. Her foot slipped under a fallen branch and toppled her into a deep pile of dead leaves and briars.

A stray branch picked up by the same gust slapped her solidly on the cheek and clung there by tiny thorns. She sat back instinctively, but the thorns hung tight and tore soft flesh. Warm blood trickled down her face from the punctures as she pulled out each thorn. The freed branch swayed freely in the wind for a second or two then affixed itself to her dress with all the others.

There was no time to peel away the briars one at a time. Richard was waiting. She pushed through the tangle of underbrush. The material in her dress tore into thin lines. One shoe was missing, and the wool blanket was gone. Of the few things she had, the flashlight in the blanket was the one thing she didn't dare lose.

She scouted the area as best she could, using first her bare foot, then getting down on her hands and knees. The flashlight could be anywhere, yards away, or just under her nose. It could be dawn before she found it, but by dawn, it would be too late.

Wandering in the night, she had taken a spill into a briar patch without the benefit of light so she could save what little power remained in the batteries. And now the flashlight was gone, and Richard would be waiting for a signal that never came.

There was no choice. She would have to go on and hope she thought of something on the way. A pat to her pocket reminded her there was something left that might work if the weather cooperated. And if the ghost of Manchester Place let her get close enough to try.

****

It would be all right now. Father wouldn't be mad anymore since the mittens were back.

Grandma opened and closed her hand around the coin Charlie had placed there. The boy had recognized his meanness and corrected it, so now everything was as it should be.

The nagging in the back of her mind started again.

An image of the boy who had stolen her mittens superimposed over the picture of another. The second was familiar, someone she thought she knew and loved. He was frightened, but she couldn't see what it was that frightened him so. She stirred in bed and touched him with her mind.

He was drawing again. The pictures flowed from some unknown source through to his fingertips and onto one blank page after another. A stack of paper, each with a drawing, told a story of what was and what would be. He didn't see the drawings or the story. His eyes were open, but he didn't see.

Look at the paper, little boy. See what it tells you. Look, and you'll know what you must do.

Gazing through his eyes with her mind, she scanned his pictures. They were disjointed, confusing, nonsense if you took them individually, but still, he drew. Together the pictures revealed a story that had yet to unfold. Or was it unfolding now?

Someone who looked like her was in a picture. Clad in a nightgown like the one Grandma had on now, the old woman in the drawing stood at the top of the stairs looking down, eyes wide and staring, mouth open in a scream. Then the boy pushed aside the drawing and went on to another one.

Grandma rolled over in the bed, tired to the bone. Things were all right now. The mittens were back, and maybe Father wouldn't be mad anymore.

He seemed a nice boy, the one with the drawings. She just wished she knew who he was.

Chapter 30

The storm wrapped Mico Island in black clouds and howling winds. Ocean waves on one side of the island and bay water on the other side crashed against the shore and brought the earth to tumultuous depths, only to send it back to shore then claim it once again.

Birds fell silent and clung to branches only to be knocked down from their roosts and buried under debris and their feathers.

Cold fingers of wind wrapped around young seedlings barely grounded with tenuous roots and pulled them free. Shrubs and underbrush leaned and bent at differential angles. Vegetation froze and cracked on the earth's surface and was whisked away like tumbleweeds.

In the distance, the wind carried the sound of a centuries-old voice. Patient and persistent, it was also restless and intolerant, having waited as long as it had. Tonight the wait would be over. The voice carried with it an undercurrent of hope that finally, things would be as they should.

Annie would complete the task this time, complete it the way it was meant to be. She saw the need through the eyes of the wind, heard it in the voice that spoke to her in her dreams, and felt it when their dreams merged and became her own.

She paced the widow's walk and looked out over

the bay with new strength. It was a power once someone else's, but now discovered as her own, and would be used to bring the light.

In the distance, the wind carried the sound of laughter.

Soon the truth would be acted on. They would look for the light coming across the bay, and their souls would know that everything was set right again.

Tonight it would all end.

Tonight it would all begin.

The branch over the walk rippled and shook, and leaned further over the edge.

Annie took little notice. Instead, her attention was pulled to the choppy surface of Lullaby Sound. There was nothing. Yet. But soon, very soon now, she would look out across the water and see the light from his boat that meant she had successfully corrected the wrongs, and he had returned for her.

Her hands touched the small of her belly.

It had started there in this belly, a mistake that threw a wedge between them. He never wanted the child, had said as much, but her loneliness and her selfishness, he had reminded her, made her turn against his wishes.

Her husband was never there for her. The child was.

It was a mistake.

The child was a part of her. He depended on her, needed her.

Her husband needed her, too, didn't he? So she walked and waited. And when the wait turned from weeks to months to years, she looked at the reason for his absence and found it in the child.

Until she had taken care of the mistake, he would wait. Then, when things were ready, her husband would come for her.

The wind whipped around her and carried with it whispers and persuasion that when the time was right when the signal came, Annie would do the right thing.

She sighed and turned to the open door that led from the walk down the steps into the house. A hint of light from the kitchen drifted up the circuitous route of the stairwell and caught her as a limping shadow heading down to the kitchen. The lights dimmed, surged, then went out completely.

Feeling her way along the edge of the wall, she stepped out on the kitchen landing and knocked over the collection of used candles. She reached for one and cupped its large, circular base in both hands. The glow in the hearth caught her attention. She went to it and carefully placed the candle on the table.

The fire burned red coals at its base and licked the inside of the hearth with dancing flames. Annie smiled as warmth caressed her body and lulled her into a peace she never remembered feeling before now. It soothed and healed and confirmed that what she was about to do was indeed the right thing. The plans would soon be realized; then, there would be peace from within.

She poked at the remaining shred of Sybil's coat burning in the fire. Flames tickled the coat, tasted it then consumed the remains in a final gulp of heat. She stretched in comfort, then settled in a chair to await the signal. When it was time, everything else would be up to her.

Annie liked having things left up to her. It suited her, made her recognize her self-worth that she was important and needed.

The wind howled, the lights in the kitchen winked on, off. Flames in the hearth surged, then reached out to touch brick and leave fingers of black soot. Heat filled the room, and the voice whispered a command.

She nodded mechanically then went to the hearth. Capturing a slender wood-piece that held a flame, she used to light a large candle. It caught immediately and cast dancing shadows on the walls. The blanket covering the broken kitchen window, slapped at the wind but held. The candle flame flickered, threatened to go out, then steadied and burned high and strong.

She stared long and hard into the base of the candle flame.

Candlelanterncandle

Then looked deep into the glowing embers of the hearth fire.

The tabby mansion had been set on fire. The lantern held high, so he might see the light from across the bay and know things had been set right. But it wasn't enough. The lantern crashed at her feet, and she watched calmly as flames trickled across the walk and set a blaze of light that would be seen for miles. She had set the fire and had burned the house to dust and ash.

The wind howled across the walk and down the stairwell to Annie's ears. It persuaded, cajoled, and told her of the way it should be done, at whatever cost.

Annie nodded, looked from the candle to the hearth, then turned to the door that would lead her to the large staircase and up to the boy's room.

She would start there.

Chapter 31

Grandma trembled under the blanket and stared at a spot on the ceiling. She opened and closed her fist around the coin the boy had given her when he brought back the mittens.

Open and close.

She knew the boy and knew he needed her now.

Did he want to make amends for the mittens? No, it wasn't that, it was something else, and someone else who should make amends.

The mittens had never been returned; after all, she realized. Father had beaten her for the infraction until she thought she would never walk again. How she hated him for doing that, and how she hated the boy for taking her mittens in the first place.

Open, close, open, close.

This boy that consumed her thoughts now was different. This was her boy, in a way, and he was afraid for his life. *She* was coming for him, the woman, one step at a time.

Open, close.

This boy had given her a present, not taken anything from her. She turned her head, squinted in the dark, and saw the small unselfish object of love pressed in her hand, its small indentation etched into her flesh. A coin. For good luck.

She remembered then. A tear burned down the side

of her face.

His name was Charlie. The baby she had held in her arms a mere few hours after his birth was her grandson. She knew he had a special gift, one shared with her, when she first looked down at him and counted his tiny fingers and toes. He was a special child, one that few understood, and it was only he who understood her and loved her for what she was, for what she had become.

Footsteps sounded at the bottom of the stairs.

The woman was coming for him.

She closed her fist around the coin, tightened her grasp until blood vessels strained at the skin then threw aside the blankets. She sat up at the side of the bed and tried to clear the fogginess.

No one would hurt her grandson.

No one.

****

Annie paused at the fourth step and looked up into the dark hallway. Shifting the heavy candle to one hand, she ignored the pain in her ankle and pulled herself up by a firm grasp on the balcony railing.

Another step.

The boy had been a mistake, one that needed to be corrected.

Step.

Soon it would be over, and her new life could begin.

Step.

She turned to the full-length mirror at the middle landing and wondered when she had gotten so thin, so pale. Her hair hung in damp clumps around her face and accentuated the drawn skin pulled taut and colorless over her cheekbones. The same clothes, worn over the past two days, had gone limp and given way to a tear here and there, a stain, and a wisp of peeled wallpaper. She pulled her gaze to the dark hallway, to the closed door of the boy's room, then returned to the mirror. A smile reflected.

The boy must be taken care of.

****

The lights were out, and still, the drawing continued. His hand raced frantically over the paper until the last sheet had been used.

He stopped. Footsteps echoed in the hallway. Heavy. Slow. It was as if a plan were still in the making.

It was *her*, not his mother, who had long since ceased to be. She was the woman in the water the day of the fishing trip. The same woman who called to him on the beach, laughed at him. She wanted him or wanted him out of the way. Now she was coming for him again.

His body trembled with fever chills and unharnessed fear. He pulled the sweat-damp sheet to his chin but knew it wouldn't help. His teeth chattered, and noise rioted through his head.

The woman, his mother, was going to hurt him. Hurt him bad.

A twinge of the darkness crept into the back of his mind and called him to safety, to look inward. Instead, he stared unblinking at the closed door that separated him from the steps in the hallway. Light from her candle flickered under the door and cast shadows in the room.

The laughing toy.

The dresser, where the toy stood just moments ago, was empty.

His stare jolted back to the door. The toy was gone. He searched through the dusky room to see where it was then froze in horror. The dark shadow was now two feet from his bed. If he tried to climb out of bed, touch a foot to the floor...

He huddled under the sheet. She was really, really mad. And now she was coming to punish him for some wrong he couldn't remember doing.

Was it because he didn't clean his room often enough, or finish his food? Or maybe she was mad because he didn't know how to read. He'd promise to do better if she'd give him another chance. Drawing a small, shaky "x" across his chest, he closed his eyes and mouthed, "I promise."

Step.

His eyes opened wide at the sound, grew bigger at the toy standing next to his bed now. It was too late for promises. It was too late for anything. The fuzzy toy shook and began to laugh.

****

Grandma stood on the landing. Her hair was a knotted tangle of gray, her nightgown wrinkled and damp with sweat from her exertion. She swayed as if her legs were barely capable of sustaining weight. Arthritic fingers strained with the grip on the handrail and glowed a dull white.

Grandma gazed from Annie, three steps below, to the candle in her hand. The flame flickered. She knew they were not alone.

"Go back to bed, old woman. You're not needed here." Annie's voice was flat.

"No." Grandma stayed, holding something small and shiny in one hand.

"I said, go to bed."

"Let me see you."

Annie's voice grew in pitch. "I said go to bed, and I mean it."

"You'll have to kill me, too."

Annie's voice softened but carried an undercurrent of fury. "Who said anything about killing? You're tired, old woman. Old and tired. Useless. You don't know what you're saying anymore."

"You won't touch me or anyone else in this house."

"I make the rules here. Not you, not anybody."

"Or anything? Who's the real rule-maker here, you or Annie? I'm counting on Annie."

Grandma's knees buckled then caught. She pulled herself to stand tall at the top of the stairs and held the railing to steady the increasing sway. Sweat popped out on her forehead and rolled down the side of her face.

"Show me who you are."

"Useless old woman! You don't know what you're talking about."

"But I do."

"Then, see me for what I am."

Grandma blinked at the confusion of shadows across Annie's face, the contortion of images that changed her face from human to something else. The body writhed and twisted then settled into the skin. A mirthless smile touched the lips of Lady Manchester.

"Am I what you saw in your feeble dreams conjured by a weaker mind?"

"You are nothing. I see that now more clearly than

I've seen anything in my life."

"Then you see nothing. Get out of my way or—"

"You'll kill me?" The old woman took a tentative step, gradually released the balcony, and stared unblinking into the eyes of Lady Manchester. "I won't let you touch a hair on that child's head. I'll do whatever it takes to stop you."

"Don't play with me, old woman. You'll lose. No one will stand in my way now."

Dark waves of Lady Manchester's anger surrounded Grandma and spun her around. She waved her arms to stop the attack and cried out in pain.

The onslaught stopped, and Lady Manchester stood beside Grandma.

"Enough?"

"You will not have this child." Grandma swung out and snatched a handful of Annie's shirt in her damp hand. Her breaths came in ragged gasps.

Twisting and turning, the ghost woman pulled loose from Grandma's grasp and threw them both off balance.

Grandma fell back a step then tottered on the edge of the landing. A final blast of dark anger touched her with no more than a soft caress. There was no sound and no expression as she looked out over the great height. The old woman reached out with both arms in a last attempt to balance herself; then, with quiet dignity, she stepped out over the edge.

The nightgown grazed Annie's hand and slid away from her touch as Grandma plummeted down the stairs.

Her body hit the mirror at the middle landing, sent a vertical crack across the face of it, and continued the fall until it finally rested at the foot of the stairs by the front door.

Annie turned away, then forced herself to look.

One leg was folded under Grandma, the other jutted out to one side under the nightgown's light floral print. It was a quick death, and in that death, her resolve, and even her eyes were clear.

Annie stood frozen. This wasn't supposed to happen.

It is better this way. The old woman was a troublemaker.

No, something was wrong. This was wrong. It was the boy who was the problem.

This wouldn't have happened if not for him. He watches even now.

Charlie stood in the doorway of his room. He stared, unblinking, at the body at the foot of the stairs, then shifted his gaze slowly from Grandma to Annie.

He backed into the room, and she matched his every step. Further and further, he went until he stopped with a jolt at the edge of his bed. Looking over his shoulder, he spotted the papers piled in one corner under the fuzzy toy. He scooped up the sheets and threw them at her.

Laughter exploded from the toy and permeated the room. Charlie cringed then shivered uncontrollably.

He gazed from her to the papers scattered randomly across the floor. Staring at one drawing then another, he saw the story.

The boy knows. He sees what is to happen. It was best that he knew.

He was a smart boy, this one. He would understand what she had to do and go willingly.

"Charlie." She reached out for him.

He stood still then looked up at her. The fear was gone, replaced with emptiness as if he had gone somewhere and left her alone.

"It'll be okay, boy. You'll see. It won't be bad. I promise."

She wrapped her long, thin fingers around his throat.

Now. You must.

Her fingers tightened.

****

Annie scanned the living room as if seeing it for the first time, and knew it would be the last.

The reflection in the cracked mirror when she returned from the boy's room smiled at her, a petite woman clad in a heavy, wool cloak. Her green eyes crinkled, and her long, red hair was carefully groomed and brushed to a shine in preparation for this night. Her voice carried confidence in the tasks that remained; her voice carried hope.

The living room would be first.

Draft from the broken kitchen window directed currents of air dancing around the room. That was good. It would make it easier, faster. Annie shielded the candle so it wouldn't go out and brushed the tip of the flame to one side of the curtain. The flame wrapped itself around the material, leaving a black residue, then caught. A tendril of fire crept up along the edge then branched out to consume other sections.

She crossed the room to set fire to a corner of the quilt-draped couch then moved into the kitchen.

The fire in the hearth had dimmed to a few embers. She toppled two of the kitchen chairs into the edge of the hearth and waited until she was sure they too had caught then took the flame of the candle to the blanket covering the window. Fire was slow in taking the blanket, but it came eventually.

Moving to the open door leading up to the widow's walk, she touched her candle to the others on the floor in the stairwell and brought them to light. She nudged the candles with her foot until they stood in an even row under the first step.

The smell of kerosene, of burned wood from years past, singed her nostrils. The old wood steps that held her weight on this last climb would go fast.

The stairs creaked and groaned. They led her slowly to the splintered door that banged and clattered with the wind and the rain.

Up she went, one step at a time, to the widow's walk and the view of the bay. For surely, the light would come now.

She fought gusting wind as she made her way across the walk to stand at the edge. This was the best place to see his light, the only place.

It was here where she would wait.

Chapter 32

Eleanor stumbled in the dark woods and quickened her pace. Something was wrong. She could feel it.

Her nose tickled with the smell. She sniffed the air. Smoke.

She hoped she wasn't too late. She pushed herself into a lope and headed in the direction of Manchester Place. The deep shadow of the house loomed on the horizon. She released a caught breath, satisfied there weren't any visible flames, and found herself counting on the reverse of the adage where there's smoke; there's fire.

Walking softly, she looked up at the widow's walk. Until today she hadn't been allowed to get close enough—the ghost of Lady Manchester had seen to that—and there had been little desire to approach. She slowed her pace to one tentative step after another.

A blast of unseen energy, angry and revengeful, sent her reeling with the onslaught. Her head snapped back, her mouth opened wide in pain at the dark presence that surrounded her. Warnings to stay away, to leave, pounded in her mind. She rubbed her forehead, pressed fingers deep into the scalp to stop the threats, but they stayed and grew stronger. She squeezed her eyes open to stare up at the widow's walk.

Annie was there, looking out over the bay in a come-and-go moonlit silhouette. It was almost impossible to be sure, but it looked like she was near the low decorative fence that surrounded the widow's walk.

Eleanor crept up on the house, pushing herself against the force that tried to keep her away. Pain seared through her head. She gasped at its strength; its will then moved closer still to one side of the house for a clear shot. Bay water glistened with an occasional burst of moonlight then slid into writhing darkness as the waves folded in on themselves.

Annie on the widow's walk with someone else.

Squinting at the figure on the walk, Eleanor saw the Annie she remembered on the beach. But there was a superimposition of sorts over Annie, of a shimmering face and body. The two became the same, separated then joined again.

Eleanor shivered in the cold rain, and with the colder thought. If Annie failed in the ghost woman's bidding, there would be another break in the decorative fence. Broken bones and open wounds eventually healed, but the mind stayed in welcome shadow for years, and heavy drapes kept the light away.

She shook her head and reached into her pocket for the box of wooden matches. She slid open the box and snatched three matches before the others fell out and disappeared. She struck the match against the side of the box. The flame blew out almost before it had a chance to start. Now there were only two matches left.

A strong smell of smoke hung on the wind from the direction of the house. She peered into the darkness. There was no fire. There was no light of any kind.

The electricity was out, but it seemed there should be some form of light in the house. Even something as small as a lit candle could surely be seen from where she was standing.

There was something very wrong in this house, so it was best she stick with the original plan. If that were lost, the rest of it would be, too.

She tore some of the shredded material from her black dress and wrapped it tightly around a stick. Using a large tree as a shield from the bulk of the wind, she cupped her hands around a match, struck it against the box, and fired the end of the homemade torch anchored under her arm. The material glowed red but refused a flame; then, a sudden gust blew it out.

Another blast of anger surrounded her and dropped her to her knees near a pile of debris. She screamed at the sudden pounding in her head and rubbed her temples to rid the pain.

The sound of a woman's laugh traveled to her on the wind then appeared deep within her mind. She writhed in the deadfall and tried to crawl away to a safer distance, but the sound followed her. The firm stalk of a dry branch hit her squarely in the palm of her hand. She grabbed it, raised it high in the air like a weapon.

"You are nothing. Do you hear me? Nothing. You will not hurt me again."

The laughing stopped then, gone as suddenly as it had appeared.

The ghost, at least for now, was gone.

With the small branch in hand, she crawled to a tree and leaned against it. Taking a deep breath, she allowed the pain in her head to ease away slowly. Loosening her tight grip on the branch, she fingered its length, felt its multiple branches with a few leaves still attached, and formed the last plan.

If it wasn't too wet, the branch might do. Eleanor pulled herself up to stand and hoped Richard wasn't a stickler for three shorts-three longs-three shorts. She waited for the wind to die down a notch then struck the side of the box with the last match.

A small flame clung tenuously to the end of the match then encircled the branch with a sputter, a crackle, and finally, a steady stream of flame. She waved the branch from side to side, but within seconds the renewed wind blew out the flame. Hopefully, Richard saw and would take it from there.

Smoke stung her eyes and made them water then flowed deeply into her lungs until she had to cough. She waved a hand in front of her face to fan away the smell, then looked at Manchester Place, and her mouth dropped.

Fire in the living room.

Flames reached almost to the ceiling. Unattended, the fire would light up the sky and gut a frame house built on a tabby foundation in no time.

And it would kill little boys and women before they knew what happened.

Eleanor stood still and frightened in the dark woods, as the sound of a woman's laughter floated from atop the widow's walk.

Chapter 33

Cold slivers of icy rain stung her face, seared her eyes. She never blinked. Winds from the maritime high forced her body to pitch and yaw with the whim of the currents. She stood tall. Waited.

The fire crackled in the rooms below. Soon the walls would be in flames, and the tidal waters would be alive with color reflecting the fire in a joust with the drizzling rain.

From across the sound, he would see that she had taken care of things. Then he would come for her.

The beginnings of heat warmed the bottom of her feet. She never wavered when an explosion blew out the window of the living room. The solid piece of glass erupted into tiny, razor-sharp shards that impaled sand and grass and underbrush.

He would come. He had to now.

A bolt of light danced across the bay then died away.

She froze, stared in hope. Her heart pounded in her chest. She was afraid suddenly, afraid that what she had summoned was not what she had wanted after all. Then the thought was gone. She smiled.

Power surged through her. She had done the right thing. The light, however brief, across the water was proof.

He would be here soon.

Staring into the distance, she willed the moon to come out and cast its glow on the water so she could see the man who had deserted her, and now was coming home.

Growing heat from the room below forced her to shift from one foot to the other.

The old wood on the narrow staircase cracked and sizzled then fell away from the walk with a deafening crash.

There was no way down now. He would have to come for her. She stared out over the water and waited. Patience grew to agitation, to doubt. She lifted one foot, slowly lowered it, picked up the other.

This had been the right thing to do, wasn't it?

Now, she pleaded, not daring to take her gaze off the horizon.

You must come for me now.

Now, please, Annie mouthed as she watched the horizon. A pinpoint of light burst through the darkness, grew larger, bolder. Its brilliance burned through the thick dark clouds like a beacon.

****

"Fire in the living room, Winston. Maybe all over. I smelled it all the way over to my place and came running."

"What about the little boy?" Winston asked. "Where is he, Stretch?"

"I haven't seen anyone."

"He wasn't on the other side of the island. I was afraid he'd be out in the water. Came here as fast as I could when I saw no one there." Winston coughed, sputtered out the words. "We've got to find him."

"What about his grandmother? Where's she?"

"Oh God, dear God. They must still be in the house. Help me get them out," Winston shouted.

"How?" Kenzie yelled. "The whole damn place is coming down."

"Are you all right, Winston?" Stretch asked. "You're as white as a sheet."

A spasm of coughing caught Winston. "We've got to get them out."

Kenzie waved a flashlight down the road. "There's help now. Those who didn't leave for the storm are coming. Can you hear them? There must be an army of them. All customers I might add."

"Open the front door through the broken window," Winston ordered as he ran to the front of the house. "Get me in, and I'll get them out."

"I'll break down whatever I have to," Stretch said, wielding a large ax. "There's more than one way to skin a cat, and there's more than one way to get into a house."

****

The light across the bay steadied. A motor surged to life.

A motor?

He had left in a rowboat. She had stood in the water to see him off in a rowboat. What little food she had was given to him, and then he faded into the darkness to the sound of oars breaking water. In her dreams, she saw it all. In her nightmares, the truth was told.

The motor from across the water screamed like a tortured animal. The light reached her at lightning speed until it jumped the shore and continued partway up the embankment and stopped.

A lean, tall man leaped from the boat and climbed the steep slope on his hands and knees.

She shook her head. This wasn't right.

He stumbled once, caught himself, and bolted across the back lawn until he stood near the eaves below her.

"Annie? It's okay. You're going to be all right." Richard looked around, spotted the large oak growing next to the house, and headed for it. "I'll come get you. Don't move."

He was wrong.

That wasn't the man she saw off in the rowboat while she stood in the water.

That wasn't the man she lived with in Atlanta.

She turned to the bay to catch a glimpse of lantern light. Darkness answered her back.

The wind howled around her and carried with it anger and a pent-up rage newly released. The voice rose high in a fury, in indignation at the events that were happening.

Spotting the fallen branch hanging tenuously from the walk, she knew what she had to do. She ran to it, leaned over to see where Richard was, and pushed the branch with her foot. Its great girth groaned, rolled ever so slightly, and stayed.

She got down on her knees and pushed harder. Her hands slipped on the wet bark, her balance shifted, and she tumbled toward the railing. It broke, and she plummeted over the side and down the narrow eaves to the ground.

Richard lunged for her from his place on the tree, caught her then pulled her in. Wrapping his arms around her, he held her tight, and lowered her to the ground into the arms of someone else then another, and another, until her feet touched the ground.

Curiosity and worry etched the strange faces that peered into hers, but when she was okay, they turned to the work of dousing the fire near the front door with bucket after bucket of water from the bay.

Richard covered her with a blanket and sat with her at the base of the tree. "You'll be all right now. Everything's going to be fine."

Annie looked at the widow's walk with the branch jutting out then to Richard. None of this was right.

The sound of splintering wood split the air.

Richard jumped up. "What have you got there, Stretch?"

"I don't know—something in the crawl space. Dear God Almighty! Someone get over here quick! I mean *now*."

Richard and a handful of others rushed to assist Stretch.

Annie closed her eyes. A shiver traveled her spine and twisted. Her breath became ragged gasps at what they would find in the house as well. And it was all her fault, all her doing.

What had Grandma done? Annie made the rules, no one else. She never meant to hurt Sybil or Grandma. Or Charlie.

She winced and dug her fingernails deep into the flesh of her palm. The wind tickled her, giggled in her ear. A woman's laugh. A wisp of a voice told her perhaps all was not lost. The voice turned to a wail suddenly.

Annie looked up through the drizzling rain and the smoke-filled air. Mann stumbled out of the house with a small bundle in his arms. He fell to his knees, sweat poured from his colorless face.

"Can't help the grandmother. Too late."

Someone grabbed Charlie from Winston's arms and carried him to the back of a pickup truck to deposit him in the arms of a woman with a splint covering her leg. The woman's face paled to the same bleached skin tone Mann had. She fanned Charlie, talked to him, and prayed and cried at the top of her lungs.

A side of the blanket fell away, revealing his small face. He still wore his glasses; the eyes behind them were closed.

Annie saw her son, her baby in the arms of the caring woman, and found no emotion she could call her own. The fingernails of one hand dug deeper into the other hand until she drew blood. She wanted to feel something, anything right now that would hurt her as much as she had hurt so many.

Her black dress torn to shreds, her bare feet scratched and bruised, and her face a maze of bleeding scratches, Eleanor walked directly to Annie. "Get angry."

Annie shook her head in confusion.

"Get angry at *her*," Eleanor said. "Don't let the pain get inside you. Turn it back on her with anger. That's where it belongs."

"I can't."

"You have to."

"It's all my fault. I can't live with what I've done."

The sound of laughter filled the air.

Annie covered her ears and cringed.

"Then it's not over," Eleanor said.

A crack split the air like thunder overhead. Annie

stared at the heavy oak branch that tottered on the edge of the walk.

"Get out," someone shouted.

"Move! It's coming down!"

"Dear God, no more. No more."

"They'll be killed if—"

Richard tackled Eleanor and carried her to the arms of a nearby man, who dragged her away. He grabbed the shoulder of Annie's shirt, tried for her arm, anything else he could get hold of. She twisted in his grasp, clawed his face. His feet slipped, throwing them both to the ground, but he didn't let go.

The wind surged. The branch swayed.

She gazed slowly upwards. Calm settled over her and filled her with the knowledge that, at last, it would be over. A final gust of wind screamed through the treetop and across the widow's walk. The branch slid off the side of the house.

Richard gasped, grabbed for her, and tried to roll away from the direct hit.

It was too late.

She screamed at the impact, then collapsed into her own welcomed darkness.

Chapter 34

Two months later

Annie turned her wheelchair away from the view of the door to the Manns' house and back toward the bay. It was a breezy day, a little on the cool side, and the sun reflected bright light on the surface of the water. A single tear oozed from the corner of her eye and slid down her face.

"Have some tea, dear. You need a little something to tide you over before dinner." Sybil pushed the steaming cup across the glass tabletop, then leaned back to caress the sling that held her other arm. She wiggled the fingers sticking out from the edge of the sling, and frowned. The broken collarbone was on the mend; it had all but healed; even the numbness in her hand was almost gone. She was better, but her sugar cookies had suffered in the meantime.

Sybil offered Annie one of the cookies and was not discouraged at her refusal.

Annie, too, was getting better. The young woman was at least walking a little bit now and improving every day. Soon enough, she would be fine, physically anyway. Her outlook was a little more stubborn. These things took time, but she was young and stronger than she thought, so maybe it wouldn't be all that long.

The little yellow pills the doctor had given her

would help ease the pain and bury the memories until Annie could better deal with them. When the anger emerged full force rather than in the drips and drabs now, Annie would do better still.

Mann coughed and sputtered, spraying liquid in small droplets across the table. "I hate flowers in my tea. Stupid little petals and disgusting yellow things that stick to your teeth like cement. Did you have hopes of being a rich dentist or something? Or maybe you're just supporting one on the side."

"Have a cookie, Winston. It'll scrape off the flowers and restore the shine to your teeth."

"Jeez, Syb. You know I hate flowers in my tea."

"They're for Annie. She needs the strength."

A flicker of amusement crossed Annie's face.

"See? Even she admits it. Don't you, honey?"

"They'll do in a pinch, I suppose," Annie said, never looking away from the bay.

"I've said it before, you know, and I'll say it as often as I can." Sybil touched Annie's arm. "You're welcome to stay here as long as you will. We love the company."

Annie shrugged. "I know you do. And I love you for it. I don't know yet. I just...don't know."

"It's not that I'm pushing," Sybil said.

Mann snorted. "You're pushing."

Sybil eyed him with a look she hoped would wither any further comment. "It's just that I, well, we worry about you. There. It's said."

"I'm telling you, Syb, you're pushing. Leave the woman to decide for herself what's best. Well, look here. Richard's back sooner than I hoped, and bearing gifts."

The young man waved, then sauntered up the rise from the boat. He brushed a hand through Annie's tousled hair, rubbed her neck, and deposited a small spray of flowers in her lap.

"How you doing?"

Annie smiled and nodded.

"Everything's handled just the way you wanted. The divorce is final in a week or so, and Mrs. Cameron's estate will be, too." Richard touched a finger to the large, healing scar across his cheek, a habit he had developed without realizing it, and reached for a cookie. "Looks like David will be a lot worse off than he ever thought possible."

"I miss Grandma." Another tear crept down Annie's cheek.

Richard leaned over and took her in his arms. "It'll be okay. I promise. I'll make it okay."

She nodded, wiped a hand roughly across her cheek. "Where's Charlie?"

Mann backed his chair out. "Took a walk, so he said. I'll go hunt him down. Need the exercise anyway."

Sybil threw herself in front of him. "You're not going anywhere. And I know I don't have to remind you what the doctor said. Rest, rest, rest. And a little extra fluid wouldn't hurt either, I suspect."

"Oh no, you don't, Sybil Mann. I'm not going that route again."

"Then leave the boy alone. He needs time to himself, just like the rest of us. I'll call him when dinner's ready."

****

Charlie stood at the edge of the burned tabby

foundation and listened. A gentle breeze carried the coolness of approaching island winter, but no sound. No voice, and no laughter either, there was just emptiness that echoed the hollowness he felt. He missed Grandma more than he ever imagined was possible, but knew, somehow, that she stayed with him, took care of him, and might even come to him in his dreams if he looked hard enough.

He stepped inside the tabby foundation and kicked at the ashes and small pieces of charred wood. This was all that was left of Manchester Place, and all that was left of his grandmother. The house would never be rebuilt, the Manns had said, and Grandma was never coming back. If only there were something to remember her by, something he could keep, could hold in his hand.

A gleam of something reflected the sunlight. He approached it cautiously, hoped that it was what he thought it might be, and picked it up. He rubbed it gently against the rough material of his new blue jeans then held it tight in his fist. The rhythmic rumble of a boat motor close to shore pulled his attention.

Eleanor nodded at him from the boat, then pointed out to the bay.

More in his mind's eye than anything else, the vision was real to him just the same.

There, in the distant waters, was a rowboat with a tiny light cast across the gentle currents like a sunbeam. The light stretched a thinning tendril toward the shore where a shadow shimmered, mingled with the wind, and carried with it the soft cry of a lonely young woman who had lost everything now.

The light caressed, beckoned. The woman reached

out, then went to it. Shadow and light swirled and danced with one another, became one, then both fell quietly into the water. The rowboat was gone.

Eleanor called out. "Charlie, listen to me. Take care of your mom. She needs you. She loves you, too. Promise?"

He crossed an "x" over his chest and waved. She waved back. The boat turned toward the mainland. In minutes it was out of sight.

Charlie took a deep breath, puffed out his chest, and headed back to the Manns' house. There were things to do now. Important things. Chores needed to be done, books needed to be read—Uncle Winston had insisted on that part—and there was a mother to take care of. Ms. Trippett was right. His mother needed him.

He brushed fingertips gently across his neck where his mother had squeezed. The darkness had come to take care of him that night. It took him deeper than he'd ever been before and lulled him to an almost breathless sleep.

She hadn't meant to hurt him. With Auntie Sybil's help and Ms. Trippett's explanation, he knew that now. And while it wasn't completely clear what happened, he had accepted their story and went back to his mother's welcoming arms.

The darkness was gone forever now. He was an almost-man, and almost-men looked to themselves for the answers.

He smiled, fingered the coin he found in the ash then slid it gently into his pocket.

They needed each other, he and his mom.

Together, they'd remember Grandma.

A word about the author...

Wendy Webb has published dark fantasy short stories and supernatural-humor murder mystery novels. After a hiatus for far too long as a professor of emergency management and a disaster responder, she welcomes the return to writing scary stuff.

She adores her husband, dogs and cats, dry red wine, theatre, and travel as long as she doesn't see a ghost.

If you enjoyed *Widow's Walk*, please leave a review at your favorite book retailer or reader website.

Thank you for purchasing
this publication of The Wild Rose Press, Inc.

For questions or more information
contact us at
info@thewildrosepress.com.

The Wild Rose Press, Inc.
www.thewildrosepress.com

CPSIA information can be obtained
at www.ICGtesting.com
Printed in the USA
LVHW030402240320
651021LV00016B/1669